Copyright © 2014 Phyllis Rudin

Except for the use of short passages for review purposes, no part of this book may be reproduced, in part or in whole, or transmitted in any form or by any means, electronically or mechanically, including photocopying, recording, or any information or storage retrieval system, without prior permission in writing from the publisher.

We gratefully acknowledge the support of the Canada Council for the Arts and the Ontario Arts Council for our publishing program. We also acknowledge the financial support of the Department of Canadian Heritage through the Canada Book Fund.

We are also grateful for the support received from an Anonymous Fund at The Calgary Foundation.

Cover design: Val Fullard

Library and Archives Canada Cataloguing in Publication

Rudin, Phyllis, author
    Evie, the baby and the wife : a novel / by Phyllis Rudin.

ISBN 978-1-77133-134-0 (pbk.)

    I. Title.

PS8635.U35E95 2014   C813'.6   C2014-905026-7

Printed and bound in Canada

Inanna Publications and Education Inc.
210 Founders College, York University
4700 Keele Street, Toronto, Ontario, Canada M3J 1P3
Telephone: (416) 736-5356 Fax: (416) 736-5765
Email: inanna.publications@inanna.ca   Website: www.inanna.ca

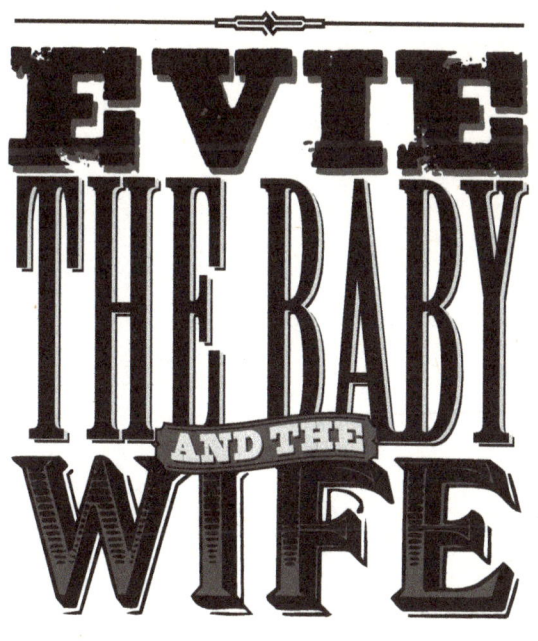

EVIE THE BABY AND THE WIFE

A NOVEL BY
PHYLLIS RUDIN

Inanna Poetry & Fiction Series

INANNA PUBLICATIONS AND EDUCATION INC.
TORONTO, CANADA

To my parents, Harold and Florence Woll

Chapter 1

EVIE WAS LOSING IT. She could still nail a target at a metre and a half, but in her prime she once zapped the kitchen door all the way from the living room sofa. Prone yet. The distance was verified by her brother Josh using the official tape measure, their father's beloved Craftsman, at 2.2 metres. It was her personal best. Projectile vomiting was an underrated talent the siblings reckoned. It belonged up there in the pantheon of athleticism alongside power farting, Josh's particular gift. As kids at the cottage they used to laze away rainy afternoons sketching out their own offshoot of the Special Olympics, one where every sport showcased competitors with wonky innards.

Evie's stomach had always been what her mother called *delicate*, though normally understatement wasn't mum's style. Its juices roiled wildly like a forgotten pot of oatmeal on the burner, eager for the slightest excuse to put on their Krakatoa imitation.

Other kids could waste their time tinkling out *Circus Parade* on the piano; Evie's intestinal party piece was always the show-stopper. Her mother was not amused. Marilyn schlepped Evie to every pediatrician up and down the slopes of Côte-des-Neiges Boulevard, trolling for a cure. She'd had it with wrapping her baby in a plastic tarp instead of a receiving blanket, a dank, fetid papoose as risky to jostle as an unexploded bomb. What she wanted was a baby like all the other babies, steady dribblers who expectorated more decorously, drop by drop like maple sap into a bucket, but instead she'd birthed a geyser. If only Evie were gushing Brent crude, the family would be fixed for life.

In fact, there was a secret agenda hiding behind Marilyn's skirts on these doctors' visits. She was seeking medical reassurance that Evie's barfing wasn't strategic, a precocious volley in a mother-daughter turf war that the baby was clearly winning. Given that Evie's belly had started rockin' and rollin' within days of her birth, the suspicion was clearly preposterous, but the notion was lodged like an ornery kimmel between the lobes of her mother's flipped-out postpartum brain and refused to be dislodged.

"Marilyn, honey. It's just gas. She's a bit on the young side to be as calculating as you make her out to be, don't you think? Her tummy just needs time to get the kinks out. She'll get over it."

"Jake, you don't understand how it is between a girl and her mother. Behaviours like these, if you neglect them at the start, next thing you know they root themselves in."

"Mare, it's not you. Get that into your head. It doesn't matter which of us is holding her. When she's fit to pop, she pops. Relax."

Relax. Ha! Jake knew that his wife's subliminal censors had black-penciled the R-word and all its synonyms from her mental thesaurus before they ever met, but in the sleep-deprived state he shared democratically with the new mother, he flung the injunction out there as if it might actually deliver. A rookie mistake. Marilyn was only able to unclench after the doctors isolated actual physical triggers in Evie's diet, which, once eliminated, stretched out the intervals between episodes and reduced their histrionic arc and reach.

Yet there remained one trigger, though duly identified, that stubbornly refused to efface itself as Evie grew older. Its origin wasn't dietary, but more environmental, or would you call it technological? In any event, it was trickier to control than food intake. Put Evie in a moving vehicle and she was toast. Ten minutes tops and the warm bile would start to puddle in her tongue's back cup. There it copulated merrily with her über-feisty saliva to synthesize the jet propulsion formula for which she alone held the patent. That particular taste, gravy cut with Javex, tipped her off that an episode was imminent in the same way that an aura tapped a migraine sufferer on the shoulder to announce, "Hold tight, bud, it's showtime."

Her mother and father prophesied that she'd outgrow this awkward tendency towards tossing her cookies in transit, but they took care never to specify a timeline so as not to be caught up in one of those parental fibs that eventually comes back to bite you in the tush. When asked by a sodden, sour-smelling Evie over the bathtub powerwash that followed yet another disastrous school field trip, "But when will it stop? When exactly?" they took their cue from the Prime Minister. They handled it like a date for troop withdrawal; a greased-pig date, a date endlessly malleable and move-offable. To give her parents their due, Evie's problem did calm down a little over the years, even if it didn't come easy to her. She had to work at it, stitching together a patchwork of feints and dodges that allowed her to tease out the distances over which she could travel with her belly in lockdown mode.

By the time she reached her twenties and was faced with a daily commute of an hour each way, Evie had finally defanged her digestive dybbuk. She discovered that as long as she didn't try to read while she was bussing it, she could manage to travel dry. Just. It was a sacrifice. So many hours shot. So many novels left untasted. So many authors left unsampled. Evie's world turned on words. The collision of adjective and noun sparked frissons at her very core that none of her feckless boyfriends was ever able to match. Those klutzes needed GPS to home in on the right spot. Even when she provided them with generous hands-on guidance in the darkness of her bedroom, the rendezvous inevitably proved to be a letdown. She always felt more like she was teaching them cursive. A socko metaphor and she would have been putty in their hands, but guys didn't seem to think along those lines in Evie's experience.

What choice did she have but to make a virtue out of necessity? At least her inability to read while heading to work and back allowed her the leisure to study the denizens of public transit on the STM's superannuated fleet. She transformed the bus into her personal Petri dish on which she performed top-level research. All her life, Evie'd been in the market for a writer. No other profession packed the same creative wallop to her way of thinking. On her daily bus rides she was on a constant lookout for clues, hoping to ferret out among her fellow passengers Mr. Write. She even had a recurring dream in which she hooked up with a wordsmith. The two of them grabbed their passports, hopped a plane, and set up a love nest in the faraway Republic of Letters where her better half toiled away on his bildungsroman.

The dream had elements that ticked her off, not that she had any control over it. The tableau was classic greenhorn. There she was, the wifey bringing in a few pennies minding the counter of the candy store so that hubby could sequester himself in the back room with his manuscript, his nib flying across the pages. Awake, Evie considered herself a feminist, but asleep her subconscious begged to differ. It inevitably cast her in the role of *baleboosteh*, the little homemaker who clips the toenails of the great man. Someday she and her analyst would go to town on her Yiddishe mama dreamscape, but for the time being she just accepted it as part of the armature of her nights.

So far her scheme hadn't panned out. She was still facing the world solo. Engineering a meeting with an author turned out to be no easy business. Writing was a solitary craft. The successful ones never poked their noses out of their apartments. Only the scribblers were plentiful, out gallivanting instead of locked up in their garrets doing battle with their muses. They yakked more about writing than actually getting down to it. Evie had to face facts. A Mordecai Richler wasn't about to board her bus at the corner of Sherbrooke and King Edward. She was forced to lower her sights a few notches and settle for a reader.

Back when she still lived with her parents, Evie was stuck taking the 105, your classic loser bus. The NDG line didn't proffer up many male readers of the type she was on the prowl for, its ridership split between the geriatric and the pubescent, missing out on the vast middle range that constituted Evie's target demographic. Sure, there was some reading going on. It wasn't a totally illiterate bus route. The retirees scanned their supermarket flyers and the Villa girls highlighted their school notes so relentlessly that barely a word escaped untinted. The odd time Evie did spy a prospect on the 105 with a novel cracked open, she always managed to find him deficient in some readerly way. Evie had zero tolerance for the slow, deliberate readers, the ones who moved their heads back and forth across the page as if they were nibbling an ear of corn at the company picnic. Ditto the lip synchers and the finger followers. She stacked them like cordwood on her reject pile across the garden-variety type drip who wore his bus pass on a string around his neck like a schoolboy sent off to day camp by mummy.

But things looked up at Decarie when she transferred to the 24. Now that was a far superior bus for her purposes, a bus that by rights should have been drawn by a plumed horse. Its pince-nez route cut straight through turreted Westmount, past the townlet's lawn bowling club, its cenotaph, and its two silenced cannons that in their glory days used to honour Queen Victoria with a birthday fusillade. From Westmount the bus trundled back into Montreal proper, letting off passengers in front of the Ritz and the Musée des Beaux-Arts before it reached the turnaround at the centre of town where its nosebag of oats was refilled. You could always count on someone riding the stately old 24 to be reading a newspaper with small dense print, one of those castrato newspapers that had cut loose any meaningful sports section. Usually it was *Le Devoir*, a serious-minded daily whose motto *libre de penser* translated freely into *the importance of being earnest*, but the pink-tinged pages of the *Financial Times* had their own set of adherents. Why had the London publishers chosen that sickish salmonella colour to begin with, Evie wondered, out of all the possible swatches presented to them? Was it some remnant of wartime rationing? Evie's mind bustled happily along once she boarded the 24, her synapses sizzling, roused from their 105 induced stupor.

So varied was the collection of reading matter on this, the Bloomsbury of city buses, that Evie might just as well have been sitting in the main hall of the city library. She took in the stapled journal offprints, the conference proceedings, and the slick artsy mags with the avidity of an industrial shredder. And all those scholarly monographs with their conga line subtitles, subtitles so rambling and word heavy that the poor little colons could scarcely bear their weight. If invited, Evie would have graciously stepped in to lend them a hand. The reading men of the 24 were either pinstriped for the downtown office towers or backpacked and crepe-soled for the faculty offices at McGill. Both categories were brimming with potential and Evie scrutinized them boldly. Her eyeballs glommed onto the likely candidates like a pair of RCMP high beams.

The gentlemen commuters on Evie's routes couldn't help but feel themselves passing through her full-body scanner. Their antennae sensed her sitting at the controls with her clipboard, tsk-tsking over their IQs, slamming their literary fetishes, and disparaging the over-abundance of lint hiding out in their belly buttons. Who was this tootsie to be judge and jury? At the terminus cafe the fellows got together over espressos and cooked up a little counter-audit of their own. All the evidence, though circumstantial, was stacked against her. In Evie they observed a young woman so vacuous that she couldn't even rouse herself to open up a copy of *Métro,* the free rag foisted on all passengers as they boarded the bus, and it was front-to-back pictures anyway. Nor, they noticed, did she bother to occupy herself with any of the other normal commuter pastimes like sudoku or crosswords. Even the dunderhead circle-the-letters game seemed beyond her ken. She wasn't on her cell, which translated to them as friendless, and the absence of an iPod signalled a totally flat EKG. The alarm should have been sounding and the ER nurses tearing in with the paddles. When you came right down to it, Evie was the solitary person on the bus not involved in some extra-vehicular activity. Even the driver was texting.

Evie counterattacked by trying at least to look like an intello. Her glasses, though non-corrective, were horn-rimmedly serious Sartrean spectacles. The canvas bag she slung over her shoulder bore the abstruse slogan of a scholarly conference Josh had attended in London. He'd been too pressed that trip even to stop at the airport gift shop to pick his sister up some of the Heathrow kitsch she'd put in for, so he handed over the conferee's tote bag as a sop. It now formed a permanent component of Evie's I-am-egghead-hear-me-roar getup. Her asymmetrical haircut was meant to convey serious but with flair, a split-level attempt to signal come hither to the poets while not spooking the academics. Maybe it had been a mistake. She feared that it might come off as indecisive. Or maybe not. She did what little she could under imperfect circumstances.

She was in a word profession now, a paying one, although it had taken her a while to find her niche. At first Evie'd gone the fiction road, inspired by movies like *My Brilliant Career.* It all seemed so simple up there on the big screen at the AMC. The heroine, inevitably a beleaguered nanny, feels the urge to try her hand at writing, a clear displacement tactic to hold her back from drowning the hellions in her charge like a redundant litter of kittens. She pens her opus at night by the light of a penny candle, wraps the sole extant copy in butcher paper and twine, and entrusts her precious cargo to a leaky mail packet for delivery to the publishing house of her choice. Bingo! Next thing she knows, it's in print. True, there do intervene a few obligatory scenes of faux narrative tension where our authoress hangs over the front gate, scanning the horizon for the postman, but essentially no potholes rut the path between the creative process and the Kindle. This storyline didn't in any way reflect Evie's own novelistic efforts. The rubber band that girded her bundle of rejection letters had snapped in resentment over the excessive territory she expected it to span. It was only a rubber band after all, not the equator.

Next up she tried studying law, suckered in by the prospect of all that Latin. *Ad hominem, ipse dixit, mens rea,* you'd need a tongue mounted on ball bearings to get through the working day. Perfect. But it didn't take her long to discover that her law school colleagues didn't get off on the ablative absolute. Their lingua franca turned out not to be Latin but Gelt. She dropped out of McGill's Faculty of Law, the bruised victim of an occupational fling gone sour. Evie was getting desperate. How many word professions were there left to try now that the tweeters had shat on capitalization and beat up on spelling like it was a drunk in the gutter?

Journalism came to her rescue. Armed with her freshly minted MFA, Evie was hired to work the graveyard shift at the *Gazette*, a designation that referred not to her hours but her position. She researched obituaries for celebrities not yet dead, and then wrote up the notices when they croaked shortly after. Newbie that she was, they didn't yet trust her to pen the bigwig obits, the Deborah Kerrs and the Claude Levi-Strausses. Not even the major Canadian obits. Evie was assigned the mid-level deaths, like the Saskatoon scientist who'd invented the hinge that allowed the Canadarm to extend and flex so it could pick the Shuttle's nose out in space; the person at one remove from celebrity, or maybe two or three.

Evie's editors had a system. They didn't have her start in on any biographical research speculatively, simply on the basis of a luminary's advanced age. Most fossils were nowhere near ready to kick off, running on the fuel of ancient grievances that wasn't about to dry up any time soon. Malcontents hung on forever. No, usually the higher-ups in her wing of cubicles, those paparazzi of doom, relied on a network of sniffer dogs to scent out notables who were in extremis, wherever on the age spectrum they happened to be parked. Her bosses' record was spot on. Once they gave Evie the green light to begin the legwork on a prospect, he keeled over obligingly within weeks. She felt like the Angel of Death, but hey, it paid the bills. The *Gazette* gig allowed her to move out of her parents' basement flat, freeing her from domestic bondage.

Okay, so maybe she was exaggerating just a tad. Her parents didn't ask all that much of her. It's not like they made her earn her keep by mucking the leaves out of the eavestroughs or flipping the mattresses. In fact, chore-wise, her contribution to the household was minimal. The real rub with this living arrangement was that her mum and dad clung like dog hair.

Helicopter parenting was the fashionable new name for the phenomenon, but why not call a spade a spade, Evie thought. It was Jewish parents who had trowelled the concept out of the grudging soil of their old-country gardens when their right-thinking gentile neighbours spurned it as a weed; Jewish parents who had spiced it and flavoured it over generations of shtetl cooking fires; Jewish parents who had distilled it and casked it, elevating it to its current state of perfection, until finally the sociologists, casting frantically about for an untapped area of scholarly inquiry seized it for their own, spaying the Yiddishkeit out of it and proclaiming its universality.

Evie's first apartment after she left home had been a disaster. So frequently did her parents drop by unannounced to check up on her that she should by rights have stuck them for half the rent. She'd chosen the spot strategically, settling deep in the bowels of a French Canadian quartier, way the hell out in the east end, a neighbourhood as remote and forbidding to her mother and father as the far side of the moon. But she'd miscalculated the extent and power of the umbilical lasso. Turns out her mother hadn't the least trouble parallel parking her Beemer SUV outside Evie's Québécois working-class digs.

The experience was instructive at least. When her lease on the dump was up, she combed every corner of Montreal to scope out the perfect building, one where her parents would feel so viscerally repelled they would never dare to pop in, lodgings that to them were so odious, so redolent of menace that her privacy would be assured forevermore. It took months of assiduous scouting until Evie hit pay dirt, a pert condo in one of the converted convents scattered around town. Too pricy maybe, but the hole in her wallet would rebound in time. There were hundreds of condofied church properties out there to choose from now that so many parishes had gone bust, former presbyteries, chapels, even cathedrals divvied up into trendy housing units. Any one of those rockpiles of religious patrimony might have done the trick, but Evie was taking no chances this time around. She opted for the structure that had been renovated with the lightest hand. Its ex-choirboy architect had taken care not to mess with the arched windows, the vaulted ceilings or the monastic corridors. He'd even preserved the chute in the convent's front wall that had allowed generations of unwed mothers to discreetly unload their newborns like an overdue novel in a library book drop. In short, he'd kept all the papal *chazzerei* that lent the ecclesiastical real estate its special *je ne sais quoi*, deconsecrated or no. It was the kayo Evie'd been striving for.

To look at them, you'd figure her parents were sophisticated, enlightened even. But she knew that if you scratched the surface of their tanning-bed biceps, it released their inner peasant who resided just beneath the skin like the Borrowers under the floorboards. Evie's mother and father were suckled on ancient taboos and superstitions. An instinctive fear of other religions and their voodoo rituals coursed through their bloodstream, doing the breaststroke alongside the globs of cholesterol. Her parents' unease in houses of worship outside the fold was acute and debilitating. Mere proximity to spires, domes, or cupolas could unleash the transmogrifying effect they'd described to her time and again in an effort to justify their blatant unecumenicalism.

First, her mother would feel a faint psoriasis itch in her scalp, right up top. Next thing she knew, a pair of horns would periscope up from her curls. A few minutes later, she experienced the feathery tickle that preceded a sneeze, and then boom, the historic curve of her rhinoplastied shnoz reasserted itself, arcing like a dolphin on re-entry. Her father's symptoms were necessarily different, the nibbled-off baguette of his shlong rising up and announcing *Heb* as if with a bullhorn. And it wasn't just the brick and mortar of cathedral or mosque that tripped the wire. Exposure to just about anything that reeked of foreign-ness, of otherness was liable to kick-start their Bruce Banner metamorphosis. Even a simple curry harboured within its tidal pool of sauce, specimen yellow, the microbial cocktail that could knock their DNA temporarily out of whack. Better to steer clear; that was their motto. Evie was safe now, impervious, cloaked in her clerical lead blanket that carried a lifetime guarantee, proud of the originality that graced her solution.

Except that it wasn't so original after all. Evie's convent-condo neighbours, a youngish crowd, all claimed to have chosen the building on the strength of its heritage architecture. Publicly, they spun their new address as a safe-ish first dalliance with the residential real estate market, but in almost every case the decision to live in a nun's cell with en suite amounted to some sort of settling of accounts parent-wise. It had more spit-in-your-eye payback than any tactic they'd tried before; more than the *keffiyah* they wore home on Rosh Hashanah, the *shiksa* they dangled in front of *bubbe,* the threat of an uncircumcised *shmeckel* on their future sons, or, God forbid, vocational school. It was the master-*zetz*. Evie fit right in.

Chapter 2

"SHOOT THE TOFU *kreplach* down this way, Evie. Would you please?"

"Okay, but only if you'll send the *cholent* back over here in exchange, *s'il te plaît*."

"Mosh, slice me off another piece of your challah. It's to die for."

"I tried the kamut this time. You don't find it too heavy?"

"No, very airy. Just right."

"It's a bit resistant to braiding, though. It keeps wanting to come unsprung." Moshe glowered at his challah as if faced with a brassy teenaged daughter challenging his parental authority. The challah's cleavage had come out more daring than he'd ever intended, exposing altogether too much virginal white between the sun-tanned mounds. With every loaf of bread he shaped, Moshe felt a Jean Valjean bond.

"I'll have to fiddle with the recipe. Or maybe I'll just go back to the spelt, like I used last week. Now that's an obedient dough. Once you separate it into ropes, you can do anything you want with it."

"Try it out sometime instead of those handcuffs you keep by your bed, why don't you?"

"Comedian. But you know the plaited rope shape is interesting, not strictly Jewish in origin at all. It goes back to…"

"Spare us your baker-shpiel for once Moshe. Have a heart." Normand took the floor. "In the beginning, there was…"

"YEAST." The assembly responded in perfect unison under his baton.

"It fermented and burbled and grew until it created the world. The earth as we know it is nothing but a giant pumpernickel."

"You laugh," Moshe broke in, honour bound to defend the dignity of the brotherhood of bakers against those who would mock, "but carbon-dated samples prove that flatbreads existed in Neolithic times."

"Yeah, we know, we know. An archaeologist dug up the remains of an ancient matzo from the site of a caveman seder."

"And he bit off a corner and it tasted just like fresh."

It all started out as a loosey-goosey Friday night potluck, an anarchic agglomeration of baguettes, spaghetti, uninspired potato salads, and cakes, store-bought; a dinner so over-starched all it was missing was a cummerbund and black tie. Evie, as hostess, took in the gaps nutritional and embarked on a personal mission to see to it that the offerings were fleshed out. She masterminded an assignment roster, and thanks to her manoeuvring the meal pulled up its socks. Now she could count on her guests from the building arriving at her door every Friday bearing on white Ikea porcelain their most audacious culinary experiments; dishes that pegged every chamber of the Canadian Food Pyramid.

It was meant to be an end of the week wind-down. That was the genesis. The fact that it was on Shabbos a mere quirk of the calendar, of no significance to the minyan of young Jews gathered round the table. But somehow, over time, the menu took a turn. The Friday night schmaltz herring of their childhood morphed into sushi, the chicken soup segued into miso, and the brisket transubstantiated into seitan. Their intention had been to set out a secular meal, one with no tip of the hat to their common heritage, but some things just can't be forced. The overall effect of a sabbath spread was too glaring to deny, so instead they ran with it, revelling in the messy signals sent out by what came to be known as their Anti-Shabbos meal.

Dr. Spock could probably have explained the schizoid need of these twenty and thirty-somethings to simultaneously repudiate their parents and emulate them, a development that should have manifested itself back when they were thirteen years old. Such a tight cluster of late-onset cases was surely one for the textbooks, but in the end, what did it matter? Here they were, settled cozily into their ex-nunnery with rules and rituals of their own devising, the Anatevka farm team on the banks of the Saint Lawrence.

"Evie, you're hogging the roast kasha. Nobody at our end of the table has even seen it up close, let alone had a chance to taste it."

"If you're plugged up, nothing beats kasha," Dizzy pointed out with authority. "An hour after eating it and everything will shoot right out of you like cannon balls." Dizzy was blessed. She had a knack for documenting a food's healing properties in such a way that removed all desire to consume it.

"Hel-lo, did you happen to notice we're eating here? Enough with the scatological talk if you don't mind," Evie said. "I'm trying to run a classy establishment here."

"A salon she thinks this is. Like she's Mme. de Staël."

"Or Oprah."

"Just a little decorum is all I'm asking. Is that so hard? I swear sometimes you vulgarians are too much to put up with."

"Excuse me O Ms. Defender of the English Language, but don't you mean to say 'you vulgarians are too much up with which to put?'"

"Remind me again, would you, why I open my door to you lowlifes every week?"

It was a while before they noticed him standing by the table. "I knocked but no one answered. The door was open so I took the liberty of coming in. This package got dropped through the slot at my place by mistake. I thought it might be important so I brought it up. I'm sorry to have barged in. I didn't realize you had a party going on."

He was a small man, trimly turned out, of an age difficult to pin down, somewhere on that sliding scale of decline between their fathers and grandfathers. His scalp, with a light cinnamon shake of liver spots, had managed to extrude a spindly ponytail of the type favoured by older men hoping to flash the signal that if their follicles were still in working order, by implication so was all their other equipment.

Everyone round the table recognized the intruder, though if pressed, none would have been able to attach a name to the face. He lived in the ground floor apartment that looked out over the street. His front door was just inside the complex's main entryway. The unit he called home was the dinkiest in the joint; that they all knew. In the days not so long past when they were staking out their respective spots in the about-to-open complex, the realtor had placed the double-rolled blueprints on her bima and unscrolled them for her clients to peruse. They uniformly pooh-poohed unit 101A, and why not? It was no more than a glorified pencil case. Back in its holy days it had probably been the domain of the convent doorkeeper. By positioning that flat should have devolved to the condo's concierge, but Mme. Côté put up an almighty flap over its beggarly dimensions and jockeyed the developer into roomier, though less practically situated quarters down the corridor. Eventually the poor little rebuffed apartment found its soulmate in the gentleman now standing tableside, holding out a parcel. He never spoke much, just a simple *bonjour* in passing. His speech to Evie represented the longest string of words any of them had ever heard emerge from his mouth.

Evie stood up and relieved him of the box. "Thank you so much for the special delivery. I'm sorry to have been a nuisance. I'm Evie Troy, like the box label says." They shook hands. "And it's not a party actually, just a little get-together we have every Friday night for some of us in the building." She belatedly remembered her manners. "Please sit down. Join us."

"No, no, I don't want to disturb. I'll leave you to your company. *Au revoir*. It was nice meeting you."

"Wait, I insist. You're more than welcome. Really. It's no trouble, and there's plenty of food to go around as you can see." She swept her arm over a table so chock-a-block with platters that every shift required a Rubik's Cube remanipulation of the entire array. She yelled over her shoulder, "ManU, go get another folding chair out of the bedroom, would you please? Dany, Judy, scootch down and make room for Monsieur...?"

"Médéry. Jean-Gabriel Médéry."

"No kidding. That's an easy name to remember. Ever meet your namesake?"

"We move in different circles."

"Well, you're in our circle now." Evie set the empty chair beside her own place and gently pulled her conscript down to occupy it. She gave Jean-Gabriel a guided tour of the table, matching every dish up with its contributor by way of introduction.

"Over here we have kugel, Désirée's specialty."

"Kugel?"

"Noodle pudding." Dizzy deconstructed her casserole for the gringo's edification. "It's non-dairy. If that's important to you I mean, and gluten free too. Certified."

"They certify such things?" he asked her.

"Absolutely, there's a governing body."

"*Tiens*, who would have thought?"

"Here's a challah, baked by our own Moshe over there." Moshe wiggled his fingers in greeting. "He's a professional baker, at the Fromentier over on Laurier."

"Apprentice." Moshe clarified. These gradations mattered to him. Only once his master-baker's diploma was conferred upon him would he allow himself to be addressed with the unqualified title. Let lowly interns refer to themselves as Dr.; let sessional lecturers sign off as Professor; Moshe refused to take the liberty pre-sheepskin. His principles forbade it. One had to respect the dignity of the appellation.

"Over there is tempeh brisket, Emmanuel's signature dish, spicy though, so watch out. It packs a real kick. ManU, take a bow. Then there's seitan chopped liver, from Zach in the corner, my arugula salad, and Diane's faux prune chicken."

"Faux prunes or faux chicken?"

"It's the chicken. Soya."

"So you're all vegetarian." Jean-Gabriel drew the natural conclusion.

"No, actually, we're not, at least not all of us, although I guess it does look that way," Evie said. "See, it all started out as a least common denominator potluck. Very egalitarian."

"It was Evie's brainchild," Judy informed their visitor.

"One of her wackier innovations," Dany chipped in, "and that's saying something."

"Thanks for that, you." Evie turned back to the newcomer and read the puzzlement behind his gaze. Clearly he was trying to figure out exactly where in the taxonomy of smorgasbords their aberrant salad bar ought logically to be classed. She undertook to explain the rules of the game. "See, Judy wouldn't eat meat, so we eliminated it from the menu, sliced it right off the top. Zach has a thing about fish, the result of some childhood malentendu with an overbony piece of smoked sable, so we axed that too, in deference to him."

"And then nuts were verboten on account of Evie." Normand added.

"You're allergic, then."

"No, although I might as well be. My father runs a nut-free catering firm. Sannoix. Maybe you've heard of it? He supplies Air Canada with guaranteed nutless snacks for all their flights. The only carrier in the country to take the pledge and he snagged the contract. It turned him into a fanatic. My mother too. For them, the prohibition against nuts was total and it didn't stop at the plant. Even at our house it was considered sacrilege to serve any. If either of us kids had ever asked for a peanut butter and jelly sandwich for lunch they would have taken it like a knife to the heart. To them nuts were the enemy. They had to be kept out at all costs. Like polio germs. Anyway, it turned me into a lifelong nut-o-phobe." Evie kept to herself all the other assorted phobes she'd picked up growing up in the bosom of that family; it was still early days.

She shrugged her shoulders at the familial alimentary quirk and resumed her explanation. "Dizzy eats nothing but organic. For Diane it's no mushrooms. Shira there's a vegan. Her we just toss a banana once in a while. But you get the picture. All those exclusions for this one and that one practically brought us down to bread and water. It wasn't exactly what you'd call festive. So we worked our way back up the food chain with dishes that most of us would eat."

"No meat or poultry, though." Dizzy, who ran a natural foods store on St. Viateur provided this emendation. "There's a level beneath which we won't sink."

A pause ensued while their visitor checked out the groaning board. "I don't eat anything that's green," Jean-Gabriel volunteered, suddenly feeling a kinship, however stretched, with his building's young stable of quasi-herbivores.

"All right. A food grudge. This we like." Evie grabbed a plate and piled it high with every entrée that lacked chlorophyll, and set it before her new acquaintance who dug right in.

Evie settled herself into her cubicle Monday morning and checked her inbox for the day's assignment of stiffs. Uninspiring as usual, a washed-up Expos player and a Liberal Party bag man. A light day. She checked their names against the newspaper's database for previous coverage and collated the high points of their lukewarm careers. After only two hours at the keyboard she'd compacted their lives into the veal pens of her assigned word limits and it wasn't even lunch time.

On spec, Evie entered *Médéry, Jean-Gabriel* into the online archive and her monitor rewarded her with a flood of hits. She limited the results to articles with photos, and pulled up a shot from the mid-seventies. The image was fuzzy when she magnified it to two hundred percent but even pixelated she could make out her sly Friday night guest. His hair had redeployed itself in the intervening years. Back then he was blessed with blanket coverage, although the sideburns and nape did carry more than their fair share of the load as the tufted times demanded. Evie patted herself on the back for her hunch. It was rare that she landed one. Jean-Gabriel Médéry, the playwright who had *le tout Québec* fawning at his feet ever since his first play hit the boards was living the Clark Kent life on the first floor of her building.

There were far too many article snippets crowding her screen to read in one sitting, so Evie picked her way through the laundry list of headlines, soaking up a detail here and there. Médéry's plays, she discovered, had gone on to be staged worldwide, garnering raves from all the top critics. Evie even faintly recollected having read one in high school, but in the way of most required reading, the content was flushed from her memory's holding tank the minute she handed in her exam. Now she cursed her teenaged bubbleheadedness. The time had come for more in-depth research so the obituarist, determined to wring all she could out of the last few minutes of her working morning, dumped her piddly locavore search engine and invoked the cosmic crawling power of her old pal Google to flesh out the picture.

"Evie, over here." Audrée from the news desk had snagged their favourite table in the staff cafeteria, the one right beside the microwave. While Evie unwrapped her sandwich, Audrée was lining up her plastic containers matrioshka style, as usual. She popped their lids and then inserted them one by one to be heated in a declension of courses from hors d'oeuvres through to dessert. Evie waited till Audrée had completed the ritualized emptying of her lunch bag before she started in.

"You'll never believe it. I had dealings with someone famous who's not dead. Or dying even."

"Ooh, that's a change for you, Our Lady of the Corpse. Who was it?"

"Three guesses."

"Evie, have mercy. I came straight here from a two-hour meeting with your bossman Aaron. I'm in no mood for games after that. I just want to shoot myself. Unless you want me to end up being the next death notice you're assigned to write up, you better tell me. Who?"

"Well, normally I wouldn't let you off the hook that easy, but seeing as how you were with Aaron, I'll cut you a break. But you owe me one."

"Fine, fine, whatever you say. So spill, who did you meet?"

"None other than the playwright Jean-Gabriel Médéry, if you please."

This would be a first for Evie. It was nearly impossible to surprise Audrée who could scoop anyone in the building with her hands tied behind her back. Her sources were impeccable, devoted, and they were early risers. Somehow, though, Evie's announcement backfired, and the surprise was all on her side of the table.

"That shmuck royale. How did you get roped into meeting him?"

"He lives downstairs in my building. And may I correct you? He's actually a really nice guy."

"Evie, you are pathetic. Just because a guy earns his living with a pen, it doesn't exonerate him if he committed crimes against humanity. Well maybe it does for you. You're a special case. But it shouldn't. The way he humiliated his wife by giving that play her name. He stripped her bare on stage. The whole world knew the intimacy of their marriage, all their private angst. She was so much younger than he was, so innocent. She trusted the bum. And now you're trusting him. That's what these guys do with younger women. It's pathological."

"Look, I'm just giving him the benefit of the doubt. I do know him personally after all. I'm sure he made the whole storyline up."

"It wasn't fiction, Evie. It was the truth. He abused his relationship with that child-wife of his to squeeze out material for a play when he hit a dry spell. I don't know how she was able to show her face in public after that. It was pretty graphic."

"And how is it that you know so much, smarty? I'm the one who's been researching him all morning. Nothing that sordid came up in anything I looked at."

"Makes sense to me. That angle wouldn't have been reported in the mainstream sources. And the Internet barely existed back then, as far as smut mongering went anyway. In those horse and buggy days, if a big name shoplifted or took drugs or hung out in men's rooms, it all ran more underground. It wasn't in your face like it is today. Your friend M. Médéry was lucky enough to have slipped in his indiscretions before the cut-off."

"That doesn't answer my question. If it was all so secretive, how do you happen to be such an expert on all of it?"

"I read the tabloids at the time, *chérie*. You were still a kid."

"And this is what you're basing your opinion on? The supermarket checkout?"

"It was common knowledge, Evie. You would have had to be brain-dead to miss it. I'm telling you, it's like knowing about gravity. A fact. Arrogant prick. And to think he raked in the bucks with that play. There's no justice in the world." Her upper lip curled back as if the spring roll she'd just chomped into had gone mouldy.

"I don't care. I refuse to judge him by what other people say, only by how he behaves towards me, and to me he's great." Evie couldn't help but champion her neighbour. This was her typical stance. Once you had the good fortune to be sucked up into Evie's orbit, her backing was absolute. You benefited from her full protection in a till-death-do-us-part relationship.

With her proclivities she could have temped as a presidential bodyguard.

"You've got it wrong, I'm telling you," Evie continued. "The Jean-Gabriel I met could never have dragged anyone through the mud like that, least of all his own wife. He's simply not capable of it."

"You've know him for what? Two days? And you're already prepared to vouch for his character? Evie, listen to yourself."

"The length of time doesn't matter. His voice was sincere."

"His voice." Audrée's tone was flat with disbelief at the extent of her younger friend's credulousness.

"You know what I mean. His demeanour. He was very up front. Very open." Evie did experience a minor twinge while conducting this defence of her dinner guest considering that he had chosen to conceal his true identity from the Anti-Shabbosites, but she decided that he was entitled to his privacy.

Audrée stuck her arms out to her sides Nixon-style. "I'm not a shmuck, I'm not a shmuck."

"Enough. Enough already. I give up. If I can't change your mind, maybe he can. I invited him back to join us this Friday night. You're welcome to come over and meet him if you want."

"No thanks. That's a pleasure I can easily do without. Trust me on this one, Granny. You don't go ahead and invite the wolf into your house. That's not how the game is played."

In a rerun of the previous week, Jean-Gabriel showed up after all the others and with his hands full. He'd cooked for the occasion. He passed Evie a foil pan whose mashed contents seemed to have carroty antecedents. "I made it as empty of ingredients as I could," he said. "I figured I couldn't lose that way. But just in case it doesn't meet your stringent standards, I brought this to pick up the slack." He held out a bottle of Bordeaux of a vintage that seldom washed down their budget-conscious meals. While his hostess struggled to find an opening on the gridlocked table, Jean-Gabriel joined the others in the living room where Moshe was pouring *apéros*. Was it his imagination or had the chatter halted with his arrival? Maybe he'd only broken bread with his younger neighbours once but he felt that he'd accurately taken their measure. If you expected to get a word in with this crowd, you had to spot your chink from across the ice and go for it. Any lulls in their rapid-fire conversations were rare, and a four-beat rest like this one probably stood unrecorded in the annals of the group.

Evie's guest's discomfiture was her own doing, though wholly unintended, an infelicitous by-product of her loquaciousness. It happened to her sometimes. Secrets she'd had every intention of safeguarding just cut loose in public like an impudent fart. All she could do on those occasions was hope that everyone who heard it would do her the courtesy of ignoring it and move on. This wasn't her night.

Before Jean-Gabriel arrived fashionably late, her regulars had trickled in with their platters and salad bowls. As usual, they headed directly to the dining room to unload them along with their weekly accumulation of gripes and gossip. Caught up in the slipstream of all their disclosures, Evie blurted out the hidden identity of their co-lodger. And once she'd gone and blown his cover, there didn't seem to be much point in holding back on the gory details, so she passed along the dirt she'd picked up from the rumour mill at the newspaper. All of them had heard of Jean-Gabriel Médéry. His name was inscribed on the peewee scroll of Quebecers who'd made it big in the outside world, though he ranked considerably lower on the fandom scale than Céline or Rocket Richard. Still, JGM, as he was known compactly in the province, was a heavyweight. Ph.D. candidates were already busy complexifying his oeuvre to satisfy the exigencies of their dissertation advisors, and translators were reworking his jangly Québécois into Georgian and Cantonese.

The revelations had her friends buzzing. The guy must have royalties pouring in up the wazoo, so what was he doing living in the merest *pupik* of an apartment? They ran the numbers. His budget had to be loft-worthy. He could easily afford the type of lavish accommodations in the Plateau or Old Montreal that they all coveted. And the wife. Now that was an interesting wrinkle. None of them had seen any evidence of one. If she was an ex, maybe she was soaking him but good. That explanation had several backers as it tidily tied up the loose ends. But she could just as well have been dead. Or maybe he kept her locked up somewhere à la Mr. Rochester if even half the hearsay were true. It was all just too juicy but they would never be able to ask him outright. The deference that they failed to show to their parents came out in their treatment of others of that generation. They were well brought up, all in all.

Jean-Gabriel sniffed the texture of the silence. It bore the familiar orchid scent of his wife's perfume. For all that his works had been jury prized, anthologized, and canonized, it all boiled down to one subject when a new crowd latched onto his name. Amélie.

The Friday night *habitués* and Jean-Gabriel regarded each other, gossips and gossipee too close for comfort. On the youthful side of the room, no one looked prepared to dispel the hush. It wasn't that Evie's company was unwilling, but they were untrained in the specialized shake-up skills an impasse of this degree of delicacy demanded. JGM on the other hand, by virtue of his age and profession, was possessed of the appropriate bag of tricks. Turning a room around was for him old hat so he cranked himself into gear, accepting the responsibility that had parachuted itself into his lap. He bowed deeply to his audience, a swashbuckling reverence. The breeze from his invisible cape was strong enough to ruffle their hair. Jean-Gabriel was pleased with the quality of his dip. Lately his sacroiliac resented sudden flourishes. When he drew himself back up, he seemed to have grown several inches before their very eyes.

"Allow me to introduce myself. *Monsieur Amélie Médéry à votre service*." He spaced the words out for maximal punch. Decades had passed since his acting days, decades since he discovered that his true talent lay behind the scenes, but he hadn't lost his timing. His accomplished delivery ventilated Evie's flat, allowing the easy atmosphere of the previous Friday night to reassert itself. The elephant was still in the room, no mistake, but he'd decided to take a brief nap on the cushion in the corner. No one so much as broached the very topic that was on all of their minds until they were digesting over tea and dessert.

"I saw the play on TV one night when I was babysitting," said Dizzy. "On Radio-Canada, I think. It would have been in the late nineties I figure. Does that sound right?"

"*Oui*, that production wasn't half bad, with Guylaine Leblanc as Amélie."

"What was your wife's name, if I'm not being too nosy." Dizzy asked him.

"Amélie."

"No, her real name I mean."

"Amélie. I liked the resonance and she was flattered by the homage."

"She was quite young when you married, wasn't she?" Evie asked in what she hoped came off as an unassuming way. "Weren't you already in your forties?" At work during the past week, on days when the deaths spaced themselves out accommodatingly, Evie profited from the downtime to do some extra-curricular fact checking. She was trying to calculate the couple's creepy factor. Josh had taught her the formula. He was a whiz on pop culture benchmarks. Half the man's age (presuming he was older) plus seven. That sum represented the cut-off beneath which any self-respecting male dare not descend. In olden days, before they'd mathematized the expression, it used to be called robbing the cradle. By Evie's calculations, the Médéry couple was in creepy territory in hip boots. When they married, Jean-Gabriel told them, not vexed in the least by Evie's inquiry, he was forty-eight, Amélie barely seventeen.

"To meet her, though, you never would have guessed she was seventeen."

Here they all leaned in over the table, expecting some amplification. They weren't prurient by nature, but when a complimentary x-rated movie came with the motel room, who ever said no? Seventeen was a Lolita-ish number, a number not long out of its training bra, a number that when faced off against the number forty-eight thrummed with possibilities, but JGM's inner thespian, roused from hibernation by his earlier impromptu performance in the living room, cut short the curtain calls and left the house wanting more. That's the way it was done.

And Evie did want more. It wasn't that she disapproved of Jean-Gabriel's May-December *affaire de coeur*, or February-December more like; she wasn't a prude, but she was curious, yes. Here she finally held captive at her own table a living breathing writer after her many fruitless years on the prowl for such a creature, and just when things were getting educational, he turned off the tap. So much for her entrée into the inner world of the artsy type. In her younger days, Evie's author reveries used to zero in on the writerly process, the creator locked in holy communion with his typewriter; a full steam ahead qwerty blitz from page one to the finish, but meeting Jean-Gabriel had loosened up the blinkers of her fantasies. Now her mind tinkered with altered scenarios knowing that even the busiest of authorial hands still found plenty of free time to venture away from the keyboard into messier, fleshier terrain than the word. This was the terrain she was suddenly eager to plumb.

Dany didn't pick up that the conversational trajectory had taken a veer. He'd been focusing all his attention on the rugelach. They really were very good. Evie's best yet. Last time she made them she'd been too chintzy with the chocolate filling but these were pleasantly plump. Only after he'd chased down every last crumb with his thumb did he lift his head from his plate and tune back in. He decided to thank his hostess for her pastry efforts by plucking out the question that was foremost on her mind and asking it on her behalf. It would be his bread and butter gift for the night. He turned to Jean-Gabriel who was deeply immersed in a discussion with ManU over the condo board's deranged decision to renew their shiftless snow removal contractor, Invisible Silvano.

"So your play *Amélie*. I was wondering," Dany interrupted. "There's a lot of hearsay floating around about its roots, let's say. You get where I'm headed. Whether it really is a work of fiction like you claimed it to be when it was staged at first. Or not. The story goes that you lifted it from your own life."

Evie showed no appreciation that Dany had expropriated her private musings and hung them out on the line, stomping on his foot under the table for his loutish presumption. But Jean-Gabriel looked serene.

"Sure I lifted it," he said. "Let's face it. I have no imagination."

The table hooted at his ironic confession. They all knew his shoulder dipped like Brezhnev's under the weight of all the medals that recognized his literary sleight of hand; the GG, the Order of Canada, the *prix de* this and the *prix de* that. Tarted up in formal attire he could match the Queen troy ounce for troy ounce.

The verdict was in. The Anti-Shabbosites came to the conclusion that their downstairs neighbour was an allrightnik. They let drop their Tribal body armour and welcomed him unreservedly into their gang.

Chapter 3

"DID YOU READ THE LABELS?" Marilyn asked.

"Yeah, Mum. Don't you think I've figured out how to check the ingredients by now? No nuts. Trust me." Evie handed over the packaged goodies she'd brought and Marilyn accepted them with the tips of her fingers. Her mother whisked them off to the kitchen to scrutinize the fine print as if a rogue cashew in Evie's trail mix could put the family at risk of anaphylactic shock. Even though the proscription against nuts in her household was strictly pro forma, the Troy matriarch had developed EpiPen reflexes over the years.

Her father's welcome was less managerial. "Hi Evie doll." His smack on the cheek was wet and warm as usual and Evie returned it in kind.

"Come on down to the rec room. We're just setting everything up. Joshie's here already."

It was the one night of the year they still gathered round the table, albeit a coffee table, in what passed for familial harmony. The Oscars drew the Troys, movie buffs all, out of their respective corners where every other event on the calendar fizzled. Anniversaries and birthdays couldn't manage to lure the kids back to the homestead, and as for the Jewish holidays, even a John Deere didn't have that level of tow-power. The Academy Awards alone could tempt Evie and Josh to fritter away an entire evening under the parental roof. It didn't hurt that Jake and Marilyn had invested in a sumo TV to sweeten the pot, under no illusions as to the night's main attraction.

Evie and her brother had reason to be on their best behaviour. This visit was the tradeoff that allowed them to snub the family for the rest of the year with relative impunity and they were determined to be agreeable, for all that their cheek muscles cried out for mercy. The siblings had even shown up early, in time for all the pre-game shlock they despised, to score a few suck-up points with their mother who was a red carpet aficionado.

Apparently Evie's snacks passed muster. They had now found their way into one of the serving bowls that Marilyn was shuttling up and down the stairs. She shouted out to her husband over the railing, "Jake. Go ahead. Don't wait for me. Serve them martinis. Kids, look what your dad learned how to do." Josh and Evie were taken by surprise. Outside a celebratory *shnepsl* now and again at a bris or a wedding, their parents didn't know from social drinking. Normally the only liquids on tap at home were Diet Coke or Ginger Ale, but Marilyn had recently won a stylish martini set as a door prize and was determined to do it justice. Jake agitated the new cocktail shaker like he'd taken a cue from the Maytag churning away in the adjoining laundry room, throwing his whole body into it. "Just like James Bond," he said. "In honour of the night." Josh begged off in consideration of the drive home and Evie followed his lead, but their mother and father imbibed happily, slugging back the kids' portions so that nothing would go to waste. In the no-no hierarchy of the Troy household, going-to-waste nearly topped the charts, bested only and forever by nutmeats.

"So, Evie, what's new and exciting by you?" her father asked. "Life treating you right?"

Since this was a night that called for generosity of spirit, Evie tossed a couple of loonies into the *pushke* her father held out to her. It was a non-movie offering that she thought would grab her parents, a vaguely personal disclosure that would leave them feeling like she'd indulged them with an intimate glimpse into her private life but would deflect any further questions; a terminal tidbit as she viewed it.

"Guess who it turns out lives in my building?" She left a theatrical pause that no one present felt moved to fill. "Jean-Gabriel Médéry no less."

"Whoa, he's pretty major," said Josh.

"Isn't he the shmuck who wrote that play about his wife, a real tell-all?" said Marilyn. "I remember it. A sort of Québécois *Who's Afraid of Virginia Woolf*. Didn't we go see it at the Centaur, Jake?"

"He ravaged the poor kid in it all right," said Evie's dad, shaking his head.

Evie hadn't realized until now that the epithet *shmuck* was screwed onto her neighbour's backside like a vanity plate. First Audrée and then her mother; what was it about that particular noun that resonated with women of a certain age when the subject of Jean-Gabriel Médéry hit the fan? Maybe it was because they'd mastered algebra back in an era when the study of math was a more serious business than in today's lackadaisical classrooms. They had both been drilled that in order to balance an equation that had Jean-Gabriel's name on one side of the equal sign, only that single honorific could stand on the other. Though this was a night for blind obedience, a night where she had willed herself to choke back every retort, Evie bit.

"For your information, he happens to be great. I had him over for dinner even. Everybody who was there loved him, a real raconteur."

"So he's still alive," Josh marvelled. Evie's brother was a big fan of the party game *Is He Canadian or Is He Dead?* Here was a factoid he could stash away for future use.

"Apparently, if he ate at my table. And he happened to be a perfect gentleman I might add."

"Well, why not? At his age," said Marilyn. "He must have been effectively neutered by all the crap he picked up off the ten thousand women he slept with on the side. Why that girl put up with him for as long as she did I'll never understand. She probably had nowhere else to go. Back in his prime, I bet you anything, he was festering with STDs."

"Mum, please."

"What? I'm not inventing his reputation. Everybody knew. I'm surprised he still has a tooth in his head."

"You're wrong about him, Mum. It was all malicious gossip, tabloid stuff."

"Who told you it wasn't so? The man himself?" Evie's mother had a good nose. "I thought you're supposed to be a journalist? Don't you do your research? It looks more like you go right to the source and ask him to tell you the truth, and then you fall for it like a ton of bricks. A reporter she thinks she is."

"I do trust him," Evie said, straining to keep a lid on, "just like I would any friend of mine. I take him at his word."

"Evie, it's guys like him who couldn't keep it in their pants who forced me to shlep across the country in the back of a pick-up truck."

Uh-oh, here it comes, thought Evie. She glanced over to Josh for some brotherly support in what was about to go down but his eyes were shooting death rays at his sister.

The overdose of martinis had Marilyn sufficiently lubed that she would have required only the slightest tap to set her careering down the slope of her favourite subject, and here Evie'd gone and whacked her one on the back. They were in for it now.

"I was barely twenty when we started off from Vancouver. Still wet behind the ears. Three thousand miles we covered. And three thousand miles meant something back then when the roads stank. Across snow-capped mountains, under the stars."

Oy. She was waxing poetic. They were in for the uncut version.

"More than two weeks it took us. And it's not like we were travelling in comfort. We didn't have an RV with its own jacuzzi and kitchen like they do today. Oh no! We made our pit stops at gas stations and if there wasn't one handy when we had to go we just squatted behind the nearest bush. Some mornings, for special, we wrapped our sandwiches in foil and stuck them on top of the engine to melt the cheese while we drove.

"Cooking, we called that. I was the youngest and since I didn't have a driver's license I wound up bouncing around on the truck bed most of the way like a bale of hay. Talk about black and blue. The others, they split themselves up between the cab of the truck, Arlene's convertible, a beauty it was, lemon yellow, and the Volkswagen bus, one of those hippie jobs.

"We were just a few at the beginning, only seventeen of us, but by the time we reached Ottawa for the protest there were more than a thousand women on Parliament Hill. You couldn't see the grass when you looked down we were packed so tight."

Marilyn's Abortion Caravan days were the highlight of her life, a blip in the otherwise invariable yenta stations of the cross. Her involvement in the cause didn't arise from any personal imperative as was so often the case; it's not like her vents had ever needed to be professionally vacuumed. A freak encounter with a true believer transformed Marilyn, in the space of just a few hours, into a hardcore member of the movement. She talked the talk and she walked the walk. No man was ever going to dictate to her what she could or couldn't do with her own uterus.

Evie and Josh were a straight-laced pair of kids. They found their mother's activist past embarrassing. What children want to hear a parent rant about placentas and fetuses in mixed company? It used to be that when Marilyn started to rev up, they tried their best to distract her. Evie and her brother would drop to their hands and knees, one behind the other, in their juvenile rendition of a caravan; more of a wagon train, really. Their references were strictly North American. They clip-clopped across the living room like a pair of pack donkeys out on the trail following Dusty and Lefty to the next watering hole. But they were too old for that now. Nor could they count on their father to cut Marilyn off. It was his habit to let his wife unreel.

Tonight, though, God was in his heaven. The red carpet chose that moment to wash across the screen in a vast scarlet hemorrhage, distracting their mother from her organ recital. Josh and Evie took great pains to participate animatedly in the Oscar proceedings hoping their stream of jabber would keep her safely off track, and in this they succeeded until they said their goodbyes. Marilyn understood that she was being handled but she played along. The same martinis that had initially loosened her tongue ended up diluting her scrappiness so she shelved her abortion monologue to placate the *kinder*. The topic never failed to bring out hives in her hypersensitive offspring. But later that night while she was drifting off to sleep, she treated herself to remembering how it all began. It must have been some lingering effect of the Oscars that had the *Marilyn Henkin Troy* story unroll behind her closed eyelids as if it were in Cinemascope.

Marilyn, April 1970

The camera panned across the frontage of Abie's Knitterie. At Abie's, like all the shops on the Main, the concept of window-dressing was at a primitive stage in its development as an art form. Essentially it amounted to cramming the window with as much stock as humanly possible. Needles, crochet hooks, skeins of wool, pattern books, ball winders, stitch holders, gauges; all were jumbled together, pressing against the glass, blocking the sun. The gentleman store owners treated their window displays like they did their marriages, as life-long arrangements. Oh, they fussed over them a bit at the beginning, adjusting this, prodding that, but then they just left them be, allowing a stratum of dust to settle on the entire business. This was the way of things on St. Lawrence Boulevard. Abie's neighbour Saul, who owned a kitchen goods emporium, was a fellow graduate of the pile high and deep school, as was Julie Levine of the eponymous Levine's Custom Table Pads. Down at Schwartz's, bloody smoked briskets were mounded for sidewalk viewing in a knacker's cart arrangement. Quantity and entropy were the guiding decorative principles up and down Montreal's premier shopping artery.

Inside the dim shop, Marilyn was sitting behind the cash, her nose buried in a textbook, allowing her father to sneak off for the quickie snoozola he fancied before supper. Abie had no compunctions about leaving Marilyn in complete charge of the Knitterie once her afternoon classes at McGill were over. It was the quietest time of day. His establishment, frequented almost exclusively by housewives, tended to be at its busiest earlier, while the children were locked up in school. Besides, his little Marilyn had grown up in the business. She knew the stock backwards and forwards, and her needlework was flawless. Marilyn's *bubbe* had observed the infant's agile fingers in the cradle and took it upon herself to tutor her in the woollen arts. Abie was duly proud of his daughter's talents in the knitting department. That girl could cast off like Ahab. He'd set her to work in the store back when she still needed to stand on the Yellow Pages to see over the counter, and she'd put in a few hours each week ever since to earn herself some pocket money.

The chime on the door jingled and a tall form filled the door. The woman who came in wasn't one of her father's regulars, most of whom she could i.d. by now. This customer strode purposefully up to Marilyn without even bothering to burrow in the twenty-percent-off bins. "Hello," she said. "I wonder if you could give me a little advice."

"No problem, I'm sure we can help you out." Marilyn adopted the royal *we* at work. To her ears it made her sound more sophisticated.

"I have a pattern here, and I'm new to knitting." The clerk plastered her face with her I'm-so-interested mask, but realistically, just how much enthusiasm could she summon up for what was sure to be the zillionth ho-hum beginner's scarf she'd end up having to nurse along since her father had drafted her into his service.

"And what are we planning on making?"

"A uterus."

"I beg your pardon?" Marilyn figured she'd misheard.

"A uterus, you know," and she pointed at the sales clerk's nether parts. She passed a pattern across the counter for Marilyn to examine. It was a carbon copy, not the usual half-page torn out of a *Chatelaine* magazine. The sketch that accompanied the typed instructions on a separate sheet was hand drawn, but accomplished, and struck Marilyn as anatomically correct based on her hazy recollections of grade seven phys. ed. where they'd covered the reproductive systems of both sexes at warp speed. The pattern's illustration even included the ovaries as a pair of perky pompoms stitched onto the uterine extremities, like the dangle balls on a court jester's hat.

"If you don't mind my asking, why would you need to knit such a thing?" Marilyn had trouble pronouncing so very personal a word aloud. "How exactly would you, you know, wear it?"

"It's not meant to be worn. It's a symbol in the struggle for women's rights."

Marilyn's eyes widened. It was clear to the customer that this guileless girl was missing the drift, and she took it upon herself to educate the innocence out of her. A bit of tough love never hurt.

"Don't you know what's going on in the world? Don't you ever read the papers?"

Of course Marilyn knew that newspapers existed and foggily intuited their purpose. Her mother lined the Pesach cupboards with them, and spread them out to protect the kitchen linoleum when she scrubbed out the oven with Easy-Off, but it had never actually occurred to Marilyn to read one.

"Are you aware, missy, that in this day and age women in Canada do not have free and open access to abortions?"

Marilyn, of course, was unaware. *Abortion* was another of those prickly words that was never spoken in her circle. It had those wash-your-mouth-out-with-soap vibrations. She shook her head in the negative.

"Do you have any idea of the number of hoops that women in this country have to jump through in order to get a safe hospital abortion?" Marilyn's blank face revealed her quasi-total hoop ignorance. Her customer bowled on.

"These women are already in a bad way, right? Here they are pregnant, desperate, and on top of that they have to grovel in front of hospital abortion committees made up mostly of men, natch. And I'm talking about the ones who even get that far. What about all those mixed-up kids who don't know the system even exists? Some system. The process is so public. It's so degrading, so long and drawn out, that thousands of them still end up in back alleys or try to do it themselves."

Marilyn was vaguely cognizant of that other furtive purpose of the knitting needle and felt a brief cramp of guilt, though she had never, to her knowledge, sold an implement to be used to such ends, but then how could she be sure? Had she ever been indirectly complicit in the criminal application of a knitting needle? Had an object that left her hands at Abie's eventually led to the mutilation or even death of some poor woman? Suddenly she felt like Mme. Defarge.

"Those TACs aren't worth shit." Marilyn's customer was wound up now.

"TACs?" Marilyn ventured to ask, her first peep since the conversation swerved away from her comfort zone of the garter stitch.

"Therapeutic Abortion Committees. TACs. Like I was just telling you about." For Marilyn's benefit she backed up a bit. "According to the Criminal Code, section 2-5-1 to be exact, women can have an abortion in hospital if their life or their health is in danger."

"And that's not good?" Marilyn was emboldened enough

to question. This section 251 thing sounded positive from where she stood.

"Aha, the catch is that women have to appear before a committee to judge if they are entitled to the procedure or not."

"The TAC."

"You got it. The whole TAC system is rotten on so many levels, I don't even know where to start. First, you have to find yourself a doctor willing to take your case up with the committee. Never an easy business. Then, assuming you do find one, in lots of hospitals the committees are stacked with members from the anti-side so it's all a dead end anyway. You're just spinning your wheels. And of course not all hospitals even have the committees. What's a woman supposed to do who lives in PEI where the closest accredited hospital might as well be on Mars? And could the committees move any slooow-er? These so-called experts, they're even dim on the biology. They deliberate as if gestation took fifteen months. By the time they get around to rendering a decision the poor woman's on to number two.

"You like stats? Try these out for size. You know how many women we figure die each year in Canada from hack abortions?" Marilyn didn't volunteer a number. The question had a rhetorical ring to it. "Two thousand women. Two *thou*-sand. And you know how many women in BC who applied to the committee succeeded in getting their abortions approved? One stinkin' solitary percent. And those women were all middle class, married. Classic. And listen to this if you can stomach it. There are estimates out there that every year 100,000 women go through an under-the-table abortion, and out of them 20,000 land in a hospital bed anyway with complications. Permanent ones some of them. Horrible. Raging infections. Infertility. Didn't they suffer enough already?

"The government and their damn TACs. Who the hell are the guys on those committees to decide anyway? What gives those obstructionists with penises the right to determine which women should be allowed to have an abortion and which shouldn't. And let's be honest. They're the ones who knocked them up in the first place. It's not like we're talking about virgin births here. Pack of hypocrites.

"I belong to a group," she said, "that believes women should have complete say, complete control over their own bodies."

This simple statement struck a chord with Marilyn. No one had the right to forbid her from doing something to her own body if she so desired. She remembered with rancour how her father had refused permission for her to pierce her ears when she was younger. It wasn't just a case of tight-assed parenting as she had thought at the time. She now saw it for what it was, a human rights violation.

"It's our goal to wipe section 251 off the books. And we're damn well gonna do it."

Marilyn eyeballed the pattern a second time. She plucked a pair of jumbo demo needles out of the bin beside her, found a half-ball of variegated afghan wool and set to work. In no time at all her customer could see the womb taking shape. This girl might be a bit of an airhead, but she was as proficient with needles as any heroine addict. She continued talking while Marilyn knit; she knit as if there were no tomorrow. "We're planning a protest in Ottawa." She could sense Marilyn's ears pricking up. Ottawa wasn't that far away, three hours max by Voyageur. "But we're starting out from Vancouver. That's where I'm from. I'm only here in Montreal for a few days, doing some advance work. I'm flying back home tonight. Do you think you can give me a quick lesson before I take off?"

"I can do better than that," she said. And Marilyn, who until that moment had been the very model of filial obedience, reached into the till and cleared it of the week's takings. Surely it was enough to cover her plane ticket to Vancouver and then some. She hesitated at the door as if she were entertaining second thoughts and then walked back into the store. She ducked behind the counter and from the second shelf down pulled out some extra large shopping bags imprinted with her father's beloved logo, *Abie's Knitterie*, written out in looping stitches using a simple knit one purl two repeat. Marilyn stuffed them with enough needles and skeins of heavy worsted to supply a regiment preparing for training exercises in the high arctic. The two weightier bags she carried herself. The other two she presented to her liege, bobbing her head slightly. This time when Marilyn reached the door she flipped the sign to *closed*, locked up as usual, and dropped her keys through the mail slot, the mantle of her future to assume.

Chapter 4

IT WAS A DOUBLE WHAMMY TONIGHT. Shabbos and the first Passover seder duking it out on the same cramped calendar square. Evie had taken the day off work to prepare for the extravaganza. Any ingrates who had the gall to die today and expect a prompt write-up would just have to lump it. They could loll around in the cooler drawer a few extra days. It wouldn't kill them. She'd check out their toe tags first thing Monday.

The Anti-Shabbos regulars were all in attendance. For most of them this was their first seder as *séparatistes*, the first one where they would lead the charge in the total absence of the elder generation. They discounted Jean-Gabriel, of course, whom Evie had included on the strength of his position as the group's Shabbos Goy Honoris Causa. Since he was totally ignorant of the proceedings he didn't really enter into the generational tally, not being in a position to correct their halting Hebrew or to grab their Haggadahs and flip showily forward through the pages to get them in sync with the speed readers who were already on page sixteen while they were busy faking it on page eight. For this seder no parent would shoo them off to the card table diaspora, refugees from the hard-core end of the table. At Evie's topsy-turvy seder, it was the young people who owned the night.

As kids they'd cursed the cosmic forces that connived every few years to plunk one of the seders down on Friday night, extending what was already an interminable and soporific affair with all the dreaded parentheticals, but tonight the crowd was pumped. They all arrived dressed to the nines, decked out in second-hand hot couture culled from the racks of the *friperies* on Saint Denis Street.

Evie'd been in the kitchen since breakfast. She had every burner on the go. Eggs and potatoes and carrots were boiling, and the broth was burbling impatiently away, wondering when she'd ever get around to dumping in its payload of matzo balls. Despite the light spring snow falling outside, she had the window cracked open for air. Dizzy was on hand to help with the prep, and Josh, ambassador plenipotentiary of the larger Troy clan, had presented his credentials at ten a.m. as head kibitzer and dogsbody. They worked flat out all day.

By the time Dany arrived at six-thirty the condo was already buzzing with guests. Evie answered the door to his kick, resplendent in her caftan, her cheeks rouged from the kitchen steam. In honour of the occasion Dany had pillaged his mother's cedar closet for his Bar Mitzvah suit, though why exactly she'd kept it for all these years wasn't quite clear to him. Was she thinking to bury him in it? The jacket was straining dangerously around his spare tire and skimpy at the wrists and shoulders, but was spiffed up with a new-to-him bow tie and pocket square. "The pants, they didn't fit at all any more. I couldn't squeeze into them to save my life," he explained, accounting for the Black Watch kilt he wore on the bottom, making him look like a cross between Woody Allen and Prince Philip. "I had to make some last minute adjustments to the ensemble. What do you think?" He twirled around to show off the pleats to best advantage and Evie applauded her approval.

"Maybe tonight I'll finally learn the secret of what's cooking under a kilt."

"That all depends on how much of a *shikker* I make of myself. Hold that thought." Dany handed over to his hostess two eight-packs of matzos and a plastic container of horseradish, homemade. "You should empty it out into a serving dish right now," he cautioned her. "It's starting to gnaw its way through the Tupperware."

"Beep-beep. Coming through." Moshe arrived on Dany's tail and kneed his neighbour into the apartment from the hallway where he was still doing pirouettes.

"So they were out of tutus, Dany?"

"They don't come in extra-large for some reason."

Moshe was balancing an epic sponge cake in his arms. Evie directed him to set the monster down on her bed. Her counters were already *Pesadik* packed, and besides, she didn't have any other surfaces vast enough to accommodate its girth. Even when he baked at home, Moshe worked in industrial quantities. With his experience and training, he found it easier to bake for nine hundred than for nine. And he was equipped for it. Moshe had visions of opening his own establishment some day and was gradually acquiring pre-owned professional cookware as it came on the market at a reasonable price. Moshe's cake moulds could sub for backyard kiddie pools, and as for his mixing bowls, in a pinch NASA could borrow one to stand in for a faulty satellite dish. His knee-high whisk and metal rolling pin surpassed the posted height limits on his kitchen cupboards so they took up residence in the living room, leaning against the wall by the fireplace like a pair of Betty Crocker andirons. By the looks of his place Moshe might have been the personal chef to Gargantua and Pantagruel.

The baker's sponge cake technique was flawless. Evie'd seen Moshe in action earlier in the day when she stopped by his apartment to pick up the cases of wine she'd stored there. He whipped his egg whites by hand. Though he owned a turbo-charged mixer, he spurned it for this particular task. Nothing beat a copper bowl, he told Evie while he worked. Copper. She didn't get it. But now wasn't the time to sidetrack Moshe with a discussion of the periodic table; he was in the zone. How, she wondered, could the same element both soothe arthritis and make egg whites stand up and salute? It was one of those ditsy substances whose alchemical properties spun off in twenty different directions. Like baking soda. She'd never understood how you could cook with it, douche with it, and scrub the scuzz off the shower door with it. Chemistry wasn't Evie's strong suit.

Moshe's rotations with the whisk were cyclonic, his arm whizzing round like the propeller on a Piper Cub. He kept his eyes fixed on the mounting foam. At the precise second he adjudged it at the perfect soft-peak stage, Moshe folded the cumulus fluff into his beaten yolks with a spatula that had previously seen action as an oar on a Viking ship. He downloaded the batter into a tube pan and slipped it into the pre-heated oven. This finished cake he now set down tenderly on Evie's white duvet. With its trail of strawberry coulis that edged the platter, it lay on her bed like a deflowered bride.

Back in her kitchen, Evie peered despairingly into the depths of her soup pot. Moshe's food channel demo cum science experiment proved to her that plain old air could metamorphose into helium if manipulated by an expert, which she clearly was not. She realized too late that she should have imposed on him, the Académie Culinaire alum, to take on the matzo balls for the soup, a task she'd arrogated to herself. Maybe the problem was that her pictureless cookbook advised its readers to make walnut-sized balls, a designation of which her mind had no grasp, considering her history. Instead she'd given them the circumference of a portly falafel, thinking to use an alternate food touchstone. As she spooned the balls into the soup they nosedived to the bottom of the pot where they were now wedged shoulder to shoulder like the Andrews sisters. At no stage in the cooking process did they show the least inclination to float to the top as Joan Nathan had assured her they would. No, her disobedient *knaidels* were earthbound. Moshe came into the kitchen and joined her stoveside, looking into the briny deep. They could just make out the skyline of the submerged *knaidels,* as if they were the domes of Atlantis.

"I tried talking to them," she said. "I heard it works with house plants."

"Maybe it was something you said."

"All I did was flatter them. I'm always a sucker for that approach," but apparently Evie's *knaidels* were immune to sweet talk. "Maybe I should have offered them a bribe," she said.

"I've been known to sing to my croissants while they're in the oven." For Evie alone Moshe bared his soul.

"Once you hear me sing tonight, you'll understand why I didn't go that route."

"You know it doesn't matter," Moshe told her. "I'm sure they'll still taste great."

"It does so matter. To me. I guess I'm more my mother's daughter than I like to admit." For her, on Pesach, the single solitary thing that counted was that the *knaidels* should be light and fluffy. It was her measure of success of the whole night. Everything else, the gefilte fish, the *charoses,* it was all just window dressing. I know I should forget all that my mother-myself business for tonight, but it just won't let go."

"Personally, I've always preferred the *al dente* version."

"No you don't."

"I kid you not, the zaftig ones that you could really sink your teeth into. There are other people out there who think like me, I'm sure. You just grew up in the wrong house."

"Don't I know it."

"Evie, come on, you don't have to think your mum's always hovering out there in the ether somewhere, disapproving. You've made something of yourself. There's no reason for you to be cowering in her shadow anymore. Leesen to Herr Doktor Moshe. He knows vot he's talking about."

"Mosh, I appreciate your trying, but you didn't live through it so you can't know what it was like. You can't even imagine. I'm telling you, not one thing I ever did was satisfactory.

Nothing. *Nada*. She was always looking down on me." She pointed into her soup pot. "This is only a symptom."

"It's not a symptom. It's just a *knaidel*."

"Same difference."

"Evie, you're the hostess with the mostess. You know we all think that. The Friday nights at your place are legendary."

"That's just because you guys have such low standards."

"Give us a little credit for taste why don't you? None of us could do what you do."

"Yeah," Evie came back. "Because I'm the only one out of all of us whose table has two leaves." She could be resourceful when she was wallowing. Evie was slipping into the quicksand of another mother-funk. Moshe had seen it before. He knew the drill. Though generally string-beanish in build, his arms, after years of carting about flour sacks, had acquired the respectable silhouette of a snake that had swallowed its charmer. They had the requisite strength to come to Evie's rescue. Moshe locked onto her flailing hands and wrested her from the matriarchal ooze with a satisfying *thwunk*. Usually the sound alone was enough to snap her out of it, restoring her to her more confident self.

The front doorbell rang. "Come on," he said. "Leave all this to simmer. You don't want to keep whoever it is waiting in the hall." Moshe started out the kitchen door thinking a restored Evie was on his heels, but when he glanced back she was still glued to the soup pot, her posture limp with failure. He caught her giving her eyes a surreptitious dab with her sleeve. They looked to be producing supplementary salt water to the amount required for the ceremonial seder dipping. Moshe returned to her side at the stove.

"Take it from a chief cook and bottle washer. It'll work out. Guaranteed." Moshe reached behind her and dared to encircle her shoulders with his arm, gentling her out of the kitchen where the bogeys of mothers and matzo balls feared to tread.

It was Jean-Gabriel at the door, his face barely visible behind a spray of peacock feathers. "I talked to one of my friends who pretends to know about such things and he said that feathers are one of the symbols you use for *la Pâque juive*. Maybe these will come in handy."

The offering didn't impress Moshe. It looked to him like JGM had nicked the clump of plumage from Montezuma's corpse, but he took note that Evie accepted the iridescent bouquet with a degree of syrupy gratitude most women reserve for roses, not bird pluckings. Evie fanned herself demurely with her chichi feather duster like she'd just stepped off the boat from Titipu. She was too gracious to point out that Jean-Gabriel had signed on with a bunko ethnicity counsellor, one with *farshtunkeneh* expertise on the lifestyle and habitat of the Chosen People. His friend had completely mangled the timing. The feather was meant to be deployed in advance of the Passover seder to flick from the kitchen cupboards any last defiling remnants of bread, not that Evie even subscribed to that medieval practice. She was a modern gal, of the J-cloth school. But for her it was the thought that counted. She latched on to Jean-Gabriel's hand and escorted him into the living room. Except for Josh, the writer had met them all before. They were used to his anglepoise posture, a davening stance that made him look as if he were considering with utmost seriousness everything they had to say. Though normally he mixed easily, tonight he allowed himself to be steered by Evie from one cluster of guests to the next.

Rightly or wrongly, Moshe had the sensation of being third-wheeled and peeled off from Evie and Jean-Gabriel towards the more welcoming embrace of the kitchen. He poked his nose into all the pots, then jiggled and stirred them with chefly *savoir-faire*. Only the soup pot failed to respond to his ministrations. Evie's slacker *knaidels* didn't snap-to under his toque of authority. Desperate measures were called for. He reached into his baker's bag of tricks for a bit of restorative botox and injected the traitorous matzo balls. In no time flat they puffed up and rose to the surface of the soup where they bounced about joyfully like boobs unbound at a Côte d'Azur beach. His job was done. He went back out to join the others.

At dusk Evie invited her guests to take their seats even though technically it was too early to get the show on the road. Seders were scripted to commence at dark, but the disobliging sun was taking its own sweet time in setting, or so it seemed to the first-timer Passover hostess. She was too antsy to hang on until the sanctioned hour so she called the seder to order while a few delinquent rays of light were still filtering through the curtains. Jean-Gabriel she placed at her right hand, while the others found their own spots, sticking for the most part to their usual Friday night positions around the table. For Haggadahs, Evie had finally settled, after considerable existential angst, on the unshowy version from her youth with its red, black, and yellow cover, Hebrew and English on opposing pages. They sold it shrink-wrapped by the dozen. She had never really appreciated back when she was younger, or cared when you came right down to it, how all the lines were numbered lest a hesitant Hebrew reader lose his way. But now, with a mature eye, she was duly thankful for the public service rendered by the marginal numbers. They were like matzo crumbs cast by Hansel and Gretel in the desert. With their friendly guidance wanderers could always find their way back to civilization.

At first Evie had figured on buying some sort of nouvelle vague Haggadah while she was browsing through the racks at Rodal's; one of those anarchist, animist, modernist, humanist, liberationist, bundist, cubist, out-there versions. What she sought was a non-discriminatory Haggadah, one that could speak to Jews of all orientations, locales, colours, and shoe sizes; a world music version of the exodus from Egypt. But when push came to shove she'd cleaved to her roots. She surprised herself by rejecting the Haggadahs that cast modern villains in Pharaoh's stead or moved the whole kit and caboodle plumb out of the desert. Even the all-English versions, though practical in so many ways, offended her sensibilities as a Quebecer where bilingualism was its own religion. Her decision appeared to be a popular one, allowing her to untense a bit. As she passed the booklets out, her guests lit up to see the cozy familiar cover from their childhood, the *Goodnight Moon* of Haggadahs.

"It's like your little black dress," Shira said. "Never goes out of style."

"And they're fresh out of the package. Not even stained."

"At our house, we each had a different Haggadah, with different translations and different page numbers. What a mess. Nobody ever knew where they were. It probably added a good hour to the whole business."

Jean-Gabriel opened up his Haggadah from the back end and riffled through it. "My mother always taught us not to read at the table."

"Well tonight you can feel free to disobey her. I'm sure you never crossed her before, good little boy that you were," Evie said.

"I was a model child. It was only later that I turned sour. Once I was out of the house. That's what comes of hanging out in bad company."

Evie reached over and flipped him to the front of the Haggadah. He stared at the serifed letters with their subterranean Morse code of dots and dashes. "I was up North once. They were putting on one of my plays there. The writing in here looks to me just like Inuktitut."

"Unless I'm very much mistaken," Evie said, "that's Hebrew. Shall we begin?"

Evie cast one final look over the table to ensure that everything was in place. Her glance lingered lovingly on her silver seder plate, inherited from her *bubbe*. It was of the type with indentations, one for each of the night's symbolic foods. She didn't want to leave any of the little hollows empty, it would ruin the effect, but she ran into a roadblock when it came to the roasted shank bone.

The bone was mere eye candy on the seder plate, a representation of the pre-Exodus paschal sacrifice. It wasn't meant to be chawed on. But its mere fleshy presence risked offending Evie's abstainer guests, so she tried to come up with an effective skeletal surrogate. Evie rooted around in her kitchen junk-drawer for inspiration. She tried out and rejected a freezer marker, a chopstick, and an Allen wrench. In the end, she went the literal route and bought a doggie chew toy, a rubber bone that mimicked the object she was after. At the store it had looked just right, but now that her proxy sat on the plate, it somehow looked more like a dildo. She hoped the resemblance was all in her mind.

After a few false starts, they fell into an easy rhythm. Those linguists among them who could manage the *aleph-bet* read off their cluster of lines slowly and clearly, and then the next person round the table recited the corresponding English translation. It went off so seamlessly that Evie's non-Hebrew-speaking guests were visited by the same illusion that they experienced while watching a Bergman movie with subtitles; they felt like they could actually understand the Swedish. There was a bit of a kafuffle, though, when they reached the Four Questions.

"Okay, so who's youngest?" Dizzy asked.

"I'm safely out of that competition, *grâce à dieu*," said Jean-Gabriel, holding up his hands palms forward in a leave-me-out-of-this gesture.

"Does it have to be a guy or can a woman do it?" Judy demanded to know, but she wasn't sure to whom she should address her question since they had decided at the outset to do away with the *master of the house*, a phallic piece of Haggadah phraseology that rankled many in attendance. It did mean, however, that the seder was rudderless.

"I've never had a chance to do it," Moshe piped up. "I was always on the high end of the age scale at our seders. What do you say I give it a try?"

"Ooh, an actual volunteer for the *fir kashes*. A historical first."

"Take it away Mosh."

"*Andale, andale* baby."

They gratefully left the field open to their resident baker who never so much as glanced down at the page. The notes wafted from Moshe's lips in a masterful, resonant baritone that sucked the residual side-chatter right out of his tablemates. The chant was familiar to all of them save one, the notes etched onto one of their brain's dustier wax cylinders since it only plopped down into playing position two days a year. Never had the melody sounded so stately. In their collective memory it was sung shakily, often under protest, by the youngest boychik in their respective families. Not that it didn't have its own childlike charm, but Moshe's rendition was cantorial. It peaked, it dipped, it paused with utter assurance. The silence when he finished clung to the table. Jean-Gabriel broke the spell by clapping, a slow, rhythmic ovation. The seder neophyte sensed it was a *faux pas;* he wasn't at the Met, but after that virtuoso performance, he couldn't hold himself back. And once he set the ball rolling, the rest of the crew joined in, plumping out the applause with bravos and the assorted whoops, whistles, and blats that they normally trotted out for the Habs. Josh, in the next seat over from the blushing Moshe, rescued the soloist from the spotlight by rushing in to deliver an English translation so dry and unleavened they all booed.

On all other fronts, Jean-Gabriel had excellent guest instincts. He recited from the Haggadah with a depth of expression the others lacked, bringing to the fore all his acting gifts. But since he couldn't participate fully in the proceedings, Hebrew-challenged as he was, he took it upon himself to be in charge of the wine. He was determined to hold up his end. Once the ritual splish-splashing for the plagues was over, he kept everyone's goblet brimming, pouring as if he were paid by the glass. ManU tried to explain to Jean-Gabriel that the amount of wine consumed during a seder was dictated by the Haggadah, limited to only two glassfuls before the meal, but such oenophilic parsimony on a festive occasion was a difficult concept for Jean-Gabriel to absorb and he unconsciously continued to pour wine whenever he spotted a needy glass. Not wanting to insult the outsider in their midst, the courteous *Yidn* at Evie's table gave in to his topping off tendencies. Besides, Evie had invested in a few superior cases of Passover wine at the SAQ. No cough syrup tonight. This wine knocked back so smoothly that even the level in Eliahu's cup seemed to go down as the night went on.

As early as *Dayenu*, the crowd was well and truly tanked. Dizzy attempted to decode for the benefit of Jean-Gabriel the significance of the song. "The refrain, *dayenu*, translates into *it would have been enough for us*. It's meant to thank God for all the different things He's done for the Jews since, well, since forever. So like even if He had only brought us out of Egypt and then dumped us like a hot potato, *it would have been enough for us*. Even if He had only divided the sea for us to scram dryshod and never done us any other fancy tricks from up in his lifeguard chair, *it would have been enough for us*. Even if he only had given us manna to nosh on in the desert and never served us any other tapas again, *it would have been enough for us*. *Dayenu*. Get it? You'll pick up the tune soon enough. It goes on forever. It's a song for slow learners. So when it comes time for *day-day-enu*, join right in, okay?" The seder singers gave it all they had. In Evie's dining room that night the lusty *dayenus* caromed off the walls and shot up to the belfry of the convent chapel where they gave the defrocked bells a playful *potch*.

The festival meal came around before anyone even had the chance to hanker for it, a first for all the expats at Evie's table who were into the printed proceedings as they never had been at their own family seders. Normally the Passover meal hunkered out there in the eternal distance like the horizon. Its refusal to come any closer had an edge to it, the same pissy recalcitrance of a tax refund. You knew it was scheduled to arrive sometime in your life span, but deep down you didn't believe it.

Evie disappeared into the kitchen and came out with her tureen. "Pesach food, the mother of all oxymorons," she announced in a pre-emptive effort to dis her own contribution, but her matzo ball soup was hailed by all present as a triumph. The remaining courses were rolled out to similar acclaim since everyone's taste buds had already booked off on their annual Passover cruise to the Caribbean. And so it came to pass that despite the absence of almost any redeeming ingredients, despite the double deprivation of leaven and meat, Evie's seder meal was toasted as the best they'd ever eaten.

Though there were no kids in attendance, Evie hid the *afikoman* all the same. Why, she decided, should she chuck the sole element of the seder that she had genuinely enjoyed when she was growing up? At the appointed time, she declared the whole apartment fair game and her guests bounded out of their seats to search for the concealed scrap of matzo as if they were contestants in a hot musical chairs competition. Moshe made a beeline for Evie's bedroom to check it out more thoroughly than he had when he'd deposited his cake. He'd had a snootful thanks to Jean-Gabriel's ministrations or he wouldn't have had the nerve to go back in there, even if it was a wholly legitimate opportunity to do a little undercover work.

While they did live in the same building, Evie's social life was a mystery to Moshe. Beyond Friday nights, their paths seldom crossed, Moshe's baker's schedule at odds with Evie's more traditional business hours. He wasn't privy to her night-time comings and goings and so hadn't been able to determine if she was attached or not. Besides, his past history had shown him to be weak in picking up the signs. He could have just asked her out to settle the whole matter, but he was one of those guys who had to work his way up to that, and he was a slow worker-upper. First he liked to be assured that the coast was clear. This was because Moshe was also a slow bouncer-backer.

Once shot down, howsoever kindly, clawing his way back to vertical was a lengthy proposition.

He found himself all alone in his chosen neck of the woods. Everyone else was focusing on the living room which was more traditional *afikoman* turf. He worked quickly, scanning the surfaces for the obvious; birth control pills, Trojan boxes, telltale photos. Zilch. Moshe restrained himself from opening bureau drawers or reaching into the pockets of Evie's robe, a silky kimono affair that was hanging from a hook on the back of the closet door. Fuzzy he might have been, but his technique was still smooth, gleaned from Philip Marlowe. Surely Evie would disapprove of his affinity for pulp, inherited from his father. He couldn't help it if his reading preferences were down in the banana boat while Evie's floated past on Cleopatra's barge. Actually both parents influenced his sleuthing approach. "Touch with your eyes," little Moshe's mother used to repeat when she pushed his stroller through the aisles at Cumberland Drug and his fingers reached out towards every shiny trinket. "Touch with your eyes." Little did she suspect way back then that she was training her cherub for a career in boudoir reconnaissance.

Moshe was trying to draw coherent conclusions from the disparate array of tchotchkes on Evie's dresser when Jean-Gabriel wandered into the room. The two men faced each other across the bed. Moshe felt possessive of the territory, but for all he knew, Jean-Gabriel was more intimately acquainted with the surroundings. The playwright was new to *afikoman* searching and felt none of Moshe's hesitation or *délicatesse*. He didn't understand that a hunt for matzo wasn't conducted like prison guards tossing a cell. He patted down Evie's pillows and prowled around under her mattress with an outstretched arm. If not for the cake inconsiderately anchoring down the blankets he would probably have stripped the bed clear down to the springs. When he came up empty, Jean-Gabriel moved on to the closet. Its closed door didn't give off the same out-of-bounds signals to him as it had to Moshe and he flung it wide open. He stood with his hands on his hips for a moment to size up the space and determine his plan of action. He started with Evie's shoes, shaking them out in the manner of a jungle old timer wary of scorpions. No matzo revealed itself. He moved on to the shelves next with their purses, albums, and hat boxes filled with who-knows-what, terrain rife with afikominial potential. Moshe, on slo-mo, was gearing up to take him in hand, ready to offer Jean-Gabriel the gentility of an Easter egg hunt as an appropriate analogy when they heard a call from Dizzy out in the living room, "found it" and they had to abandon their search.

"It was behind the dictionary in the bookcase." She held her matzo aloft.

"My mother always hid it behind the couch cushions." Evie said. "I was trying to be original. The bookcases and the hutch were always off limits, too much precious Delft for little hands to break."

"At my house it was the opposite," Shira volunteered. "My mum kept the kids corralled in the dining room. She didn't want them touching her beloved slip covers with horseradishy fingers, God forbid."

Dizzy passed out the pieces of her *afikoman* and they settled themselves back into their seats to nibble while they continued with the ceremony, but everyone jumped up just a few pages later to go open the door for Eliahu.

"What, we have to get up again?" groused Jean-Gabriel who was packed into a corner between Evie and the formidable Dany. Extracting himself was a tricky business.

"For Eliahu."

"Who? I thought it was just us regulars coming. Besides, isn't it kind of late for someone to show up now?"

"The prophet Eliahu. Elijah in English. In French you call him Élie, I think. We have to see if he came to the door. That's his cup of wine there in the middle of the table, the only one tonight that you haven't had to top off." They all angled out of their chairs and trooped to the front door. In deference to her hostess-ship, Evie was the one to open up though she was last getting to the door. They all peered out, but she knew it was unlikely Eliahu would pop by. In all the Pesach tumult she'd forgotten to give him the condo's entry code.

"What's with him?" Moshe wondered aloud. "He never calls, he never writes."

"He got lost maybe."

"What, nobody ever told him about Google maps?"

"Maybe it's because you forgot to put out the milk and cookies," Jean-Gabriel suggested, searching among his own cultural references for a logical explanation as they trailed back to their places. They picked up the Haggadahs they'd left open and face down on the table and resumed the recitative. A goodly chunk of pages beyond Eliahu Dany chanted the blessing over the fourth cup of wine, which was in fact closer to the tenth by Evie's reckoning, but then who was keeping score? She polished off her glass at a gulp, nursing her annual resentment over the prophet's no-show. As a child she always took his absence personally, like somehow the Troy household didn't rate. She deduced that if Eliahu didn't stop at her house, it was because he had preferred someone else's, someone who was kinder, smarter, friendlier, more charitable, more kosher, a more frequent flosser, who knew? There were no guidelines. It was all very murky. Jean-Gabriel was probably right. At least with Santa you knew where you stood. You behaved, he showed. You acted up, he didn't. And if he did plop down the chimney you plied him with food. That last bit sounded very Jewish to Evie. Maybe it was Irving Berlin who invented that *goyishe* custom. It would have been just like him.

Chapter 5

JAKE PASSED HIS WIFE THE STRAWBERRY JAM across the breakfast table. She shmeared enough across her mock Pesach bagel so that her lips wouldn't eject it like a dud DVD. "It would have killed them to come to our seder and spend the night with their family?" Marilyn asked.

"Honey, they want to have their own life. They're adults. Accept it."

"But to miss a seder. In every other house the kids come. You see the license plates parked up and down the street. Ontario, Massachusetts, Florida even. For Pesach the kids come home to their parents. From thousands of miles away they drive. But not our kids. Our kids couldn't even be bothered to cross town." She fumed at the thought. "Joshie would have come if Evie hadn't invited him to her seder. She's a bad influence."

"Mare, Evie's a good girl. She's just having an attack of independence. It'll pass."

"It's an awfully long attack if you ask me."

"You should know."

Jake seldom threw Marilyn's *escapade*, as her mother subsequently dubbed it, in his wife's face. Why would he? He was proud of the pivotal role she had played in the women's movement. Never would he have had the guts to embark on such a crusade in his youth, however worthy the goal. It was Marilyn who had all the balls in their family. Whenever his wife ramped up into Caravan mode and commenced to speechify, Jake listened in awe, as if he were married to Emmeline Pankhurst. But Marilyn did have a tendency to play both sides of the fence. Depending on the circumstances she chose to paint herself as either rebel with a cause or dutiful daughter, and he wasn't about to let her get away with double dipping. Jake knew full well that his wife had missed a family seder in her youth, and it wasn't just to host one herself as Evie had done. Marilyn got the point and backed off.

Marilyn, April 1970

On Pesach of the year of her twentieth birthday, Marilyn was nowhere near a seder table. As close as she could calculate, looking back, she was probably somewhere on the outskirts of Wildrose, Alberta, although to city girl Marilyn it was hard to distinguish the outskirts from the inskirts. Oh what a hoo-hah her parents kicked up when she phoned them from a gas station along the way. It wasn't enough that their daughter had lost her mind and set off on this cockamamie adventure, stealing from her father, skipping town, consorting with strangers (at least they were all women, thank God), but missing Pesach? At that point in the rant Marilyn's pocket conveniently ran out of dimes to feed into the coin slot and the call cut out.

In her mind though, Marilyn saw the Caravan as a Passover celebration of sorts. A re-enactment in a way. What was it after all but a trek through the wilderness, leading women out of slavery? For all Marilyn knew, she and Eliahu had crossed paths that first seder night when he was out doing his rounds of Jewish doorways in the Alberta foothills. She just didn't recognize him in his cowboy hat.

It was only in the fullness of time that this analogy came to Marilyn. Out on the road she was far too busy to give any thought to the Jewish holiday calendar. Whether it was the month of Nissan or the month of Sivan or the month of Brumaire, who knew, who cared?

The roughing-it part Marilyn didn't mind. It all had a summer campish feel to it. She'd been shipped off to a cabin colony in the Townships enough times as a kid to learn all the backwoodsy skills. She could portage a canoe and braid a lanyard with the best of them. But here the curriculum was more eclectic, branching out into fields of study her old camp had never thought to list in its advertising brochure; anatomy, psychology, elocution, celestial navigation, and tire changing, not to mention passive resistance and posting bond.

The new recruit liked to think she knew her way around a campfire. Her repertoire of spooky stories was vast as befitted a summa cum laude graduate of the Vindow Viper Academy, Lake Massawippi campus. But by her fellow Caravanners she was outclassed. They had melted their s'mores over the bonfires of hell. Their blood-drenched stories were more terrifying than hers could ever be because they were true; tales of women scarred, women damaged, women dead after botched coat-hanger abortions, women turfed out by their families and left on their own to take whatever hara-kiri measures were within their reach.

Marilyn couldn't help but wonder what her own parents would do if she were to come home in the family way. The easiest part of the scene for her to visualize was the initial explosion, a blowup of Nagasakian proportions. But after that she was a bit hazy. Would they zip her off to a willing doctor for a quickie scrape-scrape? Would they press her to give birth to the child and then give it up? Or maybe, like so many others before her, she wouldn't have the nerve to confide in them and would take matters into her own know-nothing hands. It was all idle speculation. She was certain the occasion would never arise, but then that's probably what all those thousands of dewy-eyed girls in maternity smocks had thought when they obligingly hiked up their skirts just that once.

Watching the highway unspool before them, Marilyn was at times beset by troubling thoughts. She didn't feel like she held up her end. Not like the other girls. (Oddly, *girls* was their sanctioned nomenclature, reserved strictly for intramural use, the Caravan's favourite in-joke.) Teaching them all to knit struck her as a feeble swap compared to the gritty lessons in life she was accruing in exchange, but the girls persuaded her that her contribution was as crucial as any of the others, and eventually she came to believe it herself.

As an instructor, Marilyn was patient and diligent. The last thing she wanted was for anyone to think her a drag on the operation. Once she'd taught the girls to decipher the kabbalah of symbols that spidered its way across the pages of the pattern books, she kept them tied to a strict practice regimen. Every night after supper, before the sun went down, they pulled out their bags of knitting supplies and picked up where they'd left off on their samplers while she circled behind them on dropped-stitch patrol. By the time Marilyn finished with them, even the most fumble-fingered would know her way around a needle.

They had a deadline, Marilyn knew. They were aiming to reach Ottawa by Mother's Day weekend. But if Marilyn had her druthers, the Caravan would never stop moving. It would keep rolling in place on the treadmill of the Prairies with Ottawa floating mirage-like, just out of reach. She was a smart enough girl, Marilyn was, but her mind was lazy. It hadn't been her habit to tax it too much. She used it mostly to memorize and spew back and then after every bout of rote learning she let it recline in a lawn chair to recover from the effort. Marilyn seldom allowed her curiosity to extend outside the borders of the week's lesson plan. What was the point? She was a solid B+ student. If McGill University in its tweedy wisdom was satisfied with her sluggish efforts, who was she to contradict? But these women electrified her as her withered professors never had. They wouldn't rest until the country was awash with government-sponsored daycares, until women received equal pay for equal work. They wanted a woman to be Prime Minister; they wanted a woman to be President; they wanted a woman to be God. The right to an abortion was only the thin edge of the wedge. These rebels she'd fallen in with had bigger fish to fry in the end. Barrelling down the Trans-Canada, Marilyn's Caravan coaches kept her engaged in non-stop rounds of devil's advocate, and they fully expected her to take them on, guns blazing. Their idea of learning wasn't bracketed or bookended. By virtue of the fact that Marilyn was there sharing their journey, they naturally presumed that she had convictions, ideas, opinions even. They figured she kept abreast of all the craziness that men were unleashing on the world.

Early on, before they were skilled at knitting, the Caravanners took the needles Marilyn had supplied them with and used them to skewer her feeble arguments. At least they weren't wasting the materiel. The first few days you could drive a semi through the holes in her logic, if you could even call it that, but little by little she started to catch on. She listened to every conversation as if her life depended on it. In her mind she served as a stand-in for the girls whose lives really *did* depend on it, those girls out there whom she'd never meet, but who counted on Marilyn being a useful cog in the machine, if only a tiny one, so that when the day came that they needed to be cared for, the system would provide for them on clean sheets.

All along the way women hitched up their wagons, veteran protesters and plebes like herself, swelling their ranks as they pressed forward towards the capital. Marilyn was proud of their increasing numbers as if she herself had converted the new troops to the cause. Early every morning when the group set out, it was the bus that took the lead. Back in Vancouver, the girls had mounted a wooden coffin on its roof, a mobile memorial to all their sisters felled by botched abortions. Only once the VW pulled onto the highway with its sorrowful headpiece would the other cars and trucks in their party respectfully fall in to the cortege. On good nights the girls had a church basement to sleep in. On bad nights, if the threats of the hecklers that hounded them rang true, they hid the vehicles away in the barn or shed of a sympathetic local and slept fitfully inside. And so they progressed. Marilyn was in heaven.

Chapter 6

THERE WAS NO HOUSEHOLD CLEANING CHORE quite so satisfying as vacuuming after a seder what with the abundance of matzo shrapnel under foot. Evie's hand-me-down canister Hoover trailed along behind her like an old dog on a leash. As it dragged over the crumbs littering the dining room rug, its dented barrel of a chest resonated with crackles, as if the beast were sucking up its own teeth.

Evie nearly hit the ceiling when she felt the tap on her shoulder. Between the vacuum cleaner and her CD player gunned up to high, both her ears were fully occupied, leaving no input channels left to pick up on Jean-Gabriel's approach.

"Don't you believe in locking your door? You never know what kind of monster might take advantage of a girl like you living alone."

"I'll take my chances. I'm protected from on high, after all, living in holy real estate. Even if I am the wrong branch of holy for the premises." Evie set down her equipment. "So tell me, to what do I owe this visit?"

"I just came by to thank you again."

"My pleasure. I hope you didn't find it too boring. Or too raucous, for that matter."

"I think it would be hard for an event to be both boring and raucous."

"True. It did get wild all right. I don't think I've ever been to a seder quite so..."

"Unfettered?"

"That's a genteel way of putting it. Anyone ever tell you that you have a way with words?"

"Well, it was my only seder ever so it can't help but set a high standard."

"It probably gave you the completely wrong idea. Usually they're much more sedate affairs."

"It was an experience, that I'll say. And now I speak so much Hebrew. I feel like a prodigy, after just one night."

"That's what endless repetition will do for you."

"I was trying to remember the hand motions to *Dayenu* this morning but they wouldn't come back to me. I guess I drank a lot more than I should have last night. You'll have to show me again sometime."

"Like Y-M-C-A. Same tune, same moves, everything." Evie did some alphabetical arm flapping to jog his memory but Jean-Gabriel looked blank. Clearly the great playwright had never muddied his tootsies in low culture. He turned to leave, still talking. "By the way, I've made us a reservation at Au Pied de Cochon for next Saturday. To thank you properly. Be ready to go at 7:00."

The restaurant selected by Evie's neighbour was a testament to *traif*, its menu selections as remote from Passover offerings as it was possible to get on this earth. Lard was the fat of choice in the establishment; it sautéed the onions, greased the bar stools to make them spin, slicked up the waiters' hair, and lubricated who knows what else that needed its passage eased.

It flashed through Evie's mind to say no to Jean-Gabriel, and not on account of the resto's bill of fare which all but oinked. It was his presumption that galled her. If that was an invitation, she'd missed out on the actual *asking* part of it. In its tone it carried an assumption of fluttery acquiescence. On the other hand, who could blame him if his hey-baby approach was as long in the tooth as he was. Evie regretted her hiccup of ingratitude and made the decision to go along for the ride.

Normally Montreal skipped spring altogether. It was more energy efficient that way. The city managers liked to harvest the heat of the summer sun to melt the residual mountains of snow. Spring interfered with the whole process and was therefore expunged from the calendar. The city shifted from arctic cold to stultifying heat almost overnight, but tonight was unusual even by Montreal standards, an April evening already Miami muggy.

Jean-Gabriel picked Evie up right on time, suavely outfitted as was his custom, and they taxied over to the restaurant. Au Pied was already operating flat out by the time they arrived. This was a bistro that didn't know from downtime, but still, amid the mêlée, the chefs, the waiters, the bartender, and even the dishwashers all went AWOL from their stations to hustle over and pump the playwright's hand. The maître d' seated the couple at a window-side table. It was the first time Evie had ever been considered window-worthy; her cool quotient heretofore had been tepid at best. But tonight she had the hard evidence, as if she really needed it, that it was all in the arm candy. Unordered nibbles materialized like magic on their table along with two flutes of champagne, compliments of the house. And now that the employees had had their turn with him, the clientele moved in on the table for a drive-by shmooze with the famous writer. Evie had never had an experience quite like it. Though her job allowed her a passing acquaintance with the famous-ish, rubbing shoulders with a live celebrity was an altogether different proposition. She could get used to this.

"So I'm guessing you come here often?" she said, once the receiving line petered out.

"It's one of my few indulgences."

Evie needed nothing sharper than her butter knife to cut through the mock self-deprecation that was Jean-Gabriel's fall-back tone. She believed his declaration utterly.

Now and again since they'd gotten to know each other she

knocked on his door after work for a neighbourly *kumzitz* and observed first-hand his monkish existence. His condo was spartan. To call it minimalist would be a wild exaggeration, implying some willful aspiration toward a named style. No, his place was kitted out punitively. His computer looked old enough to need a crank. Evie's heart went out to her neighbour who didn't strike her as a born ascetic. Though she had no proof to bolster her suspicion, she was convinced that his current way of life was a contortion of his natural, more upholstered character.

"How do you like the place so far?" he asked. "Have you ever been here before?"

"No, I've heard of it, of course. Who in town hasn't? But I've never actually eaten here. I love it already though. I'm always a fan of a restaurant that lets you see right into the kitchen."

"If I'd known that I would have had them seat us at the bar. You're right on top of the cooking action there. You could lean over and spit in the soup."

"In that case I'm glad to have a bit of distance. To remove me from temptation. This spot is just fine. I can see perfectly well from here."

"I'm glad you're happy."

They dithered their way through the night's chalkboard menu as they sipped, but they firmed up their choices by ogling the plates that whizzed past their table en route to the neighbouring diners.

The appetizer Jean-Gabriel selected came served in a mason jar. "Would you look at that," Evie said when the waiter set it down in front of him in all its rainbow-striped glory. "All those fancy layers. What did it say they were on the menu? Salmon mousse, pomegranate seeds, foie gras, yellow squash..." She ticked them off on her fingers. "There's one more layer. The dark one. What is it again?"

"Something or other with squid ink if I remember correctly."

"Right. That was it. Who'd have thunk to stack all those

yuppified ingredients in a homey little Ball jar? My grandma used to use a bottle just like that to store the *schmaltz* in the fridge."

"*Schmaltz?*"

"On second thought, maybe better not to ask."

"We used to keep our goldfish in one. Simon, he was called. We couldn't afford him an aquarium."

"Not even a fish bowl?"

"We didn't want to spoil him."

"You're a tough cookie. Remind me never to ask you for any favours."

"It's all a façade. In fact, I'm a pushover. How's your soup?"

"Fantastic. Here, taste." They performed the ritual criss-cross of spoon and fork and sparred over whose hors d'oeuvre placed first in the evening's competition.

"Somehow, I'm never disappointed when I come here," Jean-Gabriel told her. "They always manage to surprise me."

"Maybe you'll discover a layer of goldfish under the mousse when you get to the bottom of your jar. How would that be for surprising?"

"If and when, I'll be sure to share it with you."

They dug in with relish. When they finished, they polished their dishes until they showed no trace of having ever been inhabited, using the basket of baguette sponges generously provided by the establishment.

"You know, you didn't have to go to all this trouble to thank me," Evie said.

"It's no trouble at all. Besides, it gives me a lift to be seen in the company of a young, beautiful woman."

"That I believe. You do have a reputation for only going out with members of the nubility. Correct me if I'm wrong, but I suspect you're even proud of it."

"Ouch."

"Sorry. What an ingrate I am. Give me a free meal and still I show no respect."

"No, it's all right. It is. But since we're on the subject, tell me a little more if you would be so kind. Exactly what is this reputation of mine that you're so conversant with, beyond the undisputed fact you just mentioned. Enlighten me. There must be more to it."

Evie hadn't meant to lead them down this path, but when she was overly mellow she had a tendency to blather. "Don't make me spell it out. I was just talking through my hat."

"Go ahead. Tell me. I'd like to know what you and the others think of me."

"It's not necessarily what we think, only what we've heard. A crucial difference."

"Come on, out with it."

"Surely we can find something else to talk about."

"Ève please."

Some pushover. He wasn't about to budge so she coughed it up in one breath to get them past it. "They say you took advantage of your wife's innocence, that you turned her inside out in your play, put your damaged marriage on display. Like Dany said. All that dirty linen stuff. Please don't make me say more. I don't believe any of it myself."

"Well, you're in a field of one, then. When the play opened, everyone assumed I filched the content from our bedroom. An older man, a younger woman, it had to be us. If those cretins in the audience didn't have any originality, at least they could have given me credit for having some."

"You have to admit the optics weren't great."

"In hindsight, maybe not."

"So what was your marriage like then?" Evie's tongue was still stuck in overdrive. It took her a few seconds to unjam it to issue a retraction. "Never mind, never mind. Forget I asked that. It's none of my business. Please forgive me. It's not like me to be so prying. They should serve that champagne with a muzzle."

"No, it's okay. I was asking for it." He squared all the pieces of his place setting while he marshalled his reminiscences for airing. "You want a feel for our marriage? I'll oblige you. But only with the *Reader's Digest* version. Set the clock running.

"Well, probably it was like any marriage out there. Ordinary and extraordinary all at once, but then I'm just guessing. It's not like I have any other marriages of my own to hold it up against for comparison. However depraved my reputation may be, at least it doesn't involve a revolving door of weddings and divorces. My union with the young Mlle. Turcotte was my only stab at that hallowed institution.

"What you're really wondering, I suppose, is were we happy in each other? The Odd Couple. Well, you're only getting my side of course, but if I were to dump all our time together into a balance scale, I'd say it would shake out heavier on the side of the good days than the bad. Between us, at home, the age difference didn't matter. We adjusted ourselves to it without even knowing. We seemed to meet up at an age somewhere around the middle. We had our routines just like any couple does. I stayed home and wrote and Amélie stayed home and, well, stayed home."

"She didn't work? Not even go to school? Nothing?"

Evie's flurry of questions came out with more of a Betty Friedan edge than she'd intended but she had a knee-jerk antipathy for seraglio types. Prettifiers. Feh. Her mother got up, took a shower, and went out to work every day, her grandmother got up, took a shower, and went out to work every day, and she got up, took a shower, and went out to work every day. Any other model of feminine deportment was spat upon by the Troy women. How many times at the dinner table had Evie heard Marilyn revile the *farnyentas,* that clan of kept women who didn't have enough gumption to get off their fat *tuchises,* traitors to the cause. Evie caught that message her mother had pitched in her direction anyway, while countless others landed in the dirt. She'd never be a leech, a layabout, a loafer, lumpen, lazy. When her mother got bogged down in the alphabet on the l's, Evie knew she was in for a lengthy disquisition on the rightful place of females in the labour force.

"I know what's running through your mind," Jean-Gabriel said. "It all sounds very 1950s, but we didn't plan for it to stay that way. Amélie was looking high and low for a job, passing out résumés like candy, but she wasn't having any luck. She wanted to prove to me she could do something useful, bring in a paycheque, even though she was barely out of *secondaire*, had no special background in anything. Me, I didn't care. We didn't need the money. But it was important to her. That was a sore point, I'll admit. But it's not like it threatened our marriage. We were working our way through it.

"Dull as dishwater, *non*, our day-to-day? But that's the life they accuse me of setting on the Xerox machine to put on stage as *Amélie*. Only it wasn't our life up there. Nothing like." His eyes retracted from the past to refocus on his dinner companion. "Have you seen the play, Ève? I never asked you."

"I've only read it."

"So you know what was in there. Amélie and I, we didn't have any of the knock-down-drag-outs that I stuck into the script, there was none of the muck, the other women. None of that twisted crap. It all came from up here." He smacked his forehead with too much force as if to rebuke his brain for its hypercreativity.

"Then I don't get it. Why didn't she defend you against all those false accusations at the time? Why didn't she just come out and say that it wasn't your marriage up there on stage? Do the stand by your man bit." Evie tried humming a few tone-deaf bars to lighten the tone.

"Until *Amélie*, we had a quiet life, a private life. You can picture that can't you? You've seen how I live. Well, I grant you it was a little livelier when it was the two of us, but private still. Cozy. *Intime*. But then, wham, there she was, under siege, from one day to the next. All that attention, the publicity. And it was ugly a lot of it, let me tell you. Well, I suppose you don't need me to tell you, do you? That's how we got here, isn't it? It turned out to be too much for her to handle. It ate away at her that the same shopkeepers she'd always done business with so pleasantly up and down the street looked at her in a new way, a smirking, wet t-shirt way. At least that's how she felt. And she'd tell me she could feel the neighbour ladies giving her the fisheye. So she found her own way of dealing with it. She sealed herself up in the house. Stopped going to the *dépanneur*, the grocery store, the dry cleaner. Stopped answering the phone. Stopped looking for work. Turned herself into a hermit. And it was me she blamed for putting her in that situation. She figured I should have anticipated all the fallout, and I suppose I should have. The way she saw it I betrayed her, set her up for as much humiliation as if the play really had replicated our marriage. I failed in my husbandly duty to protect her. That's why she never spoke out, never denied anything, never defended me, wouldn't lift a bloody finger to set the record straight, let people go off and think what they damn well pleased. She was out of it all."

"But by doing that wasn't she punishing herself too?"

"I didn't say it was rational."

"What were you thinking, naming the play after her?"

"I've told you, she was happy I named it after her at the time."

"Was that before or after she'd seen it?"

"Okay. It was before. You could say I misled her on that point." Jean-Gabriel pushed past his peccadillo to bring himself up to the present. "So, to finish off this topic once and for all, I did get my comeuppance in the end. I wonder if it gave her any satisfaction? Maybe she never even noticed, dropped me from her radar. Why not? Anyway, the thing is, after *Amélie* I never was able to write anything half as good ever again. I'm telling you, it was like she put a hex on me. A permanent choke. And, the cherry on the cake, the whole *scandale* sealed my reputation, as you well know. Some writers who've been around the block end up in the role of emeritus public intellectuals. They get to sit on all the TV couches and spout. Not me. I end up being an emeritus public asshole."

Evie resented that punk kid Amélie for stomping on Jean-Gabriel's future with her petulant silence. What did she think she was doing standing in the way of literature, blackening Jean-Gabriel's character in the eyes of the world with her finger paints? Evie couldn't help but wonder why he'd ever picked her out of the crowd, a schoolgirl who'd hardly gotten her feet wet in life. Wouldn't he have logically sought out someone more mature, someone more cerebral, more liberal-artsy? More like herself in fact. Clearly this Amélie babe had other redeeming qualities. Men.

"Needless to say we went our separate ways after that. Or she went her separate way. And there you have it. The truth, the whole truth, and nothing but. With minor editorial revisions, a comma here and there. Now when you finally become a famous author, *ma petite* Ève, and I have faith that you will, watch that you don't make my same mistakes."

"I think we're safe there. No one so far has shown the least interest in publishing anything of mine outside of the obituary pages."

"Have patience. You never know in what direction your creative juices will lead you."

Moshe came in via the rear service entrance, the same door through which the pig carcasses reported for duty, just beside the walk-in fridges. Even though the resto had an open plan, the owners had calculated, rightly Moshe felt, that it could backfire to showcase absolutely every last aspect of the food prep to their diners. Maybe the restaurateurs didn't slaughter their pigs on-site, but they did do their own butchery, lopping off heads, tails, and trotters to the chefs' exacting specifications. Their tools were hardcore. After a good afternoon's work, the back room looked like a field hospital at the Somme. It didn't necessarily translate that an unrepentant carnivore wanted to stand ringside at the abattoir while the shochet did his business. Sometimes it made good sense to keep the children in the dark about affairs beyond their ken. So the owners partitioned off the sawdust-strewn carvery, allowing the staff to wield its cleavers in camera.

Bread delivery was outside Moshe's normal realm of responsibilities, but when the bakery's driver called in sick, it was always the apprentice who was expected to pick up the slack. Otherwise, what was the point of maintaining a food chain? Moshe unloaded the van and stashed his leggy loaves in the rough wicker umbrella baskets awaiting them under the salad station.

"Hé Mosh," called out one of the chefs from the kitchen, "Marcellin dogging it again?"

"Would you catch me behind the wheel of that heap for any other reason?"

"Come over here a minute. I'll give you something to try that will make your trip worthwhile." Moshe joined his friend behind the stove and observed as he tipped his pan toward the gas burner to set its contents alight. The two stared into the flames in culinary communion. When the blaze subsided, Moshe spooned up some of the sauce and let it rove over the topography of his tongue. His taste buds spent a few happy moments disentangling the elusive flavours, but the rest of his body didn't share their joy for long.

Moshe glanced out over the bar that separated the kitchen from the dining room. This was his kind of place, casual and convivial. As Marcellin's surrogate he'd had occasion to drop off breads at all manner of restaurants, but the eateries with a gentle hubbub like this were his favourites. He scanned the tables, every one full, and deservedly so. Clearly all the clients were relaxed and enjoying their night out, coddled in an atmosphere of expert service and earthy good food. His gaze happened to rest on one particular table where a couple was clinking champagne glasses. Who orders bubbly unless there's an event to celebrate, and he wondered what Evie and Jean-Gabriel could be feting, for indeed on second look he recognized the clinkers as his neighbours. His imagination wasn't cutting him any breaks as it ran trailers of the various possibilities on the plasma screen behind his eyes. Now it decided to pull out all the stops? Thanks for nothing.

The baker stood planted like a maypole in the centre of the action while the restaurant's employees danced around him. He drew attention to himself by virtue of his erectness and immobility. A beetle posture was the kitchen norm, hunched over sink or stove or tray, and stasis was a hanging offence. Inukshuk Moshe cast such a wide shadow over the premises that the diners couldn't help but wonder who went overboard on the dimmer, and their heads turned en masse toward command central behind the bar. It was too late for Moshe to slip back out the service door un-noticed. Jean-Gabriel was already hailing him to stop by their table.

"Moshe, *mon ami*, small world. I didn't know you moonlighted here."

His assumption was only natural, but it forced Moshe to admit that he was on truck-driver duty, endless status rungs beneath his regular occupational role. On Anti-Shabbos nights when Moshe arrived challah laden, his friends teased him for his bakerly perfectionism, but they revered his profession, that he knew. Though they never said it in so many words, translation of silences came easy to him in that affable crowd. To them he was heroic, coaxing great loaves out of the ovens with his asbestos hands. He was the creative genius in their midst, at least until Jean-Gabriel crashed the party and usurped top spot. But tonight Moshe had *shlepper* written all over him. He was still dressed in the same baker's whites he'd put on at four in the morning. The sweat crescents that his armpits normally held captive had decided to make a break for it and go free-range, scampering all the way down his torso. He probably shouldn't have even entered the bistro's dining area. However porcine the restaurant's theme, perfuming the joint with his odour of sty was carrying things too far. The owner would no doubt call over to the bakery to have him dressed down for it tomorrow.

"Join us for dinner, Moshe. I can have them set another place."

"Yes do Mosh, it would be fun." Evie seconded her table companion. "You could give us your insider opinion of everything. It would be great to eat at a restaurant with a trained foodie, almost like sharing a meal with Julia Child or James Beard."

Moshe couldn't delight in the compliment her comparisons were surely meant to relay. Instead, they left him feeling gelded. Jean-Gabriel lifted his arm to signal the waiter for an additional chair, but Moshe reached over and yanked it down with unexpected force, as if it were attached to a Vegas slot.

"No, no, I can't. Really. I have more deliveries to make."

"Can't you come by after?" Evie asked. "We'll be here for a while. They haven't served our main dishes yet. There's plenty of time."

"Thanks, but I have to get the van back."

"You can't even make it by dessert?" Evie urged him. "I peeked at the menu. They're serving tarte Tatin tonight. I know how much you love it. Come share some with us."

"Moshe, it would be our pleasure to have you stop by later. Even if it's just for a digestif."

Moshe ran his hands through what would have been his hair if he hadn't razored it down to the nub to muddy the borders between field and fallow. Would they never release him? In his current state, a complete fumigation and upgrade to civvies would take him hours and he'd still never measure up to Jean-Gabriel's sartorial standards. The guy lived an unadorned life according to Evie's recounting, but he seemed not to stint where his closet was concerned. No, better to go home and lick his wounds. He tried weakly, as he withdrew, to recoup a point or two.

"Be sure to try the *pain aux olives*," he said. "I made it myself." But later that night, when he replayed the encounter under his shower spray, his forehead pressed against the cooling tiles, he regretted his parting line that made him sound like a kindergartner proud of his lumpy clay ashtray. Why hadn't he just kept his mouth shut?

Chapter 7

"THEY WANT TO AUCTION ME OFF."

"I beg your pardon?"

Jean-Gabriel was opening the day's mail at his kitchen table while Evie superintended the pasta sauce for their dinner. He waved the letter he'd just read in front of her. "I've been asked to be a prize at a charity auction. This is what my life has come to. I'm now the turkey."

"What's the cause?"

He looked back down at the invitation. "*Sauvez le Cinéma Cinq*. You at least have to love it for the sibilance."

"It isn't very *moderne* as a concept, is it?" Evie asked him. "A meat market?"

"I don't think they expect you to get up on the podium and flex your pecs, but I could be wrong. It says here that the high bidders win a private evening with their preferred author or performer at some future date. It's all meant to sound uplifting. The winners get to feel like a patron of the arts, an honourary member of the Medici family for one night. All the proceeds go to bringing the Cinéma V back to its former glory. They'll need a bundle to renovate that pile of rubble."

"Will you do it?"

Jean-Gabriel set down his reading glasses. "I have to admit a part of me is tempted. Having women bid against each other for a *tête-à-tête* with me, it's a hard thing for a man to resist. Does wonders for your ego. But it's too risky. I'm seventy years old and I'd probably be competing against a slate of young bucks. I could end up being humiliated. It's safer to pass."

"Oh, come on. They'd be bidding on you as if you were a long-lost Picasso."

"You really think so?"

"I know so."

"You're my biggest booster."

"Always glad to provide a service. I will just ask you, though, why you assume it will be only women bidding on you?"

"Call me old-fashioned."

Evie's fingers tweezered the invitation out of the garbage. She ironed out the crimps with her hand and passed it back to him. "Are you sure you won't take part? Wouldn't you want to pitch in to revive one of the city's venerable old movie houses? Dress up all fancy? Be fawned over? What's not to like?"

"Okay mademoiselle. Since you're so insistent. Here's the proposition. It says here I can bring a guest. I'll go if you'll agree to come along with me. It's right up your alley anyway. Haven't you crowned yourself greatest movie fan in the world, or am I mistaken?"

Jean-Gabriel never missed an opportunity to ask for Evie's company on his various outings around town. *Outings* was her word. What was she supposed to call them? Dates? Anyone who kept his medications in a plastic pill-minder like the one on Jean-Gabriel's bathroom counter was over the age bar for dating. And he had other disqualifications besides. He used an extra long, no-bend-at-the-waist shoe horn. Guys who used shoe horns period were too old to date. Weren't they? Evie knew she was being unfair to oldsters or whatever the PC term was. The youth-impaired? But she was in uncharted territory. Until lately, the only individuals *d'un certain âge* she'd ever hung out with on a regular basis were her grandparents. When they leaned heavily against her and hooked arms, smelling of closed windows and Depends, it was so she could prop them up. But when Jean-Gabriel slipped his arm through hers while they strolled through Jean-Talon Market, it wasn't for support. He'd never seemed unsteady on his pins before.

Evie couldn't prevent her famously open mind from doing a bit of self-protective grey bashing. It hammered her with all the geriatric stereotypes. It saw tufts of wiry hair growing out of noses and ears everywhere it looked. And whenever Evie went to a restaurant with Jean-Gabriel, it invariably pulled a fast one on the ice floating in the water glass, replacing it with a partial plate. Evie knew where her brain was going with all this but it should have had more confidence in her. Maybe Jean-Gabriel saw their outings as try-outs for some future expanded role for Evie, but she wasn't auditioning to be his leading lady. In this pairing, at least for the time being, she was perfectly content to play Tonto.

"We watched the Cinéma V burn down," Evie told him. "From Girouard Park across the street. The whole neighbourhood was there. People were sobbing. My parents could hardly bear to look. That's where they went on their first date."

"At least the façade survived intact. That was a stroke of luck. I can't think of any other building in town as quirky looking as that one."

"I know. What would you call that style? Early King Tut? I love the way the stone's all carved up like a sarcophagus. And those twin 3-D pharaohs up top? When we used to go by it on the way to school every day all the kids kinked their arms sideways Egyptian style. A school bus ritual. If you didn't join in you'd end up having bad luck."

"You'd be haunted by a mummy?"

"I think it was more on the order of having your lunch money snitched."

"You'll come with me then?" he asked her.

"Why not? I owe the place that much I guess."

"So am I presentable?" They paused in the hotel lobby before entering the packed ballroom. Evie evened out the loops in

Jean-Gabriel's bow tie and brushed a trace of imaginary lint off his tux. "There, now you're perfect."

"You look perfect too. But then you always do. That dress. It sizzles. Red suits you."

"Save all that smooth talk for the high bidder. Don't squander it on me."

"You're a very difficult girl to compliment. Has anyone ever told you that? Are you so resistant with everyone or are you just like that with me?"

"Psychoanalyze me some other time. We have to go in. We're late."

Evie and Jean-Gabriel tacked themselves onto the end of the reception line where the paddles were being distributed in advance of the auction. The one Evie was allotted was stamped with number 455. She'd never brandish it, that she knew, but she accepted it all the same. Starting bids were set at five hundred dollars, with hundred dollar increments for subsequent bids.

Evie cased the joint. The other guests milling about were abundantly, drippingly, unremittingly jewelled, as if they'd taken their accessorizing cues from the chandeliers. She couldn't ascertain if their bangles were twenty-four carat or ersatz; she was hardly in a position to bite down on them and check for toothmarks, but she had the distinct impression that she was the only one in the room who didn't have that kind of cash to throw around.

"Anybody tempt you?" Jean-Gabriel caught her scanning the catalogue she'd received along with her paddle. Guests all over the hall were studying it like the racing form. In fact, there were a few names on the list that called out to her but she didn't fess up.

"No, no one at all. I'm content to just watch you be battled over. That's why I'm here."

A boutonniered organizer approached them. "Monsieur Médéry, sorry to intrude, but it's time for everyone on the program to come backstage. May I pry you away from your lovely companion?"

Jean-Gabriel turned to Evie and whispered in her ear. "Okay lovely companion. Wish me luck. Keep your fingers crossed that I don't lay an egg and bring in a pittance."

"I told you. One of these hot little numbers in taffeta is going to blow daddy's fortune to land an evening with you. Your *kavorka*'s still strong."

"My what?"

"Never mind. Just trust me. Now go with your handler. I won't say good luck to you. Isn't that one of those theatre superstitions?"

"Right you are. *Merde* we say in French. Literally *shit* but figuratively *break a leg*."

"Okay, *merde* it is. Go now, make money."

"And what am I bid for this fine gentleman?" Jean-Gabriel cut an impressive figure on stage when his turn came along, Evie thought, but he did look small up there, bordering on frail. It was all the fault of his position in the lineup. He was preceded on the auction block by a lineman from the Alouettes who'd filled up the stage like Paul Bunyan's ox. Any one of the other auction participants would have looked pygmy-ish by contrast, but it was Jean-Gabriel's bad karma to follow on the heels of the single bona fide hunk on the night's program. And it was no secret that the football player rang up the highest sum of all the gentlemen preceding him. The paddles were popping up so fast and furious while the temporary stage sagged under his mass that the amateur auctioneer could hardly keep up.

The bidding on the playwright took off slowly but at least it was steady. Evie surveyed the bidders, trying to gauge Jean-Gabriel's appeal in this diamanté crowd. All women Evie noticed, just as he'd predicted. He knew his market. And it was a nice age mix. He had nothing to be ashamed of. But once the bids hit the $1700 mark the younger ones dropped out, seemingly all at once. It was as if their schoolmistress had rung the bell to end recess and the girls were forced to put their paddles back in the rack beside the ping-pong balls and return to class. Only two older women were left in contention. And not just older. Jean-Gabriel was caught in a bidding war between Grandma Moses and Miss Havisham. Their wrinkles combined could carpet all of Death Valley. The audience was starting to chuckle at the spectacle. Up on stage, Jean-Gabriel smiled good-naturedly at the verve of his CARP groupies, but to Evie's knowing eye, the smile hadn't invited the rest of his face to take part as it normally did. It adhered lightly to his lips, like a post-it. With the slightest jostle from the auctioneer who stood just beside him it could easily fall off to reveal the expression it was keeping at bay. Evie had strong suspicions as to what that expression might be.

Just as her guilt over pushing Jean-Gabriel to take part in this undignified spectacle was starting to bat Evie about, a third woman saw fit to enter the fray. Bidder number 327. Evie couldn't see her clearly on the far side of the ballroom, but at least she could make out that her hair wasn't some shade of elderly. It was a nice chestnut brown. Out of a bottle, possibly, but brown all the same. The new contender brought the age of the bidders way down to a respectable mean. Or was it median? Evie's vocabulary mathematical had always been shaky. In any event, with the new, more youthful bidder in the mix, the tittering in the audience thankfully stopped.

The three-way on the bidding floor continued apace. Another thousand dollars collected in Jean-Gabriel's kitty before one of the two crones saw fit to drop out. She didn't wanted to abandon ship, but after all this unaccustomed exertion she felt a bit woozy and had to reassign her paddle hand to her walker. It was now down to the second old grey mare and the holder of paddle 327. Neither woman showed any signs of abandoning her quest for an evening with Jean-Gabriel, up-close and personal.

Evie's curiosity was piqued. She decided to move over closer to the younger bidder to check her out. It was difficult to make her way through the crush in her spiky party heels; they were designed less for walking than for aerating lawns, but once she made it to the middle of the room a fortuitous gap opened up in the crowd to allow a waiter to pass through with his tray of crostini, giving Evie a clear view of the mystery bidder. It was her mother.

All the blood seemed to drain from her body. Her ears buzzed with static and her legs went rubbery. Maybe she needed a walker too. Evie couldn't sentence Jean-Gabriel to an evening with her mother. She couldn't sentence anyone to that. She hoisted her paddle up into the air. From what seemed like a very great distance she heard the auctioneer respond. "I have $3900 over here from bidder number 455 in the red dress. The young lady's first time bidding tonight if memory serves. Do I hear an even $4000?"

That's what she'd bid? $3900? Evie was desperately trying to recall the balance in her account after her last paycheque when her mother accommodated the auctioneer with the nice round number he was soliciting. Evie's paddle flew up in hot pursuit. Her arm was moving of its own accord. Within seconds, Marilyn upped her by a hundred. The senior citizen who'd been loyally bidding on Jean-Gabriel since the beginning couldn't keep up with these two. She had to bow out. Her reflexes were shot and her frozen shoulder was starting to seize up yet again. She'd save the money to lavish on her physio.

It was down to just Evie and her mother. The audience was taking a keen interest in this contest. Somehow it smelled blood. Marilyn was going strong. She jerked the paddle above her head whenever the auctioneer threw out an amount as if she were in his thrall. And when her paddle went down, Evie's went up. Their movements mimicked each other's like a perfectly matched pair of synchronized swimmers. All they were missing were the nose plugs.

Evie wondered if her severely myopic mother could see far enough across the room to know that she was bidding opposite her own daughter. She angled in closer, planting herself directly in her mother's line of vision. Marilyn prided herself on her unflappability, but when she focused in on who it was she was bidding against, she was sufficiently discomposed that her paddle dropped to the floor with a clatter. The gallant Jake bent over to retrieve it but his wife stooped floorward at the same time and they ended up butting heads. It was a good healthy thump. They both saw stars. That happy accident bought Evie the extra seconds she needed to make the final and winning bid. She'd saved Jean-Gabriel's skin. The two of them could have their evening together in the social hall at debtor's prison.

The victor backed away and the crowd sucked her up into its anonymity as if it were a hungry amoeba. It spat her out accommodatingly at the open bar, and there she tippled her way through the remainder of the proceedings until Jean-Gabriel came to collect her. He was in high good humour but noted that her mood had taken an inexplicable slump since they'd parted.

"What happened? I only left you a little while ago. Did someone say something to hurt your feelings? Ève, tell me."

She didn't yet trust her voice.

"Come on now. Everything went well, just as you predicted. I never should have doubted you. Why don't we dance? There's nice live music. That'll cheer you up."

"I don't like to dance."

"Ève, this isn't a night for moping." He took hold of her hands.

"And I'm not moping." It was one of those bipolar negations that can also easily translate into the reverse. Jean-Gabriel trod carefully. "So what's wrong then?"

"I'm recovering."

He checked out her colouring. "You've come down with something since we've been here?"

"I'm not sick. That's not it." Evie related the details of the dramatic rescue mission she'd pulled off on his behalf while he was on stage, blissfully unaware that he was even in need of rescue.

"So it was you who won me? I'll be damned. They didn't tell us any names. But nothing could please me more. All the other guys from backstage have to be wishing they were in my shoes. Still, I'm sure your mother can't be quite the dragon-lady you make her out to be."

"Speak of the devil. Or the dragon as the case may be." Marilyn was bearing down on them with Jake pulling up the rear. There was no escape. "Now's your chance to find out if I exaggerate or not." Evie faced up to her parents. "Mum, what are you and dad doing here? It's not like you to attend a frothy charity do like this."

"Are you kidding? Us miss a chance to revive the Cinema V? It's entirely possible that you were conceived in its balcony."

"Mum, please, must you?"

"Evie, it's the plain truth. I wouldn't have missed this event for the world. What about you? I never would have thought to see you here either. Did the newspaper send you?"

"No Mum, I do obituaries, remember? Not the society page. I just came to keep Jean-Gabriel company."

"Aren't you going to introduce us to your friend?"

Evie made the requisite presentations. "It's a pleasure to meet Ève's parents, *un vrai honneur*," Jean-Gabriel said, upping the wattage on his charm to blind Marilyn in its glare. "Thank you for bidding so strenuously on a has-been, Madame."

"Marilyn, please. Oh, you're far too modest. Evie's told us all about you. She's your biggest fan. And we're not far behind, my husband and I." She waved in the general direction of her consort to acknowledge his mute presence. "We saw your play *Amélie* years back. A tour de force. That's why I chose you to bid on rather than any of the others up there. I wanted to meet the man capable of dreaming up those characters. An amazing accomplishment to spin them out of thin air like you did. Absolutely mind boggling. You would have sworn they were real people."

It was a smooth lead-in on Marilyn's part. Even Evie had to admire her finesse. Normally Marilyn wasn't one for giving the kid-gloves treatment. The formal wear must have scrubbed some of the lumberjack off her delivery. Evie waited for the other shoe to drop but the thud didn't come. Her mother continued to hide her antipathy for Jean-Gabriel behind a barrage of flattery. She was laying it on with a trowel but at least it was better than having her blurt out what she really thought of him. If a nearby guest happened to be eavesdropping on the conversation, he could only conclude that Marilyn was genuinely star-struck. But Evie was flesh of her flesh. She knew that once her mother judged someone's principles suspect, he stayed on her no-fly list until the end of time. Nurturing a righteous grudge, especially a grudge vaguely feminist, was all that made her life worth living. Marilyn was simply toying with Jean-Gabriel, buttering him up to get him off guard. Once his natural defences were down, once he was operating at only thirty-three RPMs instead of his usual seventy-eight, once she had gulled him into thinking her benign, bang, she'd plug him one.

And it was about to happen. Marilyn's posture gave it away. Her head was tilted back ever so slightly so she could scrutinize Jean-Gabriel through the bottoms of her bifocals. It was the same coiled-rattler glare she used to direct towards Evie's chin when she was about to shoot in uninvited to pop one of her daughter's blackheads. To those in the know it was a look that said run for you life, but Jean-Gabriel hadn't been indoctrinated. Evie'd never seen the urgency. Clearly her night of serving as Jean-Gabriel's personal St. Bernard wasn't over.

"We'd love to chat more but you'll have to excuse us for now. Jean-Gabriel promised that we'd dance, and he likes the slow tunes, so we better take advantage of this one. Catch up with you later maybe."

The charity prize let himself be dragged towards the dance floor. He had the wit to stay silent till they were out of parental hearing range.

"I thought you don't like to dance. Isn't that what you said?"

"I was trying to save you from my mother."

"Your mother seemed utterly delightful."

"*Seemed* is the operative word."

They wedged themselves between the other couples on the dance floor. With every spin they took Evie edged them closer and closer to the exit. "Hey, who's leading here?" he said. "You're not thinking of leaving already?"

"That is exactly what I'm thinking,"

When she wished Jean-Gabriel *merde* Evie hadn't foreseen that they would finish off the evening with it all piled up at her feet. Since she moved to the condo, Evie'd excelled at keeping the two sides of her life separate, the family side and the everything-else side. Only Josh could pass freely between them; Evie'd issued him the elite membership card. But tonight she lost all the ground she'd gained. Why was it that whenever her family made as if to merge with her friends it inevitably ended up in a fender bender? It was the family she wanted to blame, her pet scapegoat, but she suspected it was more in the way that she directed traffic. She'd have to cut tonight's connection pronto.

Jean-Gabriel made a last ditch attempt to talk her down at the doorway. "Are you sure about this? We can still enjoy ourselves, even with them here. Nice food, nice drink, nice music. The room's plenty big for all of us. And wouldn't it be a shame to waste all our finery?"

"The evening I just won with you? It officially starts now. And I say we're leaving."

"*Oui, mon général.*"

Evie rationalized away ducking out on the fundraiser. It was churlish, but then didn't charity begin at home? And that's where she needed to be. At home. Under lock and key.

Chapter 8

FUNNY HOW THE SUBJECT LINE DIDN'T CHANGE the longer you stared at it. Evie's day wasn't meant to begin this way. She had her morning ritual. A chai latte and a croissant in her cubicle while she read the *Globe and Mail* online. It eased her gently into her working day. Oh, the routine varied some. It's not like she ran on cruise control. On Thursdays she scoped out the movie listings for the weekend on the Cinema Montreal site. And on those rare Fridays when her bathroom scale smiled up at her, she upgraded her pastry order to a *chocolatine*. But discounting those minor jogs in her pattern, once she was sugared up and caffeinated, directly did she check her computer's inbox to see what dead meat she was meant to research.

Rebooting, the magic bullet of the local techies had no salutary effect on her mail program. The same subject line as before headed the list, but at least her DIY diagnostics narrowed down the source of her problem. If it wasn't in the software and it wasn't in the hardware, it all boiled down to human error, though with Aaron, *human* was a judgment call.

She rapped on her editor's door. Thanks to his semi-lofty position, Aaron occupied an office of his own with a genuine door jamb to knock on. In the cubicle farm Evie inhabited, doors were an illusion, but the little people kept up the pretense and observed an in-house visitation protocol. You were expected to bonk twice on your head with your fist and say *knock-knock* to announce your presence at a neighbouring cubby. This practice irked Aaron no end. He sensed that all the tourettish head-klopping that went on in his fiefdom was an indirect mockery of the leadership style that had earned him a private office, and in that of course he was correct.

"Aaron," she said, lingering at his threshold. "Just making sure. You positive there's no mistake about the name you sent me this morning?"

"Evie, I'm shocked. All of a sudden you're doubting me? You know that if I say someone's gonna croak, they're gonna croak. You can bank on it. Are you daring to suggest that my powers aren't what they used to be? Have my predictions ever been anything but impeccable?" Evie performed the requisite stroking. Aaron was high maintenance once you dared to engage him. What she really wanted to do was reach under that overbite of his which preceded him out of a room by a good five minutes, haul him out of his chair by those Stonehenge incisors and knee him against the wall until he did her bidding. Instead, she waited.

"What, you want I should check?" This was a hasty concession by his standards, vaulting over the entire begging stage, normally de rigueur. But Aaron didn't swivel around towards his computer to hammer away at the keys. Nor did he start punching out a number on his phone. Instead he massaged his temples with the tips of his fingers as if to reawaken his inner seer. His eyes lost their focus, blanking out as expertly as a top model's on a *Cosmo* cover. By means of grunts and moans her boss communicated with the spirit world until his vibes abruptly went on the fritz and his hands dropped down to his sides. The tightwad probably should have sprung for cable. Aaron zoned back in on his nettlesome staffer and reported his gleanings from the other side. "Jean-Gabriel Médéry. Actor, playwright, bon vivant, and all-around shit. Yup. He's a goner. Now quit wasting my time and go write him up."

Shabbos dragged its feet, so anxious was Evie to sit Jean-Gabriel down at her table and give him a thorough once-over. When her weekly dinner finally did roll around, she took care to eyeball him covertly, using the same flitting lateral glances she'd employed the Friday before to see if her guests were politely stashing their servings of her mango tofurkey under an obliging lettuce leaf. From what she could make out, he looked no different. And his behaviour gave nothing away. But then how does someone act who's just had a death sentence handed down? Strangely, for an obituarist, she'd never been very reflective on the subject. The roll of names that landed on her desktop at work every morning represented just so many stiffs. For each, she went down her mental checklist. Dates, tick. Education, tick. Marriage, tick. Family, tick. Claim to fame, tick. Honours, tick. Retirement shtick, tick. Survivors, tick. Next. She couldn't very well stop and mourn everyone she wrote up, could she? Didn't she have to maintain a certain professional distance? It was a feeble excuse and she knew it, a palliative tarp under which she swept her callous disregard for her dead, for they were *hers* when it came down to it, their legacies entrusted to her flippant hands.

For the first time in her necrological career, Evie dared to picture her own tombstone. If she were to plotz on the sidewalk tomorrow, her parents would probably opt for the hackneyed *Beloved Daughter* inscription even though *Tolerated Daughter* was more on the money. When the bereaved were churning out balled-up Kleenexes in the Berson's showroom, pricing the granite mock-ups for their late lamenteds, they inevitably favoured the platitudes and half-truths. On her weekend jogs through Mount Royal Cemetery, Evie'd never once seen a snarky monument. All sarcasm was checked at the gatehouse where the dogs were leashed and the maps handed out. The worst she'd ever observed was a naked name, a name unadorned by any ornamental *hasta la vista,* but even that was rare, a potter's field aberration in the Hallmark forest of *forever in our hearts* and *in loving memories*. Suddenly, viewed through the prism of her own mortal remains and her epitaph-challenged marker, she was ashamed of the irreverence of the newspaper's graveyard shift. And wasn't she one of the worst offenders? Hadn't it been her idea to call their softball team the Body Bags?

But the headstone was a red herring. Just what had she accomplished worth memorializing in her life anyway? Her fireball mother, shot through with the fervour of her cause, had struggled to change the world no less, to reclaim the future for the legions of the knocked up. Maybe Evie and her mother had their differences. In fact, it was all they had in common. But Evie always chalked up to Marilyn the chutzpah points she deserved for her cross-country crusade on behalf of abortion rights. She'd just never said it out loud is all. And then there was Jean-Gabriel's legacy of literature. By Evie's bookish yardstick, there existed no greater gift to pass along to future generations. Okay, so she was still on the young side. Maybe it was too early to commit to *drain on society* for her gravestone, but judged against those two go-getters Evie was already a certified goldbrick. Her mother hadn't even celebrated her twenty-first birthday when she signed on with her gaggle of uterine freedom fighters, and as for Jean-Gabriel, he'd yet to crack thirty when he raked in every award going for his first play. What was she waiting for?

Maybe she could arrange to be cremated. At least that way there would stand no monumental reminder of her washout status, just the cremains in a shoebox. Her parents could dump her out onto the peony beds at the chalet with the night's load of ashes from the barbecue. Sheesh, *cremains*, what loser thought up that one? It must have been some stumblebum funeral director who tripped over the burner pedals while he was lecturing his trainee and out it popped; a serendipitous discovery on the order of penicillin or silly putty. But then who was Evie to sneer? Whoever coined it, at least his legacy was clear, a shiny new word left behind for posterity. A word that filled a hole. Even if it did only amount to a clunky conflating, the solder job was blessed by both the lexicographers at the Oxford English and Mr. Will Shortz. Evie, on the other hand, the self-identifying wordoholic, was handing down etymological *bupkis*.

And her obituary. What could it possibly say? Even with all her prior experience tarting up the specious accomplishments of the dead and gone, Evie was hard pressed to silk purse the sow's ear grab bag of achievements that defined her own life. She mentally scavenged the dumpsters of her oeuvre for glowing phrases that might apply to herself, but she had to face facts. She wasn't obit-worthy. A just-the-facts-ma'am death notice is all she merited, fifty-five bucks for seven lines, photo extra.

"Earth to Evie," Moshe called out to her. "Come in Evie. Over and out."

At his summons Evie checked back in from the hereafter, but her brief outing left her rattled. The amateur sleuth forgot all about the sidelong surveillance style she'd been pursuing, and she shifted her eyes to pore directly into Jean-Gabriel's. Her wide-open gaze gave him entrée to slip behind the purdah curtain that hid her private fears. There he stole a glimpse of the one that stood in the foreground, the one that bore his own face. He nodded his head once in confirmation, the slightest bob for her consumption only. The table-talk swirled around the pair of them, the day-to-day blah-blah of the unencumbered soul. To prove that they were indeed paying attention they interjected a word here and there but they'd clocked out of the evening. As the guests departed, Jean-Gabriel offered to stay behind and help with the washing up.

"You know you stink in the kitchen," she said.

"It's not one of my better rooms, that's true. But I can be the in-flight entertainment."

"It's a deal."

Evie scrubbed the pots in silence while he sat behind her at the kitchen table, swiping at them ineffectually with a dish towel after she passed them over, distributing the water more uniformly around the surfaces.

"I'm okay you know," he said eventually, addressing her back. "If that's what you're worrying about. I am okay." For all that she was well versed in the lingo of death, Evie was unequipped for this conversation. Luckily Jean-Gabriel expected no reply or comment.

"Better to get hit by a bus, *paf*, and be done with it. Who needs to know the when? Still, it's not like I'm being cut off in my prime. For that I should be thankful, *non*? My father, he hung on till he was ninety-four. Did I ever tell you about him? A stingy bastard. Took his longevity genes with him to the grave rather than share them with his scoundrel son. Right on track with the rest of the family. They gave up on me way back. Ah well, all that is a story for another time. You'll remind me?"

Evie's cowardliness shamed her. She wrenched herself away from the sink and sat down to face him. "When you come right down to it," he said to her, "what have I got to hang around for anyway? Not my work, that's for sure. I'm running on fumes there. Haven't had a real success in years as you know. They just keep revamping my golden oldies. At least by kicking the bucket now, I'll be spared that mortifying spectacle where they wheel out the old codger author for a curtain call with a blanket over his knees and a rolling IV drip. Now that's something to be thankful for. I'm forgetting something here. What else is a deathbed oration meant to address? I should know, I've written one or two in my time. What is it? Ah *oui*. My Amélie. Think she'll shed a tear or two out there, wherever she is, for auld lang syne? Who am I kidding? When a shmuck falls in the forest, does he make a sound?" Clearly Jean-Gabriel had a death checklist to rival Evie's and he came out on the wrong side in every category.

Though Evie normally had a long fuse, there were a few cattle-prod topics that could zap her slow-to-blow tendencies to smithereens, and of these Amélie stood at the front of the queue. As she watched Jean-Gabriel roll over and accept the false persona his ex had thrown over him like a plague blanket, she snapped. "What is wrong with you? I don't get it. Why did you stand back and let her tarnish your image all these years? Why didn't you fight back? You're too much of a gentleman. She more than had it coming. You're entitled to your true legacy as an artist. Your true legacy as a person." As someone who'd buffed up her fair share of legacies Evie knew whereof she spoke. "Who decided that it would be Amélie's twisted, vindictive silence that would poison your memory for the world? It's so unfair. If only there were some way we could set the record straight."

Jean-Gabriel reached across the table and clasped the hands of his earnest young friend in his own. "*Dayenu, ma chérie.*"

Chapter 9

WHAT DID HE THINK, she was Ed McMahon? That she'd insinuate herself into the life of a complete stranger and then show up on the lawn with a cardboard cheque the size of a landing strip? That level of fancy footwork required a script, but for the first time in their acquaintance, the master playwright had failed her.

The doctor's forecast of six months turned out to overshoot the mark. Jean-Gabriel only hung on for three. His decline was precipitous, a jagged plunge that ravaged his body on the way down, but spared his brain. Throughout his ordeal Evie tended to him with daughterly devotion. At home until the end, Jean-Gabriel wanted for nothing. His upstairs friend made sure of that.

Evie's shame over her dearth of worldly accomplishments to fill in the crepe-swagged borders of an obituary box showed a lack of self-awareness. The trouble was that she was always so busy comparing her own qualities to the flashier ones of the VIPs she wrote up for the newspaper that she undervalued her life. It was as a friend that Evie shone, a flawless exemplar of the species. But in the grand rope line of virtues jockeying for pride of place, *fast friend* stood shyly at the tail end while other blingier attributes hogged the front and tipped the bouncer. Just because her headstone might only be incised with that slim pair of words after her name, words that could fit into the cavity of a fortune cookie with room to spare, did not mean that they were any less worthy. This was not one of those cases where size mattered, but go tell Evie.

The phone call from Jean-Gabriel's notary came through a few months after the funeral, inviting Evie to set up an appointment on the matter of the bequest. The term puzzled her, and she was one who demanded precision in her definitions. In Evie's mind, as cluttered with old novels as a quay-side bookstall, bequests were the purview of the ultra rich; lump sums bestowed on Cook and Nanny, allowing them to scrape by with dignity post great house, noblesse oblige. How could her Jean-Gabriel be following in the footsteps of those BritLit bequestors? Not that she was privy to his bank books, but surely if he had enough cash to dish out posthumously he wouldn't have felt obliged to scrimp on himself prethumously, or whatever the proper antonym was.

On the other hand, a bequest didn't absolutely have to be monetary. She'd read here and there of exceptions, ancestral portraits, brooches, a ship in a bottle. Maybe Jean-Gabriel was just leaving her a keepsake from his apartment, though there wasn't much in his cellblock abode in the way of bric-à-brac. A signed copy of one of his books perhaps? Yes, that had to be it. As she walked down the leafy NDG street that housed the notarial office, Evie felt more settled. Surely she'd be heading home with a simple memento, a sentimental token of their friendship. A sentimento. Did that word exist, she wondered? Well, Evie decided, if it didn't, it should.

Maître Miljour sat her down with a cup of tea and eulogized his late client while she sipped, easing them into the official business at hand with duly notarized decorum. He reached into his desk drawer and drew out a sealed envelope that he handed to her.

"M. Médéry charged me to give you this. It explains itself. I'll leave you alone for a few minutes to read over the contents. If you want anything I'll be just outside."

Evie tore open the envelope and pulled out a brief note.

"*Ma chère* Ève, *As you see, I have managed to accumulate a little nest egg.*"

Evie shook out the envelope and a cheque fluttered onto her lap, made out in her name. She took in the row of zeros crammed into the rectangle headed with the dollar sign. If this was a nest egg, it must have been laid by a brontosaurus. Her attention bounced back to the letter.

Now I find that I will not have the time to dispose of it as I planned. I entrust you, my dearest friend, to carry out my intentions.

Ève, the money is destined to Amélie. I know what you think of her, but I hope you can get beyond your rancour to do as I ask of you. I want her to inherit everything I have so that she may live out the rest of her life with ease.

This task, Ève, I leave to you. I hope you will not find it too onerous or distasteful, especially as there is one crucial element that I must insist upon that will place an extra load of complication on your fragile shoulders. Amélie cannot know that this money comes from me. If she sees my fingerprints staining the bequest, she will refuse it. She would starve first. Of this I am sure. I beg you to arrange it so that the money seems to come to her naturally, using whatever means you see fit.

I am sorry to have to burden you of all people with this, but you are the only one I can depend on. If you need to make use of any of the money in order to set your plan afoot, feel free to help yourself.

I can count on you, Ève. Of that I am absolutely certain.

Forgive me for leaving you alone in all this. I wish I could have been there long enough to give you the same kind of support you always gave to me, but my body is keeping me to a very stingy timetable. Use your own writ-

erly instincts to plot this through to the end, my authoress amie. I have confidence that you can do it.

With my love, my thanks, and my apologies,
Jean-Gabriel

The notary tapped gently on the door and cracked it open just enough to poke his head in. "Do you need some more time Madame?" Evie declined the proffered extension. She'd reread the missive enough times in his absence that she already had it committed to memory. With her permission the rest of Maître Miljour's body followed his head into the office. "Do you have any questions?" he asked as he took up the seat opposite Evie. The deceased's hand-picked operative was roiling with questions, but somehow she couldn't manage to articulate a single one of them, and in the absence thereof the meeting was at its end. The notary declared himself at her service, handed her his card, and released her into the fresh air with Jean-Gabriel's apartment key fob weighing down her pocket.

There was no way to avoid Jean-Gabriel's door, which fronted onto the main lobby, short of entering the complex through the cellar, a bit of childish subterfuge to which Evie availed herself for a spell after her session with the notary. She hadn't yet mustered the strength to face the outline of her friend's doorway, let alone pass over the threshold of his now uninhabited apartment. She took to looping around the building to get in through the back alley entrance, a time-sucking detour as the condo's cadastral footprint was of biblical proportions, covering an outsized city block that matched the full hectare of the property's original vocation. Evie seldom ran into any of her neighbours en route to that secondary entryway. Even if the distance wasn't enough to dissuade them, her fellow residents tended to snub the gunmetal back door since it served as the passageway of choice for the garbage cans and the recycling bins. The spillover from those containers littered the alley, turning it into a popular brunch spot for the neighbourhood vermin. For now, though, despite its drawbacks logistical and pestilential, the rear door suited Evie just fine.

The stairs inside the back door led directly to the basement. The condo's underbelly had been only minimally renovated. The space wasn't deep enough to convert into a parking garage so the builders slapped in a bank of storage lockers, brought the necessaries up to code, just, and then skedaddled back upstairs to expend all their efforts on the building's showier bits. They left untouched the flagstone floors and the arched recesses that had served the religious community as root cellars. Nor did they overextend themselves on basement ventilation paraphernalia. Two lethargic ceiling fans effectively recirculated the same cryptish air that dated from the nineteenth century. As for lighting, the cut-rate fixtures the electricians installed expressed fewer lumens than a votive candle. The ancient cobwebs, massive affairs, suffered no ill-effects in the cellar's slipshod renovation. No worker ever thought to lift a broom to them. Spun back in the day when the sisters ruled the roost, their grizzled resident spiders still sported a tonsure out of respect for their former landlords.

Evie cut through the basement to get over to the fire-stairs that allowed her to bypass the lobby. Even though her new route meant that what used to be a quick zip out to the *dépanneur* for a litre of milk was now a major reconnaissance operation, a good half-hour just to whiten her coffee, she was determined to stick with it for however long it took her to get her memories safely caged up in solitary.

It was several weeks into Evie's subterranean routine, after she'd pulled the door to behind her and taken a few steps forward into the basement, that her nerves shot her a warning that she wasn't alone. She stopped in her tracks, all her senses on high alert, but when a full minute ticked by and they detected neither noise nor movement she let out her breath. Evie figured out easily enough what had overcome her in the stillness of the convent cellar. Lately, her brain had voided itself of every subject save Jean-Gabriel's request, so her imagination had lots of extra room to kick around in. To test how far it could push its new limits it engineered a mini-hallucination to goose her one. Evie was a good sport and sloughed it off. Her joints unfroze and she continued to make her way forward, humming her way out of the quiet. But halfway to her destination the impression of another presence nearby seized hold of her yet again. No, not the impression, the surety. Acting against all her instincts that bade her flee, she whirled around to confront the lurker. A wimpled shadow flitted across the cellar in front of her. In the dim moted light Evie could just make out against its grey serge habit the profile of a scooped up apron loaded with carrots to carry up to the refectory soup kettles. So ended Evie's spelunking expeditions. She reverted to the direct route, but continued to ignore Jean-Gabriel's apartment until his keys on her kitchen counter guilted her into action and she used them as they were intended.

Someone had been in the flat ahead of her, most probably Mme. Côté nosing about, straightening up in the wake of the Urgences-Santé technicians. The medicine bottles were cleared away and the bed stripped down. Evie was relieved those jobs hadn't fallen to her. If she'd known that they'd been lifted from her plate, she might have come in sooner. The apartment had taken on its pre-sickbed aspect, hardly any different from when she used to visit with Jean-Gabriel in the early days. She checked around, assessing what needed to be done, but he'd made it easy for her. The closets, the only part of the apartment with any critical mass, had already been Salvation-Armied. All that remained of his possessions were his few sprigs of furniture, the books, and the contents of his kitchen cupboards. A morning's worth of phone calls and she'd be done. With that part of things anyway.

The computer stood invitingly on his desk in the bedroom.

Evie sat down in front of it and flicked it on. She waited while the relic roused itself, enjoying a brief flutter of cheerful expectation. Maybe there was a nearly finished play in there and she could end up being Jean-Gabriel's literary executrix. Now that had a nice ring to it. All those -ix words sounded special somehow; they were so thin on the ground. Aviatrix, dominatrix. She riffled through her brain's rhyming dictionary to come up with a couple more examples when the computer finally burped to life. The desktop was as spare as the apartment with only a few documents aligned down one side, the topmost labelled with her initials. It couldn't be the letter about the bequest. That was handwritten. She clicked to open it.

Bingo! A play it was. She hovered over Jean-Gabriel's final project with reverence before dipping in. It was her first privileged insight into the creative mind at work. If he had left it behind on paper, she would have stopped to don archival gloves.

From the outside-in her professor of contemporary literature had lectured them. Take the satellite approach, he'd said. View every fresh work you come to integrally and only then zoom in on the words. Take care to analyze at every level, not just the lexical. Lucky for her she'd been paying attention that day. It was important that she do this properly. Not only for herself. Posterity was counting on her. Evie squeezed her eyes shut for a few seconds to fuzzy up her vision a bit, and then did a whiz-through with the scroll bar from bottom to top, hoping that without the botheration of individual words, she'd see through to the secret pattern of supports Jean-Gabriel used to keep his text from getting fallen arches. It seemed to be at a very preliminary stage, that much she could gather, his draft speckled with a spilled spice jar's worth of ellipses and asterisks. There were whole clumps of dialogue coloured red, others blue, sections bolded and italicized out of nowhere. Clearly Jean-Gabriel had devised his own idiosyncratic notation style, upclassing him in her esteem, if indeed that were possible, to da Vinci status.

What exactly had he meant her to do with this, his last opus; more of an opus-let really, considering it came in at just under fifteen pages? Only one idea came to her. He'd always praised her talents as an author, though his lavish compliments on that score, as well as on so many others, were based on scanty evidence. Evie understood that this over-adulatory tic of her late neighbour in her direction was a function of his in-built chivalric style and she let it go. She'd never actually shown him her failed novel and he'd never pushed to read it. The only writing samples of hers he might ever have had occasion to see were the pieces that concluded with *survived by*, none of them a chef-d'oeuvre. In her writing group, Evie's partner, that superior bastard, had called her stories *workmanlike*. She'd been hoping he'd pick a word like *muscular* to describe her prose. *Melodic* she would have settled for. But no, he'd gone for *workmanlike*, an adjective that could only make the heart of a plumber beat pitty-pat. Mr. I've-Been-Published-in-the-*Iowa Review* hadn't been able to wrap his plow-horse mind around her distinctive style. The oaf didn't know from experimental. But Evie's unremitting non-success with literary magazines, agents, contest judges, and publishers brought her around to his way of thinking eventually. Jean-Gabriel couldn't have seriously considered that she would pick up this fragment from where he left off and finish it. And if she couldn't finish it, just what could she do with it in its current shaggy state?

A writer of his stature merited a repository, all of his works, finished and un, collected under one roof, not to mention the manuscripts, playbills, photographs, translations, and correspondence. Probably his computer and his desk thrown in too. *Realia* didn't they call that stuff? Or was the proper term *memorabilia*? Evie'd have to track down every last item, get it assembled, catalogue the lot, and then play referee with all the libraries and universities feuding over the privilege of curating it. Her executrix fantasy was rapidly starting to pall.

She didn't have a clue how to pull all this together on top of her prior obligation to Jean-Gabriel that was already sucking up the whole of her mental energy. But she was getting ahead of herself. Now was the time to cozy up and read what she had before her. She seated her mind in a loge at the theatre and let the drama on the pages unfold.

Chapter 10

ACT 1. SCENE 1.

Small, modern apartment. At c. stage a dining room with ten people squeezed around a rectangular table. It is night. The table is set festively, lit candles, wine bottles. Indistinguishable talk and bursts of laughter. A pullman kitchen stage r. Piles of dishes, pots, pans rise from the counters and the floor. Ellie is shifting them around, deckchair style. She's thirty-ish, blowsy, with owlish glasses, an old-lady smock apron over her dress. A knock at the front door. She leaves the kitchen to deposit a heaped platter on the table. The guests grab for it like piranhas and then return to their chatter. She heads to the door and yanks it open. Philippe is standing at the door holding a parcel.

ELLIE. So Eliahu, now you show up? You're way early. You're not due for another few pages. We're only at the *afikoman*. Your watch running fast?

PHILIPPE. Eli-who? No, you've got it wrong. I'm Philippe, from downstairs.

ELLIE. (Addresses her guests.) Philippe from downstairs he claims to be. What does he take us for, chumps? Wouldn't we recognize Eliahu even if he is trying to pass? Who else would come knocking on Passover?

PHILIPPE. I don't know this person you were expecting, Madame, but I really am Philippe from downstairs. 101A? This package got dropped in the box at my place by mistake. I thought it might be important so I brought it up. I'm sorry to break in. I didn't realize you had a party going on.

ELLIE. Come to think of it, you don't actually look like I've always imagined Eliahu to look. I thought he'd be dressed more desert sheik-y, you know, all turbaned and draped. Like Osama bin Ladn. But shorter. And here you show up at my front door right smartish in Hugo Boss. All right, Philippe from downstairs. I'll let myself be convinced that you are who you say you are. (She looks at her hands to assess the dirt and wipes them off on the bosom of her apron. She takes the package, sets it down and puts out her hand to shake. Philippe accepts it tentatively.) Ellie Teitelman. Come in. Please. Join us.

PHILIPPE. (Backing out the door.) Philippe de Niverville. No, no. Thanks, but I don't want to intrude. I'll leave you to your company. *Au revoir*. It was nice meeting you. I hope your friend comes that you're expecting. I hear the bridges are murder with the construction. Maybe he got tied up in traffic.

ELLIE. (Grabs Philippe by both hands and tries to pull him into the apartment. He pulls back towards the outer hall. A tug of war ensues at the threshold.) Don't go, I insist. You're more than welcome even if you are only a second stringer. On Passover we're meant to invite strangers to our table. Commanded to. It says so right in the Haggadah: *Let all who are hungry come and eat.* You wouldn't want to be the cause of our shirking our religious obligation and damning us to Hell, now would you? Do you really want to have all that on your head Philippe from downstairs? Besides there's no shortage of food as you can see.

DANIEL. You're misrepresenting it to the poor guy Ellie, calling it food. Be honest with him at least.

DEBBY. Sawdust is more like it. Or sand, if you want to keep to the desert theme.

ELLIE. I don't know what you're complaining about. A few minutes ago you were all clamouring for more.

DANIEL. They say a starving man will drink his own piss. Even develop a taste for it. The ultimate *Appellation contrôlée*.

ELLIE. Stop. You're scaring him. (She clutches Philippe protectively.) What will he think of us, his own neighbours?

DANIEL. Ellie, let him escape while the going's good. Down in 101A he probably has bread. And wine with corks. Come to think of it, why don't we move the whole enchilada down to his place? It could only improve things.

MOSE. Dump on the meal all you want, but leave my dessert out of it. It is magnifico. I guarantee it. Made with my own two little hands. Your taste buds will sing with pleasure.

ELLIE. Finally. Some encouragement from the peanut gallery. What do you say Philippe? Are you man enough?

PHILIPPE. I guess I could sit down. Just for a minute.

ELLIE. Attaboy. We'll put you right next to me. Scooch over everybody and make room. Find me a chair somebody?
(Philippe sits down. Ellie overfills a plate with food from the various platters. She serves it to Philippe from behind, leaning heavily against him.) Eat up. Don't be shy. (She hands him a Haggadah.) And here's your side dish.

PHILIPPE. What's this?

ELLIE. That's known as the Haggadah.

PHILIPPE. The what?

DANIEL. The *Haggadah*. The book we read out loud on Passover to put off the meal as long as humanly possible.

PHILIPPE. At our house we were never allowed to read at the table.

ELLIE. You obviously come from a more civilized culture than we do. Here we read while we stuff ourselves, we undo our belt buckles to make room for more, we stick fingers in our wine glasses and dribble wine all over our plates. Cloddish, I'll grant you, but liberating all the same. (She locks arms possessively with Philippe.) So Philippe from downstairs. What do you do in life?

PHILIPPE. I'm a filmmaker.

ELLIE. Oh. Yet another artiste to join our little *salon*. I myself am a writer and Mose here is a master of the flaky arts. A genius of pastry. Trained in Paris no less.

MOSE. But Passover is a rough time for me. Seeing as how it's a no-yeast season. Baking soda, baking powder, all those risers. Verboten every one of them.

PHILIPPE. Oh really? And what's the scriptural reason behind that?

MOSE. It has to do with commemorating desert cuisine or some such.

ELLIE. Desert cuisine he says. Ha! That's rich. They've been hammering the Passover story into your skull for the whole of your thirty years on earth and you can't answer that simple question? Scratch what I said before, Philippe. He's not a genius of pastry. What you have here before you is the idiot savant of pastry.

MOSE. You can never pass up an opportunity to snipe at me, can you?

ELLIE. Why would I? It's like shooting fish in a barrel.

MOSE. (To Philippe.) A writer she calls herself. A published poetess. What do they call that magazine again that accepted your piece and then promptly went under? Remind me? The one where all the poems started with *There once was a man from Nantucket*?

ELLIE. Enough.

MOSE. Or was it a haiku rag? Nah, couldn't have been. You'd never keep yourself down to ten stinkin' words. Restraint's not your strong suit.

DANIEL. And they're off! Okay you two, back to your corners. Let's put our best face forward for the company, shall we? Some more wine Philippe? (Philippe puts his hand over his glass. Daniel lifts it off.) A word of advice my friend. Take it from one who knows. In the absence of an Ativan this deadens things nicely.

PHILIPPE. (Swigs back the whole glass.) So this book, the Haggadah. Sorry if I interrupted your liturgy.

ELLIE. No, no. It's Okay. Actually you're lucky you showed

up when you did. Perfect timing. There's a pause in the reading action right now. We were just about to go search for the *afikoman*. It's a piece of matzo. That's what we call this overdeveloped cracker that we choke down instead of bread during the week of Passover. See, we wrap it up and hide it at the beginning of the ceremony, and then hunt it down at the end for a prize. Well, it's the kids that would normally do the hunting, but since we're lacking any little darlings…

DEBBY. What it boils down to Philippe is parents incentivizing the kids to pay attention through the whole tralala. In the old days they called it what it was, a good honest bribe. Now they make it sound more entrepreneurial.

PHILIPPE. A sound economic principle under either name. What do you get paid off for it? Or *earn* I guess I should say.

ELLIE. A loonie. A toonie maybe if your family's flush. High stakes poker it ain't. (She addresses the whole table.) You gotta admit, though, that there is something fundamentally screwed up here. What kid, especially a kid with the monetary instincts native to our Tribe, shall we say, would be stupid enough to consider a measly buck or two adequate compensation for having to sit still through that shitload of rabbinical hot air? Am I right or am I right? Wouldn't you think our kids would be savvier? I'm just throwing it out there.

DEBBY. An interesting ethnographic question. I wonder if the Rothschilds and the Madoffs held out for more back when they were in Pesadik short pants?

DANIEL. I can Google it if you want.

ELLIE. Put away your phone. You can save the research for some other time. For now we're going with the program.

Okay everybody. Fan out. The whole apartment is fair game. Search for the *afikoman* in any room you want. I used all my considerable ingenuity to hide that sucker.

ACT 1. SCENE 2.

The bedroom in the same apartment. Philippe is alone in the room. Taps his pockets as if looking for his cigarettes when Ellie enters.

ELLIE. Any luck?

PHILIPPE. Not so far.

ELLIE. Feel free to go ahead and smoke if you want. I don't mind.

PHILIPPE. No, I probably shouldn't after all. One of your guests will surely object. It's *de rigueur* these days. I'll head outside and contribute a few more butts to the courtyard.

ELLIE. (She plants herself between him and the door.) Come on. What's your rush to go? Are you sure you've exhausted this room?

PHILIPPE. Pretty much so.

ELLIE. I don't think you could have searched very carefully. You haven't been in here long enough to be very thorough. Tell me where you looked.

PHILIPPE. Under the bed.

ELLIE. Under the bed, he says! Don't you need imagination to be a filmmaker?

PHILIPPE. Maybe that's why I'm not a very successful filmmaker.

ELLIE. Here's an outside-the-box idea for you. Consider this. Maybe the *afikoman*'s hiding somewhere on my person. In my pocket, for instance, or down my dress. Did you think of that? A moveable feast. (She shuts the door.) I can crank up the reward, you know. Since it's my place, I'm entitled. It's a codicil in the Haggadah. I can show you the page reference if you don't believe me. Give you the exact line number.

PHILIPPE. Thanks for the offer, but my nicotine fit is having fits. I'll have to take a rain check.

ELLIE. Future Shop this isn't. I don't give out rain checks. A *no* now is a *no* forever. Weigh that carefully before you go. A once in a lifetime opportunity up for grabs. (Philippe tries to slip past her to the door while she's unzipping her apron when Mose enters.)

MOSE. Am I interrupting something? A hot 'n heavy *afikoman* search perhaps?

ELLIE. Doesn't a closed door mean anything to you?

MOSE. I didn't see any sock.

ELLIE. Go crawl around under the dining room table to occupy yourself, why don't you? Maybe you'll find the *afikoman* there and earn yourself an easy dollar. And even if you don't, you're sure to find a penny that dropped out of somebody's pocket so your time won't be totally wasted.

MOSE. (To Philippe.) You've got to watch out for our Ellie. But I'm guessing you've noticed. A fast worker, that one. You've been in here together what, two minutes already?

And you're both still upright? She must be slowing down in her old age.

ELLIE. Ignore him. As usual he doesn't know what he's talking about.

MOSE. Oh, I know what I'm talking about all right when it comes to your shenanigans. A tiger can't change her spots.

ELLIE. That's a leopard you moron. (To Philippe.) See what fuckwits I have to deal with around here? Is it any wonder I'm craving intelligent company?

MOSE. You think I don't know your MO? Let's just test it out. Philippe here can be the judge. He'll tell us if what I say rings any bells. You game Philippe? (Philippe looks longingly at the blocked door, shrugs his acquiescence and sits down on the bed.)

Okay, so to start, she lines herself up a prospect from outside her usual circle of acquaintance. It has to be that way. See, the rest of us, we've been Ellie-proofed. Learned our lesson the hard way. Want me to enter my bruises as exhibit A? (Mose starts to lift his shirt.)

ELLIE. He's crazy. I told you.

MOSE. Hold on. Hold on. You'll get your turn before the bench. Now where was I before I was so rudely interrupted? Oh right. She finds her mark and she has him between the crosshairs. Right off the bat she tries to bedazzle him with zingy chit-chat, hoping to establish her credentials as a brain, a wit. This is a crucial step. She has to land it just right, because clearly a body built like that can't be expected to carry the show. I mean I ask you. Isn't that what they call on *Law and Order* prima facie evidence? Or do I have that wrong?

ELLIE. Quit putting on airs. You should stick to Pig Latin, your native tongue.

MOSE. Withdrawn. So this stage can't go on for very long since, like I said, her pool of repartee is shallow. Once the yakking dries up, she has to get physical. What else is there left for her to do? That's when she goes into her patented clinging vine routine, hangs all over the poor sap. All hands on deck. Wraps herself around him as tight as Saran till he can hardly draw breath from under that tarp of flab. It's usually around now that he's getting it into his mind to make a run for it.

ELLIE. Aren't you tired of this game yet? It must be taxing your short attention span.

MOSE. Patience, patience. I still have a ways to go. Philippe, you know that sinking feeling you get sometimes when you pick up a girl who's sitting alone at a bar and before you get to the olive at the bottom of the first drink you clue in to why everyone else gave her such a wide berth? Well it's like that, if you need me to paint you a picture.

But Ellie here, she's blessed with a good shnozzola. As soon as she sniffs out that she's got a flight risk on her hands she dispenses with the preliminaries and jumps him, bang, in her inimitable way. You're lucky I walked in when I did. Once she has her mitts on you it's like being humped by a gorilla. Do I have it right so far, Bwana Philippe?

ELLIE. (To Mose.) Look who's talking. Passover defines you to a T. We all know that without any leavening powders acting on you, you'd never manage to get it up. I can match you point for point little man.

* * *

"Evie, you in there?" Moshe was yoo-hooing to her from

Jean-Gabriel's front door. "Hello-o. Evie, that you? Anybody home?" She didn't respond, but he took the open door as an invitation. She could hear his footsteps padding towards her through the living room. She shouldn't have left the door wide open after she let herself in, but she'd dreaded being entombed in Jean-Gabriel's apartment. She figured that with the buzz of the building's hallway traffic in her ears she'd feel less confined. Wrong choice. Why was it that hindsight never kicked in early enough? She should have picked claustrophobia. If only she'd closed the door and locked it Moshe wouldn't be about to glimpse the smears goose-stepping across the screen before her. And once he started to read there'd be no going back.

There was barely time to rectify her bungling, but she had to spare him. She owed him that. Evie clicked to snap the file closed just as Moshe was coming into the bedroom behind her, but Jean-Gabriel's arthritic computer was slow to comply. She clicked on the X again and again but the overdose of the *close* command addled the machine. Evie'd flooded it. The file just hung there, its dialogue blaring in the bulked-up font Jean-Gabriel's clouding eyes had resorted to those last weeks. She fumbled with the monitor button but her fingers were limp. She couldn't press hard enough to do the job on her first try. Moshe had his hands on the back of her chair and was leaning in to read over her shoulder. As a last resort she closed her eyes and willed herself to vaporize but when she looked down to check on her corporal status she was still sitting in front of the computer, as visible as ever. Moshe hadn't reacted yet. How could he hold it in? She dared to lift her eyes back up. The screen was blissfully blank. In the endless instant since she'd looked away, Word 1922 had finally managed to sort out her manic multiple messages and given the file the hook.

"I was worried when I saw the place left open," he told her.

"It's only me straightening things up."

"Glad I don't have to wrestle with a burglar. I wasn't really prepared for that. Boy, when you clean up a place you don't fool around. Even neatening up the desktop. Anything interesting?"

"No, just junk."

"Need any help?"

"I'm fine thanks. Be done in a minute. Just leave me here to finish it off so I won't have to come back."

"You know where to find me if you change your mind." He headed out but Evie called him back.

"Mosh. Thanks for the offer."

"No problemo. Don't work yourself too hard, now."

She didn't have to. It was open and shut. Jean-Gabriel had learned his lesson well since he'd fouled his own nest with *Amélie*. After that, when his gimpy imagination needed a crutch he foraged further afield for inspiration, preying on acquaintances of the disposable type with which he was so richly endowed, individuals whose exact relationship to him couldn't be as easily pinned down. He didn't risk offending anyone of significance with his new approach, just the poor sods who recognized themselves on stage. Their humiliation was internal, their rejection private. He'd landed on a fail-safe system. Chew them up, spit them out, move on to the next lot.

Evie strained to contort the evidence in an effort to give her friend his due. It was her habit of a lifetime. This time she couldn't make it work. Jean-Gabriel would simply have called his practice *fictionalizing*, but Evie wasn't sucked in by the innocuous sound of that word. In her mind, the playwright's technique was right up there with euthanasia; it sounded right-minded unless you were the one whose face was on the wrong side of the pillow.

She pilloried herself instead of the proper victim. She'd been too arrogant to accept the warnings of her mother and Audrée. Oh no, she knew better. Her gut instincts were infallible. Who did they think they were to knock her judgment? Evie'd forged ahead despite them and welcomed the snake into her own home for God's sake, welcomed him with open arms, delivered her friends up to him like some Shabbos pimp, the easier for him to defile them. But her, her he'd singled out for special attention. In heartfelt recognition of her boundless *naïveté, stupidité,* and *honnêteté,* Jean-Gabriel nobbled Evie for an extra credit assignment. Of course she'd have to carry it out unsupervised as he'd be inconveniently dead, but she'd follow it through to the end. She was such a straight-arrow, Evie. He had her pegged. She'd never tear up the cheque and walk away. He'd trusted her and in exchange she'd slog her way through the slime of his posthumous commission somehow. If only she could forget what she'd seen while she was scrambling to close the file and her eyes skipped ahead to the list of possible titles. She'd just had time to absorb the first one in the column, the one with the two red asterisks. It would stick in her craw forever. *The Village Idiots' Buffet.*

Chapter 11

SO WHAT DID AARON WANT WITH HER after all this time? According to the voice-mail he'd left her while she was at lunch, she was being summoned to the boss's office to discuss the Médéry file. There was a file? It was news to her. Normally Aaron wasn't one to rehash, let alone months later. Why disinter and dismember previous prose? It was an abomination. Besides, even if he had suddenly found syntactical fault with the paper's sendoff of Jean-Gabriel, Evie hadn't been involved in the end product, as he was well aware. Despite all her prep work, JGM was too big a fish to toss into Evie's skillet for a simple garnish of butter and parsley, so at the last minute Aaron flipped the playwright over to one of his maître-sauciers for a more lavish final treatment. A good thing, probably. For once Evie was grateful that all-stars didn't fall into her hands.

Before heading over to Aaron's office, she gave her colleague's write-up a professional once-over. In fairness, it covered all the bases without descending into hagiography. Quebecers liked their defunct heroes a bit raggedy, and the text duly portrayed Jean-Gabriel with his halo chipped.

Her editor was leaning against the doorframe, waiting. He pointed Evie towards the single guest chair with a gracious gesture that his tongue didn't know how to match. "Park your butt." Evie balanced herself on the edge of the seat. "Coffee?" He poured some for them both from the insulated carafe beside him. Only once Evie witnessed him drinking from his own cup did she dare to drink from hers. You couldn't be too careful. The head of the graveyard shift was making an effort; politeness to him didn't come easy having been raised by wolves. His obsequiousness threw her off balance. If she hadn't reread the union contract the week before, she would have sworn he was gearing up to give her the boot. Aaron passed her a vending machine danish on a scrap of brown paper towel and leaned comfortably forward as if he routinely invited the peons in for a chummy kaffeeklatsch.

"I solved a little mystery for myself today and I'm feeling pretty good about it." Evie dismissed out of hand the possibility that he'd finally cracked the classic walking-while-chewing-gum conundrum. The office odds on that one were too long. She waited patiently to let the twerp have his big reveal, if that's what his little mind was set on.

"Remember a while back when I emailed you Jean-Gabriel Médéry's name as a dead duck and you double checked with me on it?" Evie nodded her recollection. "I wondered at the time why you were so curious about him. You'd never second-guessed me on anybody before, let alone an old fart. Why that old fart, I asked myself. It's not like he wasn't due to check out. I mean the guy was up there. Well now, out of the blue, I have my answer. A little bird told me this morning that you knew him. Not knew of, but actually knew him, on a personal basis." He could barely squelch his excitement.

"That's right," Evie said. She'd already decided on her strategy. She'd keep her responses to the minimum. Why pay out enough rope for him to hang her with? For surely, though she couldn't fully grasp why, a scaffold with her name on it was hiding behind his coat cabinet. She resolved to bite off her replies while they were still exiting her lips, locking the gate on the full story. The problem with this approach was that Evie's open personality didn't take well to conversational pauses. She always felt obliged to fill in awkward silences. Such was her character. Like nature she abhorred a vacuum.

"We were friends," she added. With her artless description of her status vis-à-vis Jean-Gabriel, Evie felt Aaron's eyes making the rounds of her body in a reappraising way, one that made her crave a proximate fig tree. It was obvious their definitions of the term *friend* didn't jibe. She had no alternative but to clarify, hoping to shift his mind from the Lotharian sense of the word that he'd fished out of his remaindered dictionary.

"Neighbours," she fed him. Aaron digested her revision. For some reason he seemed happier with this chaste reframing of her relationship with the writer.

"I don't suppose in the course of your neighbourly acquaintance that you ever had occasion to meet the wife, Amélie?"

Et voilà. He'd gotten to the point. "No, we never did meet."

"Strange, don't you think? All these years and she's never opened up. A regular sphinx. No one's ever been able to get that broad to spill her guts for the record." Aaron was picturing a better office for himself, one on an upper floor. With a secretary of his own. Maybe one of those ergonomic chairs. And the increased email quota the newspaper allotted to managers, the better to redistribute his porn. His employee's connection to Amélie Médéry was tenuous, practically non-existent, but that thread was all he had to loop round his waist so she could hoick him out of the death biz where he got no respect.

"It would be quite a coup for the paper if you could land an interview. A coup for you if you could pull it off. Who knows where it would lead?"

As if she needed reminding that Amélie shunned all interviews. It was the very fact Evie had cursed her for in the past. But now, with her revisionist perspective, she had nothing but admiration for the woman's *sang-froid*. No way on earth would she intrude on Amélie's privacy on that simian Aaron's behalf.

But on second thought, was this meeting some kind of cosmic wake-up call? Evie'd been stalling on the Amélie front, the cheque burning a hole in the GIC where it was parked. She reran in her memory the crystal ball divertissement Aaron had put on for her when she'd questioned the presence of the playwright's name on his soon-to-succumb list. Now she was viewing his performance with a less jaundiced eye. Evie's understanding of occult machinations was vague, but supposing Aaron genuinely was a channeler between the spirit world and terra firma. Could it be that Jean-Gabriel was giving her an otherworldly kick-start using her boss as an intermediary? No, she rejected the notion just as quickly as she came up with it. What poltergeist in his right mind would choose to communicate with earthlings using Aaron as the middleman. Talk about scraping the bottom of the psychic barrel. But then again, maybe wherever it was that Jean-Gabriel was consigned you couldn't pick and choose your emissary. She pictured a Shawshank setup where you go collect your laundered jumpsuit and blankets from the trustee and find a name slipped between the folds in exchange for two packs of Luckies. Evie decided not to obsess over procedural matters. The important thing was that this dispatch from the beyond had successfully played dodge ball with the meteors and the comets and the dead sputniks littering the highways and byways of outer space in order to reach its designated addressee. It was time for her to act.

On this street the pigeons had the better view. The modest rowhouse facades were nothing to write home about, refrigerator boxes, samey and symmetrical. But somehow the rooftops hadn't gotten the memo. They were decked out for Ascot, sporting florid headgear meant to redirect the eye from their flat-chested undercarriage that would never snag a suitor. The rooflines on the east side of the street aped the Middle Ages with enough crenellated castle towers to shield a regiment of archers, while the houses on the opposite side were more eclectic in their roofery, more pacific in their appurtenances, decorated variously with Aladdin's lamps, funerary urns, and beavers. Number 6738, though, lacked any rooftop puffery, thrown up by a builder armed with no more than a T-square and a deadline.

To get to the back yard, which was evidently their destination, they passed through a side hallway that gave Evie a clear view of all the rooms on the main floor. Though the owner wasn't really that much older than she, the décor was all sensible shoes and support hose, everything squared to the corners, nothing out of place. In the hospital kitchen, one plate and its matched mug snoggled in the drainer, their frisky intimacy at odds with the priggish aura of the house. No doubt they'd be reprimanded later by matron.

But if the house was spinsterish, the garden had flung off its corset, scattering its stays like buckshot into the mulch. No edged plots here; no trace of the manic alignment that blighted the home's interior. In the secluded yard, a merry anarchy of flora belied its master's restrained intervention. Amélie and Evie sat down at a tiny wrought iron table shaded by a grape arbour. Their chat lurched along, pausing after each of Evie's serves that couldn't seem to get a steady volley going.

"I've never seen such an amazing garden. Sitting here, you'd swear you were in Provence."

"That was the plan."

"Was there much back here when you moved in?"

"No. *Rien*. Just packed earth."

"So you created it all from scratch?"

"Pretty much so."

"It must take up a lot of your time, even though it looks so natural."

"Yes, but I enjoy making things grow."

"Not me. My thumb is so black, I've been known to kill a plastic geranium."

"*Ah oui?*"

The excess of conversational dead air had by now coalesced into a mini-climate that clamped itself onto the postage stamp garden, choking off Evie's gift for small talkery. Usually she was able to coax the most buttoned-up interlocutor into giving out. It was one of her hostessy skills. But in these peculiarly oppressive conditions, with all her sallies falling to naught, the intervals in between efforts began to stretch uncomfortably long. It must have been the FedEx envelope sitting on the table between them that had her off her game. Even though Evie had sent it herself; even though its presence accounted for her visit, it disconcerted her to see it in these unfamiliar surroundings.

Amélie came to her rescue. She pulled from the envelope the copy of Jean-Gabriel's unfinished play that Evie had printed out and set it on the table. Her index finger drummed the text.

"This Ellie in here, this is you I presume."

"It's me."

"And the others? Outside of Philippe I mean. Made up?"

Evie shook her head. "My closest friends. They're more than friends really. They might as well be my family."

Silence reigned again, but of a different tenor; a deeper, more contemplative quiet. Amélie passed the pages back and for a second they both clasped them from opposite ends. It amounted to the secret handshake, the proof they were members of a support group of two that met in the same church basement. The realization that they were sisters under the skin freed Amélie to hurdle over several levels of trust that ordinarily would have been the work of months, even years. She plunged in with no preamble.

"It was the kids, you see."

"I don't follow you, what kids?"

"The kids I failed to have. If not for that who knows how things would have ended up between us. Funny, for someone who defied her parents to marry an older man, a *bohémien* like they called him, my dreams were as traditional as they come. I didn't want a career for myself. What could I do anyway at that age? A home full of kids. That's what I wanted. It's what we both wanted."

Evie could easily imagine the barney if at the age of seventeen she had brought home for pre-nuptial inspection a beau who, if you stopped to count his tree rings, was closing in on the mid-century mark, outranking her own father in longevity and paunch. But à la Amélie she would have plugged her ears to their warnings. Such was the way of daughters in love. Parents, however modern they saw themselves, however many generations removed from the old country, never twigged that nowadays these visits were mere formalities. By the time mum and dad were meeting the hoary reprobate who was in any event already shacked up with their daughter, resistance was futile. According to the script, now was the moment for them to negotiate with the *alta kocker* who'd mesmerized their daughter as to the number of goats they'd contribute to the ménage.

Amélie went on, "But the babies didn't come, and they didn't come and they didn't come. Who imagines that kind of thing when they're young? I thought it would be instantaneous. You know, like it is when you *don't* want them. Well, it didn't take long for things to go sour after that. And they soured with a bang as you and the whole world now know."

Evie was processing this missing link when Amélie added, "To be fair, it wasn't just Jean. Neither of us handled it very maturely."

"But you weren't mature," Evie jumped in, eager to support the overgenerous Amélie with all the firepower at her disposal. "You were hardly out of your teens at the time." Ever since Evie had unfriended Jean-Gabriel post-mortem, she needed someone else to put in his slot on her tool belt. Otherwise she was off balance. Replacing him with Amélie would restore her equilibrium. She struck Evie as eminently deserving, short acquaintance be damned.

The facile ageist out that Evie tendered on a salver was shoved aside by its intended recipient. "Let's just say there was a lot of blaming going around. He was certain it was me, that it was my equipment that was defective, shall we say."

Evie wasn't sure if pushing the gynecological line of inquiry was going too far but apparently she was her mother's daughter in the end. She snapped on a pair of latex gloves and dove right in. "Was it true?"

"We never had tests. Can you believe that? Nothing so practical. We just yelled louder. That was our way. Who knows, maybe we would have worked it out eventually. But once he wrote the play, well, that was it. What was private became public."

"You could have denied that it was true, given a few of those *our life together is just peachy* interviews. That's all it would have taken. Spared yourself the humiliation."

"That's exactly what Jean wanted. For me to lie. Just like you, he said it would serve me well. Serve both of us well actually. But I preferred to crawl in a hole. Another example of my mature thinking."

"You never married again?"

"No. I never met anyone else who I was willing to take a chance on after that. I never reconciled with my family either. But the worst was that I never had the kids I'd always longed for. And that's about it for me. I cope."

It was an ugly example Amélie held up to her, looking back to see your entire existence defined by nevers. It cut dangerously close to the bone, threatening to dump Evie back into the funk of headstone mode, where she had a tendency of late to wallow, picturing the feeble inscription that would sum up her no-account life. Suddenly all the remaining questions she'd had at the ready dried up; all those petty whys and wherefores were overshadowed by more fundamental issues that seized control of her brain.

The meeting was unravelling just as fast from the Amélie end. Shedding the reticence of a lifetime had taken its toll. Her composure was starting to crack around the edges. Evie recognized the signs. It was as if she were looking in a mirror. Though she'd barely arrived she already sensed that she'd overstayed.

She was struggling to conjure up a plausible exit strategy but Amélie was quicker on the draw. She reached behind her to grab the wicker moses basket that was sitting on her stoop and then pointed toward the garden plot by the back fence that was apparently calling out her name, demanding her attention on a matter of some urgency. Surely her guest understood her obligation as first responder. She left Evie alone at the table with an apologetic shrug.

Amélie knelt down at the far bed in a practiced garden crouch that her knees were only lately starting to resist. She cast her eyes over the gathering of plants before her. They went way back together, Amélie and her shrubs and flowers. They were tight. She'd grown them from seeds and slips, most of them, nursed them along in her tumbledown shed until she adjudged them ready to stand on their own two feet in the outside world. She knew their characters inside out. There were the bullies who would take over the whole bed if she didn't play hall monitor, the diva bloomers who dropped their petals any old place; the maid would come along to pick up after them, and then there were the old guard perennials who nervously peeked out from behind their curtain of blossoms as the first nervy annuals started to move in to the neighbourhood.

There wasn't really much to be done at this time of day, but since she had an audience she made a show of deadheading a couple of roses and pulling the straggler dandelion that she'd missed on her early morning bed check. She was satisfied. Everyone looked comfy, watered and clean. They'd all gone beddy-bye in the afternoon sun. Amélie took her sweet time loading her basket up with strawberries, checking over each one for imperfections. Then she turned to her blueberry bush over in the corner and repeated the one by one inspection routine that served to separate her all the longer from her visitor.

Her visitor didn't mind the separation. She sat in welcome solitude at the table, unwinding just enough to let herself fully appreciate the spectacle of colour and perfume that was Amélie's thumb-print garden. Evie's own talent for gardening was nil, her earlier admission to her host unexaggerated. She'd once given it a stab at her parents' house, a backyard dilettante with a designer straw hat and a spade who was aiming to outbloom Giverny behind the carport. Her parents, supportive as always of her whims, gave her carte blanche. The way it went, she was industrious enough in the sunshine, but neglectful in the damp or when she had a better offer. She didn't last out the season. Marilyn called a halt once she discovered that her daughter had somehow managed to kill her precious rhubarb plant whose resilient root ball dated from the big bang.

That experience wised Evie up. Now she understood the infinite patience it took to nurture plants to maturity because she didn't have it. And she understood to her shame the tenderness and devotion a thriving garden demanded of its custodian. So while she lingered at Amélie's, it interested her to observe an expert at work, someone sprung from the opposite end of the cultivating continuum to herself. Strangely, it didn't actually seem to be work to Amélie whose pinched shoulders disengaged as soon as she knelt down, as if she were safely bowered among old friends. Evie was intrigued by how touch-y she was with her plants, fondling them, tickling them, nosing them. Maybe that was one of the many ways she'd muffed it in her parents' garden. Evie'd only handled her plants on an as-needed basis, to plunk them into the soil or to pinch them back. She wasn't one for kitchy-coo, at least not with begonias. But Amélie stroked the velour ground cover with her open palm for the pure pleasure of the sensation. She jiggled her fuchsias to set their cascade of flowers dancing, and she waved her fern fronds lazily back and forth in front of her face as if she were fanning sahib.

The lush greenery, the radiant blooms, the boughs pendent with fruit; all of them conspired to give Evie a jolt of inspiration. In the time it took Amélie to run her harvest under the hose and bring it back for them to share, the idea grabbed hold of her with full force. It was a snap decision, but Evie was convinced of its essential rightness. She was rolling in cash. She could make it happen.

Chapter 12

"**D**OES ANYBODY KNOW how you'd go about buying a baby?" Evie's contributions often sheered off towards the loopy so no one in the Friday night crowd found her question any farther out of left field than usual.

"You could check out the ads in the *Penny Saver*," Dany offered. "That's what the kid did in *Juno* when she was preggo, remember? And she wanted to find a good set of parents for her baby?"

The silver screen was Evie's Wikipedia, her first point of consultation whenever she needed information or advice, so her friend's suggestion amounted to cinematic coals to Newcastle. Evie'd long since gone the *Juno* route and paged through all the pulp circulars that were delivered to her door in the weekly Publisac, but she came up empty. Nothing but deals on blade roasts and Rice-Chex. Just to cover all the bases, though, she borrowed Moshe's bike and made a tour of the Island, collecting a copy of every community newspaper printed in a decipherable alphabet until her pannier was crammed to bursting. None of them had a child trafficking column. Go figure.

The regular adoption process was out. The waiting lists were light-years long, and besides, there was probably a proscription in the agreement you signed against flipping babies like you would a residential triplex. Evie's plan, so promising, seemed stillborn.

Even with Jean-Gabriel's personal ATM at her disposal, her hands were tied. But then, in an Evel Kneivel leap of logic that had her sail cleanly over all the negatives lined up bumper to bumper on the infield below, she landed on her solution. It was deliciously simple. She would have the baby herself. Evie's mother had made one grand humanitarian gesture in life, and this was going to be hers.

So her plan was a bit out-there she had to admit. Maybe more like *way* out-there. And it wasn't what you'd call a quick fix. She was signing her uterus on for the long-haul. In the extended history of their acquaintance, Evie's womb had never pegged her as an extreme do-gooder. And it certainly never expected to be so intimately involved in any philanthropic mission. That wasn't in the owner's manual. But it was in no position to resist. With this decision Evie had found peace, so they were going forward as partners.

Evie determined to keep draft two of her birth scheme a secret until she was too far along for anyone to try to sway her from her chosen course. Once her side view announced full occupancy it would be too late to turn back. How exactly she'd field the eventual questions her bump would provoke she hadn't quite worked out, but she'd have concocted some sort of cover story by then. In the meantime she was taking a one-step-at-a-time approach, and step one was implantation.

For sober second thought she had no leisure. Amélie wasn't getting any younger. Evie moved ahead full throttle and set herself up with an appointment at a donor bank she'd once read about in a magazine at her dentist's office. The name had stuck with her, J-Sperm: For the Infertile *Frum*. Okay, so her choice of clinic made no sense. This she acknowledged to herself even though woo-woo decisions had become her stock in trade over the past few days. The baby, after all, wasn't destined to a Jewish home. Still, the surrogate mother-to-be, as unreligious as she was, felt a certain queasiness at the prospect of having one of her kosher eggs mating with *traif*. It was like the ham and cheddar on a bagel they sold at the paper's staff cafeteria; there was something fundamentally wrong in the commingling. Evie didn't want her *kishkes* harbouring a fetus at war with itself; a fetus that come December would be nagging her to buy it a Chanukah bush. Maybe Evie was non-practicing, but she was still a non-practicing Jew. She didn't hold with those phony baloney mashup holidays that cherry-picked the best bits from different traditions. Even though she presumed that Amélie would raise the child as a Catholic, if indeed she raised it churchy at all, at least the peewee Crypto Jew Evie handed over gift-wrapped would be all of a piece.

The waiting room was crowded with couples. They sat on the couches, quietly conferring, filling out the medical questionnaire on a clipboard. Often they referred to files they'd brought along, heart-wrenchingly thick. Only Evie was all alone and without a paper trail. She made short work of her form and handed it in to the receptionist. When her name was called she was led into a small consultation room and settled in at a desk.

The walls were papered in baby pictures, OU-certified graduates of Evie's chosen stud farm. The receptionist handed her one of the binders from the bookcase to browse through prior to her meeting with the doctor, and invited her to help herself to further reading material if nothing in the first binder appealed.

Evie turned eagerly to page one. The entries were arranged spreadsheet style. The first column assigned a unique code to the sperm posting its candidature. The next provided a brief biographical note (with all identifying details redacted, *comme il faut*). The remaining columns, C through Q, were devoted to the father's physical attributes; eye colour, hair colour, straight hair vs. curly, righty or lefty, swarthy or fair, lanky or runty. None of the notations regarding appearance mattered much to Evie who wasn't in the market for a bespoke baby. She accorded them only a cursory glance. Whether the baby was likely to emerge freckled and pudgy or blue-eyed and lean was to her irrelevant. Her goal was not to match the baby up to the parent, coordinating them like drapes to the wall-to-wall, so that one day off in the future the checkout girl at Provigo could remark to Amélie, "Oh Madame, your baby looks just like you." Only the column with the potted biographies piqued Evie's interest. Her profession had turned her into an aficionado of the genre.

She began to read the vitae in column B. Evie worked her way down assiduously, but after a few pages she had the distinct impression that she hadn't advanced at all, that the character sketches had cloned themselves. Maybe it was just that the clinic was using some buggy version of Excel with a duplicating fetish, but it gave her pause nonetheless. Alarm bells started to go off in her brain concerning the quality of the donor pool. Now that she belatedly stopped to consider it, what future doctor or lawyer (and they were all future doctors or lawyers according to the listings) would present himself at a clinic and pump out his plutonium grade semen benevolently? He had to have a screw loose somewhere. Any normal guy would write a cheque as a charitable donation, not jerk off into a cup. Evie shifted gears. She'd shifted gears so often in the last few days that she barely know if she was coming or going. But at least now she knew this much; she'd flip through her personal Rolodex to find her donor, someone who would upload his chromosomes onto her welcoming placental shores using the old-fashioned method.

It had not escaped Evie's notice that Moshe kept his eyes trained on her in a hankering kind of way, but she'd never given him any encouragement. Why exactly she wasn't sure, except that withholding was its own aphrodisiac. Moshe didn't deserve it, but somehow for him she'd never lowered the drawbridge that would have permitted the crossover from friend to lover. God knows she'd been a lackadaisical gatekeeper in the past, allowing to pass unchallenged an embarrassing number of iffy types, yet before Moshe, the most worthy of pretenders, Evie was determined to play the martinet.

Still, she knew without reservation that it was Moshe who would ante up her egg's better half. He was a mensch, Moshe was, a good man. If she were hired to ghostwrite his bio for the binders at the clinic, that's all she would say. His sperm would fly off the shelf. So maybe he was on the shy-ish side, Moshe; so maybe he was a lunch-pail type, no doctor or lawyer; so maybe his authorial talents didn't run to sonnets or novellas. The only writing he did, as far as Evie was aware, amounted to piping *happy birthday* onto chocolate ganache, but she wasn't in the least disdainful of this hole in his résumé the way she might have been before her recent disenchantment with a certain member of the writing profession led her to radically revise her rule book.

And even if not bookish, Moshe was cerebral. He was a flour and water intellectual, one of those baker-philosophers as revered in the Hexagon as the deconstructionalists and the phenomenologists; a new-world offshoot who, once he started in on the subject of bread, inevitably ended up linking it to life, the universe, and everything. Evie went on to consider her choice on a more earthly plane. Moshe was as solid as the day was long and funny in his quiet way. And hadn't he lifted her out of the dumps more times that she could count? Yes, here she had the *beau idéal* of a donor, and one who had always shown himself pliable to her desires to boot, a veritable Gumby. She was about to offer herself up to him holus-bolus on a silver platter, a Pippin stuffed in her mouth. He'd jump at the chance.

"I'll have to sleep on it," Moshe said.

Sleep on it? That wasn't what he was programmed to say. Moshe's backbone, never much before in evidence, had taken its good old time in making an appearance. Evie had invited

Moshe over for drinks in order to decant the plan in which he was meant to play a seminal role. He listened without interruption while she backed up to the beginning of it all, her meeting with the notary, the letter, the cheque. If Evie were adhering to a strict chronology, her discovery of the file on Jean-Gabriel's computer would come next. It had a certain big-picture relevance she supposed, but she stuck with her initial inclination to hold the play in protective custody. In her bowdlerized recounting of the events for Moshe, Jean-Gabriel's unfinished scenario bit the dust. Evie picked up her account with her visit to Amélie, and her ultimate decision to acquit her moral obligation to Jean-Gabriel with the fruit of her own loins. It was the first time she'd shared the secret of the bequest with another soul, and it was clear to Moshe, who was attuned to her every shift in tone, that Evie had suffered in the burden of its sole ownership. He absorbed the story as it unrolled, first over sips of his wine then over slugs.

That JGM had left Evie a bankroll with a cat's cradle of strings attached wasn't all that much of a surprise. The guy always struck Moshe as a taker. But the naked fact that Evie had singled him out to father this child had him reeling. He tried not to betray his shock, administering to himself a couple of mental slaps in the face to bring himself around to the job immediately at hand. He knew what he had to do, but his heart wasn't in it. The baker wanted nothing more than to acquiesce to Evie's off-the-wall proposal. How often in his dreams had she opened his bedroom door and slid between the sheets beside him, and now that it was on the verge of happening in the flesh he felt compelled to resist, compelled to force her to see reason. What a nuisance a conscience turned out to be.

Her plotline was so full of holes he hardly knew where to start in. "Evie, come on. This plan you've cooked up is way beyond the call of duty. Way beyond, I'm saying. It's a minefield. Don't you see that? And on top of everything, it's all just based on a guess, a feeling you have. How can you presume to know Amélie wants a baby?"

"She told me so."

"But that was years ago, back when she was still with Jean-Gabriel. What is she now, fifty?"

"No, she's only thirty-nine. Plenty young enough for a baby. My cousin Andrea gave birth at forty-three. You know how it is with women now, they wait till their clocks are almost at their last tick and then they jump for it. Thirty-nine, that's nothing."

"Well if she did want a baby so desperately all this time like you say, wouldn't she have done something about it herself? Why does she need you, a perfect stranger, to come along and do it for her?" This line of reasoning Evie had difficulty countering in so many words since there was no actual reasoning involved in her calculations. She was simply convinced that she had decoded the signs correctly during her visit, that Amélie's longing for a baby was undiminished, but her barrenness had withered her to the point that she had no strength to fight against it. She was trapped, it seemed to Evie, in some kind of reproductive catch-22.

"And this grand conclusion of yours, it came to you just by studying her house and her garden? Evie, give me a break."

"I studied her too, Mosh. Of course I did. What do you take me for? Do you think I'd go ahead and put myself through the whole upheaval of a pregnancy on an off chance? This is almost a year gouged out of my life we're talking about."

"How do I know what you're capable of? Never in a million years would I have imagined you coming up with a stunt as loco as this, but here we are considering it."

"Mosh, you just have to trust me on this. I swear the vibes were there. That house of hers was crying out to be cluttered up with toys and diaper pails. Its order went against nature. She's only surviving in there, not living. She still wants a baby. I could sense it."

Moshe considered this spacey Evellian analysis of all the available non-evidence and decided a change of tack was in order. He took a stab in the dark. "It's your mother, right? You're trying to outdo her. Make your own selfless contribution to womankind."

"So what if I am? What's wrong with that?" Her testiness here indicated that he'd struck a nerve.

"Evie, your mum's gesture was impersonal in the end, a glorified joyride. Yours couldn't be any more personal. How do you know you'll even be able to give the baby up in the end?"

"This baby, when it comes, will have Amélie's name on it. I would never dream of kidnapping it to keep it for myself."

"How can you say that? Your entire body will be tangled up in it. It's not like snipping off a loose thread. You think you can just have a baby so lightly? This is an actual baby we're talking about, a real flesh and blood baby."

"You think I don't know that?"

"You don't sound like you do."

"I am only having this baby for her. That's the only reason. For her."

"Well, what if HER baby is born with something wrong with it?" Moshe started to pace.

"The baby will be fine. I'll follow every rule, take every test on the books. I won't stand in front of the microwave or eat unpasteurized brie. Scout's honour."

"Evie, quit being flip. It's not the time. You know as well as I do that things can happen even when parents do everything right. There're no guarantees."

"I'm healthy, you're healthy. The baby will be too. I can't explain how I know this to be true. I just do."

The would-be father was making no progress in his program of dissuasion but he still had a bottomless stash of what-ifs to plow his way through. What if you have twins? What if she clues in that the baby is yours? What if she figures out Jean-Gabriel's hand in all this? What if it turns out she doesn't want to take the baby when you go to hand it over? What then?

"Amélie will take this baby. I'm telling you. She'll take it."

How could he argue against brick wall come-backs like that? What was it with Evie? Was she noble or was she nuts? It was a fine line he supposed. Had history ever made its mind up about Napoleon?

"So how do you know she's really decent, this Amélie, based on one single meeting? Deep down decent I mean. If she's anything like the character in the play, I wouldn't leave a cockroach in her care, let alone a baby."

"Forget the damn play. Forget it, will you?" For someone bent on selling, Evie's injunction was overly snappish, but lately even the merest allusion to the Médéry dramatic output was all it took to set her a-sizzle. She caught her flub and tamped herself down in short order.

"Amélie's a real person, Mosh. I liked her. More than just *liked*, I respected her. You would too if you'd met her. In all those years since Jean-Gabriel she's changed, pulled herself up by her bootstraps. So maybe she's a little buttoned-up, but that's the worst I can say about her. If you can crack that shell she straps on every morning and take a peek in, you see that she's kind, she's good."

"What does she do for a living? Is it steady?"

"She has a great job. She works at Toronto Dominion. She's been there for years. But the job won't matter, right? When I hand over the baby, I'll hand over all of Jean-Gabriel's money too. It'll be like she landed on free parking. She'll never have to work at the bank another day in her life if she doesn't want to. She can be a stay-at-home mum and still send little he/she to Harvard when the time comes."

Here Evie hesitated, and for the first time all evening Moshe could make out the fault line of insecurity she'd tried to powder over in primping for their meeting. "Okay, I will admit to you that I haven't quite worked out how I'll actually manage the hand-over without revealing where everything came from, but it'll come to me. I have plenty of time to come up with a plan. And you'll be there to help me. If you agree that is."

This gentle poke towards a quick resolution didn't have its desired effect. Moshe rolled on with his interrogation like the Energizer bunny. "How will you explain a pregnancy that results in no baby to your family and at work? Huh? What will you tell them? That you're swelling?"

Evie had never known Moshe to be lippy, but then again she'd never pushed him this far. In fact, here he'd hit on another aspect of the project she'd yet to resolve and she confessed as much. Moshe's insistent probing was starting to find chinks, but still she was unshakeable.

Their to-ing and fro-ing went on late into the night and play only broke when Moshe went home promising to sleep on it. At least this hitch in her plan Evie could handle. That night she appeared to Moshe in his dreams, more obliging than ever. She did everything he'd ever wanted and then some. By morning Moshe knew he was a goner, that he'd give in to anything Evie proposed in the end. But before he caved ignominiously, he had some banking to attend to.

She worked in one of the glass 'n glam downtown office towers, not some dusky corner branch with a golden age wicket that packed in the crowds. Moshe had a bit of trouble tracking her down at first. She didn't go by Médéry, of course. It should have occurred to him. In Quebec, women carried their birth name for life by law. A few ladies here and there tacked monsieur's name onto their own with a hyphen, but it was a rarity in the province to curtsy to hubby in this way. A little web research turned up that Amélie's surname was Turcotte. This whole name business worked to her advantage, Moshe figured, masking from the prurient public her relationship to the notorious playwright. Furthermore, Turcotte was a garden-variety surname, the Smith or Jones of Quebec, its ubiquity padding her privacy in an extra layer of mattress ticking.

Amélie wasn't a teller. He'd learned this much on the phone. Her name plate hung on the door of one of the private offices on the mezzanine identifying her as a small business advisor. This Moshe interpreted as a good sign. Clearly the bank trusted her as someone who could grow things. She stood up to shake hands and he took the opportunity to study her. She was dressed corporately. Her desk had softer edges. No way could this be the vixen who had bewitched Jean-Gabriel. Her posture was firmed up with rebar, and her chignon winched her cheeks back so tightly her nose had to pick sides. Moshe tried to envision the two of them as a couple, but even by rolling the calendar back in his mind to photoshop out the toll of the intervening years, it struck him as a miscegenetic pairing, unless of course they'd had some sort of Helga the Hausfrau number going. What was Evie smoking the day she'd met her?

Moshe and Amélie sat down to discuss the proposal he'd fabricated for the occasion and she started right in without any of the usual climatological foreplay. Mme. Turcotte was all business. He was looking to set up his own bakery, he told her, a cover story that was true, in fact, but years in the offing according to the modest passbook he set before her from a rival banking establishment. He was thinking of transferring his allegiance to the TD if she could advise him more soundly than the apathetic counsellor over at the Royal. She took his humble account seriously, and guided him through an investment strategy that would, she assured him, see his bakery plan take shape far sooner than he'd expected.

The awning fluttered in the breeze, his name splashed across it in gold against a wine-coloured field. It sheltered the rattan chairs on the terrace out front where his loyal customers watched the world go by sipping their *café au laits* and crunching on *palmiers* made with the finest Quebec butter. Local ingredients, nothing but. Moshe had studied the output of the competition.

On busman's holidays around town he'd bought his share of flaccid baguettes and yesterday's croissants reinflated with a bicycle pump. Not in his *boulangerie*. Nor would he sell any of the charcuterie or cheeses that polluted the counters of the other bakeries in town. Moshe was against the dilution of the bakery. Breads, cakes, and pastries. Period. Everything baked on site under his personal supervision. He'd take on an apprentice or two every year. Give back to the profession. And he'd stick to just one location. Okay, so maybe off in the future he might expand, but not too soon. He'd seen it happen all too often, a cozy little neighbourhood bakery, puffed up by its own success, expanding itself into mediocrity. He would resist the temptation until the time was ripe.

So impressed was Moshe with Amélie's monetary acumen that gave the bottom line of his future a nice yeasty lift that he almost lost sight of his primary mission. He tried to snap himself back into gumshoe mode, but he just wasn't cut out for the investigative life. Why had he even come? What did he think he would find out by actually meeting Amélie face to face? All he'd managed to discover was that she was financially savvy, but dexterity with figures did not a mother make. The appointment was clearly over and Moshe rose to leave, no farther ahead than when he'd arrived. Amélie joined him at the door of her office to see him out. She stood directly in front of him. "Monsieur Benshimol," she said, looking into his eyes with a warmth that had been invisible from across the Saharan expanse of her executive desk. "Save the first croissant for me, won't you?"

Chapter 13

EVERY MORNING EVIE TOOK HER TEMPERATURE and studied the distribution of red x's marked in her bedside calendar but she needn't have gone to the trouble. When it came to putting a bun in the oven, Moshe was a pro. Here was a case where his expertise afforded him no satisfaction, cutting short an exercise that gave him pleasure beyond any he'd ever known.

Evie figured it would be a slam-bam-thank-you-ma'am kind of operation when she dared to picture the actual event in her mind. How else could it unfold between two friends who had inked their procreative arrangement with a handshake? It would be a business boink, nothing more. She dreaded the arrival of the agreed upon optimal day. It wasn't that she was inexperienced, but in every previous instance, the route that led her into bed with a new partner was hormonally not contractually paved, loosening up the garters of her inhibitions as nature intended. Now that zero hour was approaching, Evie feared that her mating with Moshe would be like sex between a set of Ken and Barbie corn husk dolls, their pumping so tinder dry the friction risked setting the bedclothes alight. And who could predict how many months of parched repetition it would take until their respective gametes made up their minds to boogie?

Moshe foresaw their rendezvous differently. On the evening of the twenty-third, the date on which she deemed the stars of fecundity in perfect alignment, Evie arrived at his door tied up in so many knots she could barely shuffle her feet to step over the threshold. What precisely it was in this leaning tower of *mishugas* that accounted for her current tension he couldn't pinpoint. She gave nothing away. In fact she scarcely spoke, barometer enough of her inner turmoil. Moshe's heart ached to look down into her face, so bravely unsure, her unaccustomed geisha gaze fixed on the territory of his shoelaces. It was Evie who had choreographed this whole grand scheme. He'd only been Mr. Along-For-the-Ride, but he sensed in her fragile silence that she yearned to cede him the sceptre for this crucial step, and in this his instincts turned out to be correct.

Moshe reached under Evie's chin and tipped her head upwards. He'd hardly ever touched her before. Not officially anyway. Sure, there had been a few accidental hip-bumps at the stove and innumerable two-cheeked pecks of greeting and farewell, but they barely counted except to stir in him the desire for expanded opportunities. So now that he was licensed, Moshe treated himself to a leisurely tracing of the contour of her jaw, a delicate outline which he had long since committed to memory from across the Shabbos table, the better to reproduce it in his dreams. He lifted his hand to brush away the bangs that were caught in her eyelashes. How often in the past had it taken all his strength to hold himself back from clearing his view of her hazel eyes in just this way? He kissed her forehead gently at the vacated spot, and matched it on the other side. His hands slipped back to entangle themselves in her hair, anchoring him against the future, for he was convinced that any minute Evie's guardian angel would swoop down from the clouds to grab him by the scruff of the neck, remind him he wasn't allowed on the bed, and slap him on the nose with a rolled up newspaper. But now that he'd come this far Moshe knew no force could prise him away.

His lips skimmed down to explore the neighbourhood of Evie's eyelids. Moshe's tongue trilled back and forth along those pesky long lashes. Their silkiness was such that he forgave them their former trespasses. He let gravity ordain his route and meandered downwards, bestowing kisses on all the hills and valleys of Evie's face that he'd coveted since first they met, marking time in front of the broken elevators.

Back when the refurbished building opened, the elevators were on the blink more often than they weren't. For some reason, the nineteenth-century structure resented this retrofit in particular that gutted it like a fish, while accepting with equanimity every other modern incursion the construction crew inflicted upon it. Moshe and Evie found themselves stranded together in the condo lobby. They chatted while they waited patiently, sucked in by the *repair in progress* sign that they later learned to be a cruel joke. By the time Sir Galahad had carted Evie's retinue of grocery bags up four flights of stairs for her and stopped in to collect the coffee reward she was offering, he was hooked. Nothing had changed since.

Moshe's exploration of Evie was different from anything she'd ever experienced before, more on the order of a *dégustation*. He licked, he tasted, he sniffed her bouquet. He bit lightly on her earlobes as if testing their degree of doneness. He might have been evaluating her for a third Michelin star. That Moshe relished his feast couldn't have been any clearer to Evie. With the pressure of his parted mouth against her, she felt his urge to swallow her whole.

While he was taken up with savouring the V of her throat, nuzzling its buttery hollow, Evie bestirred herself to wonder just how Moshe might taste. All evening she'd been sleepwalking; her mind stuck in neutral, her body Moshe's marionette, allowing herself a brief sabbatical from the directorship. It would be left to Moshe to make every last decision tonight, which suited her down to the bone. She'd done altogether too much deciding lately, and the burden of it had depleted her. When was the last night she'd slept all the way through? And as for eating, her stomach had hopped itself up into a state of rebellion that harkened back to its misspent youth; Evie could do no more than pick. Suddenly, though, she found that she was downright ravenous.

Evie commandeered the fingers of Moshe's left hand and sampled them one by one, extracting their essence. What she'd anticipated was a tangy sourdough, but instead spun sugar melted in her mouth. Evie couldn't resist a sweet table. She drew Moshe's t-shirt up over his head and dropped it on the floor. She was eager to gorge unimpeded. Children were starving in China.

Moshe rubbed her belly in lazy circles, marking out the property lines of their project's future abode. "Do you think it took?" Evie nestled in closer as she asked the question. "Maybe we should have another go. You know. For insurance." Moshe was a firm believer in extra coverage. At the rental car counter he always shelled out for the collision and liability even though his credit card purported to offer the same protection.

Evie's request made good sense and he complied happily. In fact he continued to comply for the rest of the night and all through the following day. Moshe knew full well that they were meant to be focused, working towards a specific embryonic goal, but even though he'd signed on he wasn't prepared to play the lapdog. He dared to shake things up now and again with manoeuvres that weren't strictly speaking reproductive, and Evie embarked on his scenic detours with matching enthusiasm. They'd get there in plenty of time.

"Mosh? You awake?"

"No."

"I know that trick."

"Can't get anything past you." Evie doled out the pinch he deserved though on his lank frame, it was a challenge coming up with an appreciable wad.

"Tell me..."

"What?"

"Have you been with many women before?" He was silent

for a while, but Evie had the feeling he wasn't using the interval to count up on his fingers and toes.

"No," he replied eventually. "I wouldn't say many. A few is more like it."

"A few. Now that's an answer I approve of. I wouldn't want to think that the father of this baby is a love 'em and leave 'em kind of guy. Genes count."

"Yeah, that's me all right. A Class-A womanizer."

"Serious, any of them?" Moshe didn't look overeager to proceed with this line of questioning but he came clean. "One was, I guess. Serious-ish, you could say."

"Meaning?"

He expelled a let's-get-it-over-with breath and compressed the entire relationship into one unadorned sentence calculated to stifle the subject. "Well, if you define it by how long it dragged on, and that we lived together for a little while in there, then yes, I guess it would qualify as serious."

"And that would be Maïté, right?"

"How in the world do you know about Maïté?"

Evie's mouth sometimes shot off without her prior consent. Why had she felt the need to toss out this morsel now? She'd had it stored away for months, never meaning to bring it out into the light of day. She could read Moshe's distress through her hands, his muscles clamping shut like security gates. She tried to massage away the damage she'd done. While she stroked she divulged her source, her journalistic scruples flying out the window.

"Oh, you know Dany. He's such a blabbermouth. Besides, that's what you get for missing an Anti-Shabbos. Then everyone yaks about you. Don't pretend you don't know the risks." She was a bit ill at ease with this blame-the-victim approach, but Moshe accepted that this was the way of things in their little community. The bylaws were unambiguous on that point.

"Well, remind me never to skip again even though there's nothing much left in my dull past that's gossip-worthy. If that's the best they could dredge up it must have been a slow night."

She could feel him starting to loosen up, so she pressed a bit further despite herself. "Can I just ask when it was?"

"It's been a while now that it's over. Before I moved in here."

"What was she? I mean what did she do for a living?"

"She was one of the thousands of unemployed actresses on the Plateau. They're a dime a dozen. You know that."

"And what was it that went wrong?"

She'd probed too far now, and with a ragged fingernail. "Look, I don't really want to go into all that, Okay? This bed's too small for three." Moshe hesitated, and then kissed the tip of her nose to blunt the sharpness of his tone. He lay back down to remember what exactly had gone sour.

What could he say to Evie, that they'd broken up over the clock? No, that wasn't really the reason, although it seemed like it at the time. Everything always waited to blow until they were setting their alarm clocks for the next day. Maïté's life took off as darkness fell, while he shared a schedule with the city's garbagemen. They might as well have been living in different time zones. Moshe was lashed to his ovens by apron strings that she could never convince him to cut with the result that he was always too whooped to squire her around to her night-time haunts up on the Plateau. So she found someone else who would; someone who, if you saw him out on the street at five a.m., was more likely to be trailing home than heading out to work his shift. It was surprising, now that he mulled it over, that they'd been able to get together long enough to effect the break up, so rarely did they inhabit the same room awake. All their other problems, and they were too many to catalogue, somehow seemed subsidiary to the clock which took on Big Ben proportions in Moshe's mind, its chimes tolling out the doom of their coupledom.

"I'm sorry," Evie said, interrupting his flashback. "I shouldn't have asked. I was out of line."

"Forget it." They had retreated to their respective sides of the bed, the first time since they'd started in on Evie's game plan that the mattress had seen any distance between them.

"And what about you?" Moshe asked after a spell. "Many guys?" He turned on his side to face her, propping up his head with his hand. "Even though I guess you reserve the right to remain silent since I was so stingy with the particulars."

"For me, not many either."

"Come on. Someone like you. I bet you had to beat them off with a stick."

"I'll take you to the clinic tomorrow to have your eyes examined."

"Thanks for the offer, but I see fine."

"Well, however few or many there might have been, none of them was ever serious."

"Why not?"

Fair's fair. If Moshe preferred to keep the grisly details of his past liaisons to himself, so would she. Besides, why should she direct his attention to all the flaws in her nature that her exes had flung in her face on the way out the door? He'd find them out soon enough on his own, surely. That's the way it had always gone. Evie's men tended to be quick on their feet in the put-down department. They normally struck first, lighting into her while she was still stumbling to articulate in the precise terminology she favoured just how exactly they were duds. They always had the edge because they weren't so hung up on phraseology.

Maybe it would be different with Moshe, though. After all their Friday nights together, he'd seen into most of the corners of her personality and survived to tell the tale. Still, Evie saw no reason to itemize her defects just in case he happened to have blinked and missed any.

"Well, usually," she said, "just when things are on the verge of getting serious with somebody, I start to fixate on some fatal character flaw that I'd let slide at the beginning. And eventually that bug, whatever it is, forces me to dump him."

"Such as?"

"Oh, truly reprehensible stuff I'm talking about. He'd be a toothpick chewer or a gum cracker. Wear a pinkie ring. Something like that. What else could I do?"

"Well at least I'm safe on that score."

"I never would have given you a tumble otherwise. A girl's got to have standards."

They'd exposed enough of themselves. Better not to stir up the sediment of their respective pasts at this stage in the game. What would it gain? In silent agreement the two of them went back to what they did best. Everything else could wait.

It was rough going at the office those first weeks. Luckily Evie hadn't made any serious slip-ups yet, but it was only a matter of time. She couldn't concentrate. All she wanted to do was shove her keyboard out of the way, pillow her head on her crossed arms and snooze. The only thing that stopped her was that she was a snorer, and big-time. When they were growing up Josh always mocked her for blasting like a locomotive at night, but she figured he was just trying to get her goat. Wasn't it the prerogative of older brothers to torture the kid sister with bogus slurs? She wouldn't fall for it. Evie was no sap. But later in life her boyfriends confirmed that Josh had it dead on with his Orient Express simile. Besides, how could she explain away her sudden narcoleptic tendencies? Nope, napping on the job was out.

On top of being dog-tired she was wrung out. Even for rock-bottom grooming Evie had no energy. Her arms lacked the primal oomph to repeatedly hoist the curling iron the marathon distance from the dresser to her head for styling. Instead she gathered her hair up like table scraps. How could a fetus the size of a raspberry (she was reading all the books) sap her strength so disproportionately? Evie hadn't been planning to announce the pregnancy before it showed, but the grapevine was buzzing overtime at the newspaper when she started to turn up at work in her new roadkill look.

Over lunch Audrée sized up her colleague with motherly concern. "Evie, you can tell me if anything's wrong. You know you can confide in me. I would never let on to anyone. It would be just between us."

"I'm fine, I'm fine. I've just got some things on my mind. That's all."

Audrée was unconvinced, eyeballing Evie's blouse that looked to have been dug up from the bottom of the dirty clothes hamper, and her face which was a coordinating shade of battleship grey. "Well, my lunch table is always open if you change your mind. Only a penny per consultation, cheaper than Lucy even. A steal."

Aaron was less circumspect. "You look like shit." It was a measure of Evie's meltdown that she walked away from his remark with no riposte. Her brain was too dulled from her sleep deprivation experiment. She would have taken a strop to it if only she could summon up some dregs of her old zip. The comment rankled, though. She reported it to Moshe that night after work while he was stocking her cupboards with the rice cakes and rusks that she craved. He nibbled on some melba toasts to keep her company. To him it was like eating picnic tables, but since they were all Evie could stomach he kept his own counsel.

"I wouldn't say you look like shit exactly."

"Gee, thanks for your support."

"Come on Evie. That didn't come out like I meant. He stood behind her and kneaded the tightness out of her back. "But you do look, you know, kind of droopy. That's good, though. You're right on schedule according to chapter two. Excessive fatigue is perfectly normal in the first trimester."

Moshe had been keeping up on his side too. For the past few years his reading had run mostly to food books, but ever since Evie knocked at his door with a bottle of fizzy apple juice to announce liftoff he'd set aside *The Chemistry of Gluten*, not exactly a page-turner anyway, in favour of *What to Expect When You're Expecting*. It was the same book Evie swore by and he wanted them to be on the same page.

It struck him as a very complete tome. Moshe read it as attentively as if he were going to be quizzed on the content. His copy was already so dog-eared you would have sworn he was on to kid number three. He paid particular attention to the last chapter which dealt with pregnancy loss in all its heartbreaking manifestations. Every one, that is, except theirs; a surrogate mother giving her baby up to a woman who doesn't have the slightest inkling that she should be out shopping for a layette. When it came down to practical advice that was the only chapter they really needed. This baby would be born whether they learned about Braxton-Hicks contractions or not. But Moshe never drew Evie's attention to this gap in her chosen book's coverage. He'd noticed she seldom read ahead. So in the meantime Moshe shared what he'd gleaned from the early pages and kept his fears to himself.

"Jake, I've got a job for you."

Marilyn had dropped in at Sannoix with no prior warning, exhorting her husband's secretary to summon him in from the floor; her visit was of a pressing nature. She cooled her heels in the reception area, checking out the bulletin board on the wall labelled *danger*. Pinned to the corkboard were close-ups of almonds and macadamias head-on and in profile, looking as if they belonged on a wanted poster at the post office. When Jake tarried too long in the factory for her liking, Marilyn made for the guts of the plant though she knew full well that such a move was a no go. The secretary barred Marilyn's way, splaying herself out like human caution tape across the door. No outsiders entered the sterile area of the flight kitchen without the boss's say-so. Not even Madame. Jake had his apparatchiks well-trained.

Something was gnawing away at his wife, that much was

clear to Jake as soon as he heard the page. Marilyn's normal driving circuits seldom took in the arid industrial tract sheltered under the wingspread of Trudeau International where his plant ticked along in perfect symbiosis with the airport.

"What, I don't work enough to suit you? I need you to give me more to do?"

"Come on Jake. This is no joke what I'm here asking you. It's important. About your daughter. Have you seen her lately? Well, it may interest you to know that she looks like hell. She deigned to meet me to grab a quick lunch downtown today since I had to hand over Joshie's keys, and I couldn't believe my eyes. I want you to convince her to make an appointment with Dr. Irwin. Maybe we'll be lucky and she'll listen if it's you doing the suggesting. Me, forget it."

"You're exaggerating, Mare."

"When have I ever been prone to exaggeration?" Jake let that one pass. "I'm telling you, she looked like something the cat dragged in."

"The kid probably just needs some sleep. Must be burning the candle at both ends. Nothing's wrong with her. She's healthy as a horse."

"Jake. I'm not dreaming this up. She was so pale you could see right through her. And she kept yawning like she couldn't get enough air in her lungs."

"Maybe it's a reaction to something she ate. You know how finicky her stomach can be. Remember how she used to blow? Wow! That kid had some range. Nobody in the family could outshoot her."

Marilyn wasn't in the mood to put up with her husband's reminiscences about Evie's puking prowess. "Enough Jake. Listen to me. This has nothing to do with food. Her hair was barely combed. I'm not even sure it was washed. And she wasn't wearing any makeup. Her clothes were a rumpled-up mess. She looked like she didn't care how she looked. That's not like her and you know it. Remember how many hours she used to spend in front of the mirror? She had to be put together perfect before she'd so much as stick a toe out the front door."

"What are you trying to say? Our Evie's on drugs suddenly?" He'd seen the public service ads on the busses.

Marilyn was making no headway with her list of nebulous symptoms. She didn't have all day. "Jake, she picked up the bill."

"Okay. Okay. I'll talk to her."

The Anti-Shabbosites were forced to make a change of venue. For the first Friday in recorded memory Evie would be attending the event as a commoner with Moshe assuming the hosting headship. But by the time that night rolled around, Evie had ducked out of the proceedings entirely, too whomped from a week of work to make even a token appearance. Moshe delivered the trumped up excuse whose missish Victorian wording appealed to Evie's literary sensibilities. She was indisposed, he reported, and hoped they'd move on, but her absence loomed over the table. Something major was up, not just your run of the mill cold or cramps which in any event had never held her back from presiding before.

"Burnout maybe?" Dizzy proffered her theory over soup.

"Nah, she doesn't work that hard." To this truism they all nodded.

"Some sort of allergy?" ManU put in his two cents. "Maybe after all this time she's allergic to us," a suggestion which had its own logic.

"Swine flu?" Dizzy posited. "They say our age group is the hardest hit."

"Then she'd be dead, not just dead tired. Besides, we went together to get our shots, so that's out."

"What else would make her look sucked dry that? Mono maybe? Chronic Fatigue Syndrome? Lupus, God forbid?" The quacks at the table chronicled all the wasting maladies suffered in their wider circle of acquaintance, an exercise that entertained them pleasantly all the way through dessert.

"Maybe she's pregnant." Dany threw it out there over the apple crumble, provoking the biggest poof of laughter of the night.

"Well, then it must have been by spontaneous combustion," said Shira. "We all know she's had nothing but downtime as far as guys go since that Steve last year."

"No, no. He wanted us to call him Stephen, remember? He was very adamant about that."

"You're right. I stand corrected. Stephen with a *ph*, not a low-class *v*. What a stuffed shirt, that one."

"I don't know. I kind of liked him," Zach said.

"I did too." Dizzy backed him. "He was very well spoken."

"Presentable."

"Well off."

"Polite."

"Married."

"Well there was that. Remember how she found out?"

"Yeah, that wasn't pretty."

"Whatever. The real point," Judy said, drilling down to the crux of the matter, "is that with him out of the picture, Evie has now officially worked her way through every last guy on the Island of Montreal who knows enough to say *to whom* instead of *to who* and there's no one left for her to go out with. She's doomed."

How was it that Moshe was always out of sync on the scuttlebutt? Here he was, though incognito, the deepest inside of all Evie insiders, but still he was blank on great swaths of her life that to everyone else were public knowledge. It only served to confirm to him that their intimacy was a temporary construction on the order of a kissing booth at a county fair, earmarked for dismantling at the end of the season.

Dizzy was forced to tap her water glass with her knife to wrest the others' attention away from the faithless Stephen. "Hey, hey, forget about the putz from Bountiful you guys. He's dead and buried. Let's keep our eyes on the ball. Now

I've been thinking about what Dany said and it's not as stupid as it sounds. Everything fits. Evie's completely wiped out. I'm saying zonked. Right? And when we met at Myriade the other day she ordered decaf. Can you believe it? Decaf. There. It was so embarrassing."

"And last Friday night she didn't drink any wine," ManU volunteered, warming to the pregnancy postulate. "I noticed because I brought a really good bottle for a change, a Bordeaux worthy of Jean-Gabriel, *olav hashalom*. Not plonk. Has anyone ever seen her pass up on the vino before?"

"She didn't eat any of my carrot *cholent*," added Judy, eager to pile on "She said that she was feeling queasy."

"We can't count that as an official symptom, it makes me queasy too."

The table quieted. To the amateur diagnosticians' own astonishment, the jigsaw puzzle of circumstantial evidence they were piecing together interlocked tight and clean. Their conclusion was incontrovertible. Dizzy declared Evie pregnant in absentia, and the chat shifted direction. They were eager to move on to provenance.

Chapter 14

THERE WAS AN UPSIDE to feeling like she'd been flattened by a log truck. It reassured Evie in a way, that when it came time to give this baby up, she'd be happy to part with the sadistic little bugger who had suctioned every last particle of energy from her body. Good riddance. She'd sleep for a month straight once it was all over.

Now she'd gone and done it. The Evil Eye had been dozing at the controls but when his radar belatedly picked up on Evie's unmotherly brainwaves he snapped back to attention. Soon that deb would look back on complete and utter exhaustion as a walk in the park. He toggled a switch and brought Evie's ADD innards back from the gulag. The Upchuck Queen, as Josh had dubbed his sister in their youth, was restored to the throne.

Evie started hurling like there was no tomorrow. She let rip like a fire hose aimed at a burning orphanage. If she didn't grab at the towel rack for purchase, the recoil threatened to kayo her. And there was no predicting what would set her off or when. At least as a kid she could count on being able to keep the cork in as long as she wasn't on wheels. There was a certain degree of comfort, back then, in understanding her tummy's mindset. But now the episodes were random, capricious. She reviewed every step of her day, every food that crossed her lips, but she could extract no pattern. Her stomach was rogue and out of control.

To Evie, these two crippling conditions intertwined constituted the ne plus ultra of torture stylings, the double helix from hell. If only she had the power to petition Torquemada for a change of method, she'd put in for evisceration. From where she stood it sounded easier to tolerate. During her few daily intervals when she was neither green around the gills nor catatonic, she marvelled that any woman on earth would consent to bear more than one child. Why wouldn't she just call the Abloy guys out to the house while hubby was at work? It beggared understanding. Her mother had it backwards all these years. Evie twigged to it now. It wasn't that you could take control of your uterus. Oh no. It took control of you. Evie's womb grabbed her by the hair, yanked her head back and had its way with her. There were times when she genuinely wondered how she'd survive. She hauled herself home from work at the end of the day and collapsed into the first chair that presented itself. The bedroom, however tempting, might just as well have been at the North Pole.

A nun stood opposite the chair in which Evie was slumped, surveying the living room proprietorially. She wore an old-style habit of the type that never cruised the streets of Montreal anymore, the full monty. The Sister's cornet was a grand sculpted affair, its starched white wings extending from her skull like the fins of a '59 Caddy. She made herself right at home once her inspection was complete. She kicked off her shoes, plunked herself down on Evie's sofa, and propped her feet up on the coffee table to massage the matched pair of killer bunions that adorned her big toe.

"So *nu* Evie? You're thinking you might want to get rid of it, the little pisher cooking up in your hibachi down there?" She stared pointedly at Evie's stomach region.

"I beg your pardon?"

"Evie, Evie, Evie. From me you can't hide anything."

Evie was trying to make sense of her apparition. Just who

was this home invader who looked like Sister Bertrille but talked like Tanta Freydl?

"It's a mitzvah you having a baby for that poor soul, that Amélie. A good girl. She hasn't had an easy life. Her good-for-nothing husband shtupped every skirt with a pulse. Lucky thing he was pumping blanks. Well, maybe not so lucky for his wife. But anyway, you'd be doing an act of, oh what did your *maman* call it back when she made her fancy protest up at Parliament Hill?" She struggled though her senior moment until the fugitive expression popped out of its hidey-hole. 'Guerrilla feminism.' That's what Marilyn used to say."

"You know my mother?" Here was a collision of cultures Evie had difficulty imagining considering her mother's propensities.

"Well, not personally, more by reputation, let's say."

That her mother's notoriety was such that it had managed to slip behind these cloistered walls stashed under a barrow-load of potatoes was beyond Evie's comprehension. No girl really knows her own mother, but Evie seemed exceptionally clueless in this regard. She was reconsidering for the first time in her life her mother's brush with activism when her visitor slipped in the zinger. "And that way the little matzo ball you're carrying wouldn't have to die."

The word Evie had been turning over in the boudoir of her mind lately was *termination*. It gave off only businesslike reverberations. It was a word that she felt she could act on, a bloodless, bureaucratic word. But not even to Moshe had she confessed her recent inclination, so how could this spectre, or figment or whatever she was, have weaselled its way into the private preserve of her brain?

"Evie, *bubeleh*, it was your decision to bring this baby into the world. No one forced you to do it. The idea sprang into your pretty little *kop* and you acted on it. Fine. But if you change your mind now, it's not like returning a sweater to the Bay."

"I'm scared." The admission burst out before she had a chance to quarantine it.

"About what?"

Evie was embarrassed to continue. She was confiding in a ghost? But somehow she couldn't restrain herself. The reading on her pressure gauge was perilously high. If she didn't hurry up and perform a prophylactic venting she'd blow, her body parts splattering the length and breadth of Mile End.

"The mechanics of it all, you know."

"At your age, no one ever explained to you how it all works?"

"No, not that. Everything else. The secrecy, the paperwork, the handover." An underscore of panic entered her voice. "How will I arrange it all? There're no rules. What was I thinking?"

Evie's procrastinating had caught up with her. So consumed was she by the baby solution she'd come up with that she pushed off any consideration of the inevitable fallout. But the time had come to face up to the fact that duck and cover wasn't working.

"You're right. It's not like a wire transfer. Ask your *maman* for help with having the baby and all that other stuff that's worrying you."

"Are you crazy? Oh, excuse me, *ma soeur*," Evie tried to retract her protocol gaffe. Her guest gave her an exculpatory wave. "I meant to say, with her track record on abortion?"

"Didn't you ever listen to her when she explained to you about her past? She's not pro-abortion, she's pro-choice. Boy are you *tsedrait*. If she knows that you want to give birth to the baby she'll come on board. You heard it from me."

Evie and Josh never really had listened when their mother launched into her Abortion Caravan reminiscences. In fact they'd made it their life's work not to listen. So her drop-in phantom was right. Evie was a trifle vague about the finer points of her mother's philosophy, never having absorbed the story from cover to cover. It didn't matter, though. This nun, however tuned-in to Marilyn's psyche she thought she was, couldn't understand better than Evie what made her mother tick.

"Impossible. She'll try to talk me out of it. Convince me she knows better, like always. I don't have the strength to be lectured at right now."

"Give the woman a chance Eveleh. Would I lead you wrong?" Evie's spook heaved herself up from the sofa, her intervention over. "This was my cell, you know. I like what you've done with it. The recessed lighting is very effective."

"Thank you, Soeur…?"

"Marie de l'Eucharistie. Now think over what I said, *maidel*. Confide in *maman*. Well, I have to be off. Got any of those spinach knishes left from Friday for the road?"

Chapter 15

IN AN EPILATORY MISSTEP of epic proportions, Marilyn had her eyebrows reapplied mid-forehead back in the seventies when everybody was doing it. After the procedure, her bare brow bones jutted out like Gibraltar, purged of their reason to live, while her two perma-pencilled replacement brows, perfect circumflexes, lorded it over them from on high. The problem was that the arc of her new brows and their move to an upper storey gave Marilyn the appearance of looking down on the world. They changed her mien utterly and to no good effect. Marilyn's face was now a mask of perpetual disapproval. Those brows had Evie and Josh confused the whole time they were growing up. They were convinced that no matter how stellar their report cards or immaculate their bedrooms, their mother's gaze held a reproof. No doubt the kids of facelift parents suffered similar miscues. Poor Marilyn. She never understood why her relationship with her children was so fraught. But now here was Evie sitting at her kitchen table, reaching out to her. Marilyn listened coolly to the whole story.

"We'll have the baby at your father's factory," she said. "You can eat off the floor there. Most hospitals aren't that sanitary. I'll call Sarah to get her going on forging the birth certificate. I don't know if she has any experience with Quebec documents. I don't think so. But she still has contacts all over the country. And Arlene can tear herself away from her practice long enough to do the delivery. She's semi-retired now anyway. I bet you Laura and Virginia will be willing to come along to assist. Everybody can stay at our place. We have plenty of room to put them up now that you and your brother are both out of the house." She paused to consider any angles she might have missed. "Let me be the one to break it to your father. I think it'll be easier coming from me."

Marilyn, she of the Humvee personality, was taking charge. Her Abortion Caravan comrades would come to her Evie's rescue, of that she was absolutely sure. Alone among her Montreal friends, when Marilyn talked of a sisterhood she didn't mean Hadassah.

The tidal wave of maternal support overwhelmed Evie. Robust mothering she was accustomed to, but in every previous instance Marilyn had been trying to propel her in a direction she didn't want to go. This was the first occasion, as far as she could recall, where her mother would be working the room on her behalf. Marilyn wiped away her daughter's tears. "Don't worry, my sweet girl. Don't worry. Mummy will take care of everything. You just keep yourself healthy."

Why Evie had decided to confide in her of all people, Marilyn couldn't fathom. There was certainly no genetic predisposition for it. Marilyn had hardly been so up-front with her own parents in her radical days of yore. She'd simply cut and run, the donkey kick of *tsuris* she'd hammered them with on her way out the door just so much collateral damage. A wave of regret washed over her. She made up her mind to go visit her mother up at the Waldorf that very afternoon to apologize. So maybe making amends forty years after the fact was a bit on the tardy side, but she figured there was no statute of limitations on *mea culpas*.

Evie tried to pull herself together. She'd lost the veneer of self-possession she liked to maintain in front of her mother, her Halloween costume of adulthood slipping off her shoulders and falling to the floor. "You really know forgers?" she asked.

"How do you think we got the passes that let us past the guards and into the Parliamentary gallery all those years ago?"

The RCMP Security Service had a rap sheet on Marilyn as long as her arm. Evie would have known as much if she had ever once tuned in to her mother's Abortion Caravan recital, but contrary to her time-honoured pattern, Marilyn decided not to rebuke her daughter for her habit of inattention. She didn't want to raise any hackles at this delicate juncture. Nor would she pose any prying questions though they were piling up within her as they rolled off the assembly line, begging for egress. This *rapprochement* with Evie was too fragile and she didn't want to risk shattering it with an ill-considered remark. She even self-censored the million dollar paternity question. It would all come out in the wash she supposed. She need only be patient. For now, she'd concentrate on rounding up the old gang and getting them on board for one last post-parliamentary bamboozle in the service of a good cause.

Even the baby seemed to calm down now that Marilyn was at the helm, wreaking less havoc on its mother with each passing day. Moshe, who had thus far been spared the pleasure of meeting the redoubtable Marilyn, dared to suggest that this reprieve was in fact attributable to Evie entering her second trimester, that placid eye-of-the-storm era of pregnancy. *What to Expect* spelled it all out. Evie let Moshe go ahead and think what he pleased. She knew the truth of the matter.

Delray was thriving according to the ob/gyn. It was Moshe who insisted upon giving the baby a name-in-progress, plucked out of his head in honour of his delayed vacation. Before he'd imposed the moniker, Evie referred to the baby as *it* or *the fetus,* which lacked a certain warmth in his mind. Moshe came from a demonstrative family. At his house, a return from the trenches or from the grocery store called for a greeting of equal amplitude. According to family lore, Moshe only topped six feet because his diminutive parents squeezed him so emphatically when he was growing up that he shot up like toothpaste from the tube. It was only natural that with his gushy upbringing he'd choose to lavish as much love as possible on Delray, even if the baby was only theirs in escrow.

Every evening after Evie came home from work Moshe dropped by to lend her a hand. He generally found her just inside her door, wedging off her shoes. This project she attacked even before she'd shucked her carryall off her shoulder or removed her coat. It superseded in urgency every other activity. Once she freed herself, she stared down in despair at the pair of rugby balls that had yet again latched onto her legs down where her feet used to hang out. The switcheroo occurred every afternoon at work when she wasn't paying attention. One minute she had the slim little tootsies she'd come to know and love, perfect seven-and-a-halfs, and next thing she knew, poof. They'd been snatched and shipped off in a container car for resale in Russia and she was left with cheapo knockoffs sized for a sasquatch.

Secretly, Moshe was impressed by their circumference. Evie never did anything half-way. But he wisely stayed mum on the subject while he puttered around her apartment making himself useful, encouraging her to stretch out on the sofa to let the culpable juices redistribute themselves. He propped her feet up with pillows and settled her comfortably in while he whipped up a dinner from the ingredients on this week's tolerated list. Once he had it at the simmer, he went back to the living room to attend to Evie in his usual way, shimmying down her trousers to bare the porthole through which he delivered his nightly talk to Delray. It was a choppy narrative, a stream of consciousness stew of genealogy, fatherly advice, and unadulterated schmaltz depending on his mood, but it always began with his signature line. "Once upon a time Moshe and Evie decided that they wanted a baby to love." He'd never intended it to be picked up for serialization the first time he spoke into Evie's tummy to their son, for they sensed that she was carrying a boy, but Evie fell under the spell of his tale and demanded that he carry on.

Moshe traced the various branches of the Benshimols around the world for the baby's edification, using his finger as a pointer and Evie's swell as his globe. His own parents had opted for the well-worn pipeline that started out in Morocco and debouched in Israel where they fully intended to settle permanently. Not so the remaining relatives. Free thinkers. When they left Safi behind for good and all, they tried out more far-flung destinations, Montreal, Caracas, Durban, London. Uncle Daniel ended up in Yokohama, God alone knows why.

But the Benshimols were a close-knit family, and eventually the separation started to wear on them. They began an epistolary campaign that kept the post offices on five continents in business, each cluster of relatives trying to persuade the others of the superiority of its chosen city, hoping to prod them into repacking their chattel and making one last move so that they could all be reunited. Moshe's parents didn't have much to offer to promote the case of Tel Aviv. Forced military service for their beloved nieces and nephews? They didn't waste their ink. Inexplicably, it was Montreal that won out. Years later Moshe's father showed him the Montreal letters, written by his brother André, the poet, so-called, who'd self-servingly elided the whole subject of winter.

And so it came to pass that the Benshimols installed themselves *en bloc* in Montreal. They pulled up their delicate roots that had been coddled for generations in the toasty subsoil of North Africa to transplant them into the Quebec permafrost, and against all laws of agronomy, they took.

Evie eavesdropped on Moshe's belly button monologues and wondered what it must be like to come from such a tight family, a family that so yearned for togetherness that its members crossed oceans as if they were puddles to recreate the *mishpocheh* without borders that they had grown up with. And from his telling, the aunts and uncles sounded so loving.

Their worst crime, she heard in a later installment, was that they pinched your cheeks with excessive zeal.

Maybe Moshe was just uncritical by nature or was romanticizing his childhood for the benefit of Delray's tender ears, but could it be that his family was genuinely so affectionate, so easygoing? Evie considered the hard evidence, what she herself had witnessed outside the boundaries of story time. Moshe was the only one of the Anti-Shabbosites who didn't gripe about living near family. His mother was gone now, but he had dinner with his father and sisters every week, and willingly from what she could gather. Evie's relationship with her own family, by which she meant her mother, who steered the Troy ship of state, was less bumpy now than it had ever been, but still she thought it the norm that there be tension between parents and kids. It was a fact of life. How was it that Moshe's family sounded like the Huxtables but in Hebrew?

"Okay, Delray," he said, "Listen up. Don't forget when you're crossing the street to look out for cars turning right on red. It's against the law in Montreal, but sometimes drivers from out of town don't know and still do it, so be extra careful at corners. Got it?"

"Why are you wasting your breath on advice that Amélie's sure to deliver? I grant you that she won't be likely to give him your designated hitter speech, at least not with the same passion, but I'm pretty sure she'll warn him not to run out between cars or chase a ball into the street."

"I know, I know, but I can't help myself." Now that he'd started, there were so many more lessons Moshe wanted to download into his baby's noggin while it was still at a stage where it was willing to play sponge to pearls of parental wisdom. Nine months wouldn't be nearly enough time. Tonight he'd only managed to cover multiplying with zeros, the *passé composé*, and that hollow thump you should hear when you tap a perfectly baked bread on its bottom in the oven. He'd shaped his lips into a tight round O and flicked his fingers against the kettle drum of his cheek to simulate the exact sound. Moshe was trying to confer to Delray, simultaneously, the full battery of leg-up tips that would vault him over the stumbling blocks of growing up and a lifetime's supply of fatherly affection. It was an ambitious program.

Maybe the baby couldn't hear what his father was saying, Moshe knew that Delray's ears weren't fully wired up to the generator yet, but he was confident that the missives he was sending his son's way were being taken in one way or another and stored in some remote depository of his brain until the proper trigger, sometime off in the future, tickled them out of dormancy. Only very occasionally did Evie chip in. "Tell him not to feel like a failure if he can't climb the rope, even if he can't climb the knotted rope."

"You don't want to tell him yourself?" Moshe asked gently, trying to coax Evie into taking a direct part in the conversation, but as always she demurred, happy to let Moshe serve as their communal mouthpiece. The way she saw it, there was no need for her to speak to Delray. The baby had intravenous access to her every thought. Unfortunately the flow was reciprocal. In the middle of the night, in the quiet of her bedroom, she could hear Delray sticking it to her. "You're giving me away? You're handing me off with a crib blanket and a cashier's cheque hidden in my diaper? What kind of mother ARE you?"

All Evie could do in her own defence was recount to him the child-proofed version of the saga of Jean-Gabriel and Amélie, including her role, as if it were a bedtime story. Some nights she had to tell it over and over again until he quieted down and fell asleep, and she could never change the wording from one time to the next because he didn't like that. Once she had him safely bedded down, Evie spent the rest of the night praying that he'd eventually understand that giving him up was its own act of love.

And they wondered why she was tired.

Chapter 16

"Our Evie's having her baby at the factory? My factory?" In the space of a nanosecond Jake's complexion ratcheted down the colour chart from ruddy to putty. Marilyn tried to arrest the descent before it landed splat on dead white.

"Stay cool honey. Calm down."

So far, all had been going according to plan. Jake predictably reared up at various points along the way. "She's pregnant?" "We don't know who the father is?" "Our first grandchild, maybe our only chance at one ever, and she's giving it away?" At those spikes in the conversation his wife just grabbed him by the reins, patted his flanks reassuringly, and eased him back down until he eventually fell in step at her side in a gentle trot. It's not like she hadn't done it before. But now she'd reached the point in the account where it could all hit the fan. Though Marilyn esteemed herself a gold medal meddler, coming between a man and his livelihood was an exceptionally risky move to attempt. She couldn't just steamroller along and hope he'd kowtow to her best judgment. Even a man like Jake had his limits. His pristine factory was going to be contaminated. Blood. Fluids. All manner of shmutz. If she didn't know better, she could easily come to the conclusion that this birthing incursion onto his de-germified turf pained him more than the fact that his daughter had gone and knocked herself up on behalf of some stranger.

Jake racked his brain for a respectable out. "Don't you need, you know, machines, monitors? High tech stuff?"

"Arlene'll be doing the delivery. She's brought so many thousands of babies into the world in her time she can do it standing on her head. Besides, Evie wants her to do it midwife-style. Not high tech. Mellow, she says."

"If that's the case, then can't she just do it at our house? Or over at her place?"

"What are we Jake, savages? Don't we want our Evie to have all the advantages of an antiseptic environment?" Marilyn paused, hoping he'd come round to the foregone conclusion without having to be pushed too hard. She essayed a gentle repetitive *noodge* in the right direction. "Well, don't we?" And just that quickly he signed off. She'd feared worse.

Jake pushed his Barcalounger back to a 45° angle, the optimal tilt for mulling. Therein he digested the state of affairs slowly and methodically, as was his wont. The Troy women had to act out. It was in their blood. In a surge of benevolence he hoped Evie would give birth to a boy. It would be a blessing to the future parents, whoever the hell they were.

"Is she doing everything, Evie?" Now that Jake had reached the acceptance stage, he edged forward in his thinking.

"What everything?"

"Screening, vitamins, all that stuff? What do I know anymore, it's been so long. Lamaze? Whatever needs to be done."

"Of course she is. She's following her doctor's orders to the letter. Don't you have faith in your daughter to have good sense about something as important as this?" Mrs. High-and-Mighty was only able to deliver this *zetz in* good conscience because she had already elicited satisfactory responses from Evie to the self-same questions. Marilyn was still keeping the deal she'd made with herself at the beginning, to hold back on a wholesale inquisition, but she sneaked in a few baby enquiries from time to time nonetheless and Evie obliged her with replies just fulsome enough to silence her for a decent spell.

"You're going to go for prenatal classes, aren't you?" she'd asked Evie.

"Don't worry. I'm all signed up. We've been to a few sessions already."

"Who's *we*?" Marilyn hoped that with these two words that offered themselves up ever so naturally in the conversation daddy's mask would slip, revealing his secret identity, but no such luck. Evie kept her partner's face as securely shrouded as Igor Gouzenko's.

"You know my friends from the building? The ones I have Shabbos dinner with? One or another of them goes with me every week. They take turns. They've been a terrific help in all this."

"Aren't you embarrassed to show up every time with somebody else when the others are all couples? They don't look at you funny?"

"No, I just told them the first night when we were all introducing ourselves to each other that my husband is off doing humanitarian work in Guatemala."

Evie wasn't a born liar. Evasion was more her style; tap dancing around the truth, but somehow she'd whipped this Latino smoke screen out of thin air for her mother so that Moshe could retain his silent partner status. The parents-to-be were both adherents of the loose lips school of thinking.

But, of course, it was Moshe and Moshe alone who accompanied Evie to all the classes and huffed and panted at her side. It was Moshe who watched the video of a delivery along with her and shielded her eyes from the episiotomy scene, and it was Moshe's back that supplied resistance to hers when the mommies rolled out the mats to do their pressure exercises against daddy. The two of them had even gone on the tour of the hospital delivery room with their classmates though for all the relevance it had to Evie's particular birthing venue they might just as well have toured a Chips Ahoy plant.

For every doctor's appointment, for every bloodletting, scan, and weigh-in it was Moshe who sat beside her, providing Evie with the second set of ears she craved for the subsequent kitchen table rehashes. When it came time to watch Delray's heartbeat on the screen Moshe was right there, and he took home from the matinée his own souvenir glossy. Even though he would have liked to magnet it to his fridge like Evie had done, that position was too public, so he hid it away in his bedroom in an androgynous yellow frame since they had agreed beforehand not to pose the S-question of the ultrasound technician. At times they regretted their decision. On the not so infrequent nights when their curiosity got the better of them, Moshe would unstick the picture from Evie's refrigerator door, bring it over to the couch, and hold it up between them. They turned it this way and that, but for all their scrutiny the sooty moonscape offered up no clues to their untrained eyes. The word on the street, though, bolstered the parents' inkling. All the black-clad *nonnas* in the fruiterie who stopped Evie to apply a caliper gaze to her bulge were in accord. Since she carried samovar style, a boy they decreed it would be.

The full-length mirror was just one more instrument of pregnancy torture as far as Evie was concerned. Used to be she didn't mind checking herself out in it mornings, stripped down. Maybe she wasn't what you'd call a beauty, but on a good day she could turn a head or two. Ancient history.

The new Evie was a bloater. Her skin could barely contain her. Her ankles puffed out like cinnamon buns. As for her other body parts, they had their own tales of abuse to report to the monitoring agency. Her cheeks and nose had darkened until they looked like they'd been brushed with an egg-wash, and her *pupik*, an innie under the *ancien régime*, now protruded from her belly like a coconut macaroon. Evie chalked it up to poor planning. It must have been because she'd mated with a baker that she looked as if she'd been popped into an oven at

350. If she'd wanted to bloom in pregnancy she should have hooked up with a florist.

Evie was growing time-lapse style, the layers of fat accreting as if she were a candlewick God was dipping and redipping in tallow now that he'd gone off modelling with clay. In response to her unaccustomed bulk, Evie's hip bones rejigged themselves and their new configuration had her walking like she'd forgotten that she'd left Trigger back at the stable. Apropos, you couldn't even say that her legs were fully operational as tools of locomotion. They still carried her between the bedroom and the bathroom and the kitchen, but at distances outside the demarcation of that triangle they balked. This trickledown effect of Evie's girth put a crimp in her well-laid plans, rendering her housebound far earlier in the pregnancy than she'd anticipated.

The mother-to-be clocked off on leave from the newspaper and settled in to wait for Delray to make his appearance. She hoped that her hasty departure from work would scupper the surprise shower she'd overheard was in the works. There were no secrets in Cubicle Land. It was the etiquette that had her stumped. What do you do with all the presents when you have no baby to show for your efforts at the end of the nine months? Not even, *kaynahorah*, a dead baby for which at least there were rules. Emily Post didn't have a chapter that applied to Evie's particular situation. She'd checked. In a pinch, she figured she could extrapolate from the advice on how to dispose of the wedding gifts when a marriage was called off at the last minute, but Evie was just as happy not having to deal with this eventuality. Didn't she have enough on her plate?

Not that there was any assurance that the home front would be any more of a shower-free zone than the office. None of the Anti-Shabbosites was aware of Evie's plan to farm out this baby. Her friends naturally presumed she'd be keeping it, otherwise why wouldn't she have patronized the clinic down on Jeanne-Mance Street that Judy's pristine southern hemisphere could personally vouch for? No other explanation made sense.

So far though, the subject had yet to be broached directly and Moshe hadn't picked up any outside rumblings. The forecast looked clear.

It was a relief to Evie that she no longer had to appear in public draped in so many metres of fabric that she felt like a yurt. Moshe tried to convince her to step outside on his arm to breathe in some fresh air. It wasn't healthy for Delray to be cooped up inside all day and her crampy legs could do with a bit of stretching, but Evie was having none of it. Overinflated as she was, she saw herself as a grotesque. She refused even the shortest of excursions that Moshe proposed, to the shaded bench in the park just one street over where she feared to be mistaken for an installation. No, she and the couch were sticking together for the duration.

Isolation wasn't a problem. Anti-Shabbosites from the distaff side popped by in a steady stream providing Evie with goodies and gossip and lotions.

"This bag balm is great. You're gonna love it," Dizzy assured her. "It prevents stretch marks and moisturizes like nobody's business. Guaranteed. My customers all swear by it."

"You can't prevent stretch marks." Evie corrected her friend's deceptive sales pitch. "Once you have them, you have them for life."

"You know what I mean. Make them less visible. For lots of guys stretch marks are a turnoff. You can't be too careful."

"Funnily enough," Evie paused to resettle the Quonset hut of her belly, "guys are the least of my issues right now." Still, Evie scrutinized the fine print on the container. She'd always been a serious label analyzer by virtue of her no-nut childhood, but since Delray moved in she'd become downright obsessive.

"It says here that it's meant for veterinary usage only."

"You can ignore that. Trust me. Just go ahead and slather it on your stomach. While you're at it you can put it on your heels, your elbows, anywhere it's dry or scaly. Why do you insist on reading all that disclaimer stuff anyway? You know if you ever read all the possible side effects listed on the brochures that come with your pill bottles, you'd never take anything and drop over dead probably."

Evie was unrelenting. "It says here it's meant for udders."

"Look, I use it all the time on rough skin. And not just me. Millions of women can't be wrong. Why else would the stuff come in such a cutesy little tin? Explain me that. You think the farmers buy it that way for Bossy's sore tits?"

"You really use it yourself."

"Absolutely."

"You use it instead of all the other stuff from the cosmetics counter."

"On my hair even, when it's sun parched."

"And you never noticed any negative side effects?"

"Mooo."

These neighbourly visits were necessarily more constrained than in the old days what with so many half-truths to keep properly aligned in Evie's mind, so many wildfires to stomp out. It was only with Moshe, her co-respondent, that she could let down her guard.

"You'll have a lot of time on your hands once Delray's born and gone, Mosh. What'll you do with yourself?"

Moshe was in the midst of painting each of Evie's toenails a different colour. His job was a tad sloppy. He didn't know from cotton balls. He thought that maybe he should tape them off, like when you're painting crown moulding, but lacking any procedural guidance from their owner, he went ahead and did them free hand. Evie wouldn't complain even if he did make a hash of it. She couldn't reach them herself to do the job; she couldn't even see them.

"I don't know. I hardly remember how I used to spend my time before all of this."

He didn't tell her the truth—that he never wanted the pregnancy to end. Evie could keep right on ballooning until she dwarfed the Orange Julep. It wouldn't bother him. He wanted their intimacy, however artificial, to go on forever, but Delray's arrival would mark the end of their cozy domesticity. They weren't living together, strictly speaking, but Moshe had established a bit of an outpost at Evie's place the more sedentary she'd become. It was daddy who did all the nesting in this pregnancy. But soon Moshe would have to unpartner himself, unfather himself, and generally unmoor himself from everything that mattered in his life.

"What about you?" he asked back, hoping for a hint that Evie might be harbouring comparable inclinations.

"Pick up on my old life, I guess. Put all this behind me."

No way could he wring any comfort out of that reply. Moshe's position in her old life was discretely measurable, across the dinner table and one seat over where the place card read Challah Man. And that's where he'd wind up again. Moshe knew himself. It was his very goodness that had snagged him this gig, but goodness didn't work to his advantage in the long haul. In his experience, women liked a trace of the no-goodnik to jazz things up a bit, but there were no dark corners to his character that would lend him a bit of broody interest.

"You really don't think all this will leave any dent on you? That you'll just be able to walk away?"

"I guess my hormones will have a word to say about that. But in the end I have to walk away, Mosh. Otherwise what was it all for?"

Moshe had a healthy male respect for hormones. He'd already observed their random abuse of power over the pregnant Evie, and he dreaded the postpartum havoc they might wreak. Since day one he'd been trying to steer her onto the subject of the immediate aftermath, to get her to open up. He feared that if she didn't talk it out now, down the road he'd be dealing with a postnatal train wreck, but as she often did, Evie flipped the conversational focus over to papa, hoping to stave off that discussion for a while longer.

"You've been a good father, you know?"

"Come on, I haven't had to do any heavy lifting. That all comes later."

"Don't demean yourself. You've done plenty."

Moshe blew on her toes to avoid facing her compliment head on. "Thanks," he said, then looked back up at her. "To be honest, it does worry me sometimes that Delray probably won't have a father while he's growing up, no man there to lean on, but I guess Amélie will figure it out."

Moshe had the makings of the best kind of father in Evie's estimation, a motherly father. What a waste that he wouldn't have the chance to take his blossoming paternal skills out for a spin with Delray once he was born.

"You know what I worry about?" she asked him.

"Tell me."

"Promise not to laugh?"

"Promise."

She didn't continue until she'd checked out the set of his face, hoping to size up the sincerity of his oath. "Well ... it's that he'll inherit my ditz genes."

Moshe was relieved that it was a low-level worry that she chose to pull out of her over-stocked pantry this time around, easily counterable with a bunt, or so he thought.

"You're no ditz. And I qualify as an expert here. Have you ever met my sister Dina?"

"See, I knew it. You're not taking me seriously. And I trusted you to. But I am a ditz. More than that. An idiot, an imbecile. Demented. Call it what you want. It's all the same. Someone who'd come up with a wacko scheme like this? I deserve to be put away and have them throw away the key. And what do you do? You deny it. Maybe it's your head that needs to be examined, not mine."

The escalation took him by surprise though it shouldn't have. Ever since Evie'd been off work she'd been stuck on an overthinking jag in terms of the whole Delray initiative. It was an unproductive line of reflection since it was too late to close that barn door but she couldn't stop herself from questioning every choice she'd made along the way, chewing herself out over every self-perceived mistake in an endless tormented loop. In the movies, Moshe thought, this was where the hero would slap the heroine in the face to snap her out of it and she'd thank him for it, but since he wasn't the physical type, he went behind Evie's back to enlist the aid of her dictionary to douse the flare-up.

"You're on the wrong track. I wouldn't label your behaviour as *ditzy*, strictly speaking. I'd use a term like *inventive*, or *avant-garde* maybe. Besides, I don't think a boy can be a *ditz*. Definitionally speaking I mean."

"You know what I'm talking about."

Her tone had downgraded to merely pouty. The word-y talk was starting to work its magic, but it could only go so far. Moshe took her hands between his own to rub away the last bit of distress that they held, "Amélie strikes me as pretty grounded. If Delray has his head in the clouds, she'll anchor him."

"So you're a nurture over nature guy?"

"I pick and choose according to my mood," Moshe said.

"Me too. On the one hand I like to think that maybe nature will out and he'll grow up to be like us in the end. We're not so bad, I don't think. As parental material goes."

"High praise indeed."

"On the other hand, things might go easier for him if he isn't all that different from Amélie."

Moshe could sense her probing on her person for a phantom third hand to keep the topic rolling. He arrested her search. "Evie, we just have to accept that it's something we'll never know and move on."

"You're right. I know you are. But Mosh, before we leave the subject of things we'll never know, do you ever wonder what kind of mother she'll be, Amélie? Not that I'm implying that she'll be anything but a good mother. I don't mean that.

More her style of mothering. *Laissez-faire,* smothering, super strict. What do you figure?"

He let himself be drawn in. "*Laissez-faire?* I think somehow no. If I had to guess, I'd say on the strict side, I suppose. No-nonsense. Fair. But it's hard to pin down that kind of thing. There are probably as many styles out there as there are mothers. Take your mum as an example. How would you qualify her style of mothering?"

"Mine? Easy. *Ess, ess.*"

"Well," Moshe said, "I think we can safely cross that style off our list."

Chapter 17

EVIE DIDN'T COME BY HER HOSTESSING PROWESS via the milkman. Her mother's parties were legendary; no event went unsung on her watch. And now Marilyn had an excuse to strip the bubble wrap off the punch bowl and spit polish the platters. The idea of a party only came to her gradually. At first she'd figured on bringing into town just those few Caravan alums who would be directly involved in Evie's delivery, the medicos from the original group. But she caught herself thinking small and recalibrated. Here she had the perfect opportunity to parlay a minimalist gathering into a full-blown reunion of the core gang of seventeen. They were getting on, after all. At sixty, Marilyn was the youngest. When if not now?

Her party planning juices started to burble in earnest. The only possible snafu she foresaw regarded the timing of the affair. It had to fit neatly around the baby's arrival and go know when that would be. After communing with her calendar, Marilyn fixed on the Saturday night of the week preceding Evie's due date. It was a safe-ish bet. The Troys were late for everything. Their tardiness was notorious in their circle. Any baby claiming that family's horological lineage would surely be locked into the same pattern, unless of course the pokiness genes were recessive.

A dinner party she pooh-poohed. Too pedestrian. A cocktail party ditto. This bash needed an angle to lend it some of Marilyn's name-brand sizzle. She tossed and turned all night trying to come up with the perfect gimmick — she did all her best thinking asleep — and sure enough by morning she'd come up with it. A costume party. Marilyn threw on her robe and headed straight to the computer. Breakfast could wait. She sat down at the keyboard and composed an e-invitation that spelled out the sartorial regulations for the night. "Modern garb forbidden," it began in bolded caps. "Come dressed as you were on Monday May 11, 1970." The Caravanners were now of an age where details were starting to drop off the edges; the names of all those grandchildren, where they set down their glasses, why they walked into a room, but that date in May was incised on the brain of every last woman on the guest list. All of them recalled precisely what they were wearing on that particular spring afternoon forty years before, those housewives-off-to-a-bridge-luncheon costumes that allowed them to infiltrate Parliament disguised as cream puffs, those prissy getups that snookered the Hill commissionaires into dismissing them as harmless wee ladies come to observe their government in action. Oh, they remembered all right.

Marilyn's party dress code was inspired. Sixteen RSVPs zipped into her inbox before the day was out. The invitation sent all her old companions chugging up their attic steps to dig up the outfits that they had wrapped in tissue paper and sani-boxed the way other women preserved their wedding gowns. They shook them out and held them up by the windows to assess the damage the years had wrought. All in all the clothing had weathered the interval in decent enough shape, creased and faded maybe, but then so were they. A trip to the seamstress to let the side-seams out a bit and they'd be good to go.

Jake worked at the airport. He was accustomed to the thunder of low-flying planes overhead. But the din of seventeen women tarting themselves up in his second floor bedrooms outgunned those 747s easy. He was thankful he'd been assigned to kitchen duty so he wouldn't have to witness the chaos upstairs, where he would be in any event unwelcome. Marilyn shielded Jake from all the tumult with intent. She didn't want him entertaining any second thoughts about his decision to let her Caravan cohort loose on his factory. True, they were professional women now, and grannies most of them, but somehow tonight, with forty mental years shed, these babes were gearing up to party. Oh yeah.

"Are those jalapeños I smell frying? And onions?" Arlene was powdering her nose in front of the mirror in Evie's old bedroom, but she retracted her puff to free up her nostrils for a verificatory sniff. Sure enough, they recognized that vaguely flatulent aroma of her old nemesis. Chili. The other girls' slowpoke noses took a few more seconds but once they nailed it they hooted over Marilyn's crock-pot homage to all the church basement suppers their succession of hosts had simmered up for them as they wended their way across the country. Back then it had seemed as though an epidemic of chili was overtaking the country in lock step with the Caravan. Chili of one variation or another glopped into their bowls every blessed night as predictably as Oliver's gruel, and occasionally, when their meals were split between two different towns, it sneaked in a guest appearance at lunchtime too. Only at breakfast could they count on being spared. By the time they reached Ottawa most of them had OD'd on the dish that looked like vomitus and stank like Tijuana. But tonight, by washing it down with massive lashings of beer, even those girls who'd sworn that they'd never be able to look another kidney bean in the face for the rest of their lives found that Jake's Chili Vegetariano slid down just fine.

Evie wasn't in attendance, though she'd been invited. Her absence was calculated. She worried that the get-together had the potential to turn too liquid, and if it did, she didn't want to be on hand to witness her personal medical team playing chug-a-lug. It was a good call. Even though no breathalyzer would have deemed them drunk, all the other euphemisms applied. They were loose, they were happy, they were relaxed. These girls knew how to party and they knew how to protest.

Marilyn, May 1970

It didn't matter how often she watched them. The ragtag skits her comrades put on in all the cities and hamlets en route moved Marilyn to tears every time. Her assignment as prop manager prevented her from assuming a role onstage, freeing her to sit in the audience and blub. But even if Marilyn wasn't included among the dramatis personae, her contribution to the pantomimes was critical. It was up to her to acquire the gear the actors needed for their performances and to position it according to the script demands.

Most of the props had been easy to round up, purchased at one sweep through Canadian Tire for under twenty bucks. No fuss no muss. Marilyn rolled her cart purposefully down the housewares aisle where she helped herself to some shish-kabob skewers and kitchen shears. She caught sight of her actions in the store's overhead anti-theft mirrors. The reflection was all innocence, a prettyish young housewife in a car coat stocking up on equipment for the evening's barbecue. A security guard monitoring the mirrors would never imagine that instead of threading the skewers with marinated chicken cubes and pineapple chunks she was planning on going home and sticking one of them up her snatch in the upstairs bathroom where she would subsequently bleed to death on the octagonal tiles. An honest mistake on his part. Marilyn herself was new to the underbelly of innocuous objects, but she was learning fast. In fact, as a solidarity move, she was maintaining a personal boycott against the sharp and pointy. Irrational maybe, but Marilyn had found religion and was carving out her own level of observance. For the rest of her life, Marilyn would shun ballpoint pens, stiletto heels, and carrots. Such was the zeal of the convert.

The prop master hung a left down the cleaning products aisle and pulled some supersized containers of drain cleaner and bleach off the shelves, adding them to the kitchen gadgets that were clanking about in the bottom of her basket. The knitting needles she required had already been supplied gratis, courtesy of Abie's of Montreal, sparing her a trip to the yarn-goods aisle. A quick zip over to the toy department for a plastic stethoscope and assorted sundries and she'd be ready for the checkout line.

The Abortion Caravan troupe had a limited, summer stock repertoire, but its audiences didn't come out expecting *Fiddler on the Roof*. Its morality plays cut to the chase. Marilyn's favourite, if you could call it that, was the one starring Arlene in the role of the desperate teen. Arlene begs the doctor on bended knee for an abortion, emoting her little heart out as if she were Lillian Gish. One look at her bare feet and shabby attire and the doctor boots her out of his office. In sweeps Martha dressed to kill, clearly bent on the same procedure. She opens her purse and fans out hundred dollar bills like a winning bridge hand. The doctor pockets the cash and leads Madame by the hand into his examining room to check out his curettes. On her way out of the doctor's office, all smiles, she steps neatly over the teenager's body so inconsiderately splayed out across the threshold, blocking her way. Curtain.

These skits primed the pump for the public meetings that hitched onto their coattails. The women in the audience, emboldened by the Caravan theatricals that echoed their own experiences, stood up and spilled out stories they had never before dared to share; stories that fuelled and fanned Marilyn's nightmares. Every tale was harrowing, but one in particular burrowed into her heart, therein to take up lodgings for the rest of her life.

They were gathered in a Saskatoon school gym that night. A willowy young woman rose from the bleachers when Arlene opened the floor to the turnout. "My younger sister Jesse committed suicide," she began. "Four years ago. I was the one who found her. She was hanging from a beam in the garage. I went to get my bike and there she was. No note. Nothing. But I knew she killed herself rather than tell our parents that she was pregnant. She couldn't make herself say it to them. I begged her to. She wouldn't. She was only sixteen. A top student. She wasn't wild. She wasn't a bad girl. Just the opposite. Maybe it's hard for all of you here to believe in this day and age, but she only half-understood what was happening. Sex-ed, what kind of joke was that? And words like *contraception, abortion*. A foreign language to us. She asked me to help her, but I didn't know what to do. I couldn't tell her where to go. I didn't have a clue. What kind of sister was I? I should have told our parents myself. That's what I should have done." She paused to collect herself in the stone silence of the hall, righting her shoulders and straightening her flowered blouse that must have concealed a back stripped down to the bloody sinews after so many years of self-flagellation. "Our family. It's ruined. Nothing can change that. I saw your poster, so I'm here now. I don't want this to have to happen to one more girl."

Jesse's ignorance was not at all difficult for Marilyn to comprehend, in fact. She herself used to be one of those girls, colossally innocent, a reproductive *dummkopf*. How old was Marilyn before she understood that drinking from the same Coke bottle after a boy had already touched it to his lips wouldn't make her pregnant? No degree of unknowingness could shock her. Her heart grieved for Jesse who would have been her exact age had she lived. A girl like Jesse, Marilyn might have shared a hall locker with her or studied for geometry tests beside her in the school library. Marilyn could see her so clearly she could have reached out and touched her. In that chilly Saskatchewan gymnasium, Marilyn co-opted Jesse as her sister, the dedicatee in invisible ink of all of her future Caravan endeavors.

Regina, Winnipeg, Thunder Bay, Sudbury. At every stop they came out to testify; women who would never be able to bear children, their insides cut to shreds by backstreet boys, women infected by instruments so dirty they wouldn't have used them for garden tools, women berated, bullied, blackmailed, women reviewed by the TACs and branded by them as SLUTs. Marilyn listened to them day in day out, but no matter how often their stories repeated themselves, never did she become inured to their outpourings.

The engorged Caravan closed in on the capital. Some of the extra vehicles they accumulated en route didn't belong to the committed. Ever since that incident in Thunder Bay, OPP squad cars took it upon themselves to ride shotgun. The Caravan had buffeted skirmishes aplenty with tail-gating anti-abortion militants who shouted down their message and sabotaged their meetings, but until that night they had never descended to violence. The bloody punchout erupted in the audience after a brief oral preamble. Of all the subjects the girls had covered to prepare themselves for potential misadventures their odyssey might throw their way, they'd never touched on refereeing, but it probably wouldn't have mattered, Marilyn supposed. Even Arlene with her swim team shoulders couldn't have prised those two apart.

One of the officers who arrived on the scene informed Arlene, who had an I'm-in-charge look about her, that for the remainder of their journey through his province, they would benefit from a police chaperone.

"Thank you constable," Arlene said, "but you don't have to babysit us. It's all over. Just a dustup. We can look after ourselves. This just sprang up too fast, before we had a chance to get a handle on it. Don't worry. It won't happen again."

"Ma'am, trust me on this. It's not just a question of the odd punch being thrown or your tires being slashed. Before all this is settled, people are going to get hurt, maybe killed. I don't want it to be one of you. You ladies will be babysat."

This wasn't Marilyn's first time in Ottawa. She'd been to the capital before on a school trip, a yawn from start to finish. It was one of those pedagogical jaunts promoted as an end-of-the-school-year treat, but the teachers at her high school were clearly a bit hazy on the difference between reward and punishment. The expedition was a monumental shlep. Maybe Ottawa was the country's seat of government, but it was a hick burg with nothing much to redeem it as far as she could see. Everything was so fusty, the Parliament buildings, the MP who shook their hands, their box lunches. And the debate they watched from the gallery over some bill to amend an amendment to an amendment; even shul wasn't that mind-numbing.

But today when the Caravan swung into town like a cocky new sheriff and the verdigris towers loomed into view, she approached Parliament Block with a new sense of participation, of ownership. Finally she got it. This is what Monsieur Coulomb had been trying to drill into their resistant skulls in Civics class. She, Marilyn Henkin from Côte Saint-Luc, had a genuine role to play in the governmental process. Well, to be completely accurate it was a role at one remove. The other girls would be doing all the negotiating after all, the girls from the Vancouver inner circle who had set the Caravan in motion, but still they would be funneling Marilyn's inchoate thoughts. And look who they'd be talking to. Marilyn could hardly believe it. It was all arranged. Prime Minister Pierre Elliott Trudeau himself would be at the table.

Now Pierre had it in his power to redeem Marilyn's view of politicians, and she was in good company. When Trudeau stepped out from behind the wheel of his sexy little two-seater, his signature black cape swinging, a rose in his lapel, all the women in the country swooned over the Elvis of world leaders.

He was both Canadian and cool, two words that before his time had never been caught canoodling. Pierre was forging a new prime ministerial model that Marilyn could get behind. He was a modern guy.

Before the girls on the Caravan undertook to inject some political smarts into her, all Marilyn really knew about Trudeau's activities was that he was dating Barbra Streisand, but the fact that he was squiring around a Broadway diva didn't cut any ice with them. They'd informed their protégée early on in the trek that it was her Ottawa heartthrob who was the very author of their discontent, the Frankenstein who'd unleashed the Therapeutic Abortion Committees on the country in 1969, him and no other. Pierre was committed to the TAC system. It was his baby. Let Marilyn ruminate on that for a while. So she did.

Maybe Marilyn's reasoning was faulty, she still distrusted her fledgling analytical skills, but the way she saw it Trudeau had tried to do some good. Before he came into the picture, abortion in any way shape or form had been illegal. Period. She'd been coached on the history. For a hundred years it was either do-it-yourself or be-done-to. Some choice. Leap into acid or leap into flames. But then Trudeau stepped up to the plate. He ushered a bill through Parliament that allowed women to have a safe hospital abortion if a Therapeutic Abortion Committee deemed them needy. Okay, so the committee system was flawed. Even worse than flawed she was prepared to admit, it was downright stinko. But in her eyes, after a century of nuthin', Trudeau had made one small step for womankind and for that she gave him credit. Not full credit, but maybe a C+. The girls, though, they red-inked a D- across his bill and considered themselves generous. To them he was the wuss who had the authority but hadn't gone far enough. Marilyn couldn't help but notice that no one ever went far enough to suit them. On any subject. It was part of their lefty charm.

A lifetime ago, before they ever left Vancouver, the girls had shot out telegrams to the Prime Minister, to his Minister of

Justice, and to his Minister of Health and Welfare, setting up the meeting. A sympathetic MP booked the girls the Railway Committee Room for the parley, right up on the Hill, a serious venue for a serious discussion. Saturday, May 9th, 1:00 p.m. At long last it was about to happen. This is why they'd barrelled across the country listening to the voices of Canada's women all along the way. For this encounter. They would all sit down and thrash out an abortion program that made sense if it took until doomsday.

Chapter 18

MARILYN, MAY 1970

The bastards stood them up. Turns out they were previously committed. Right hand left hand. Oops.

The girls regrouped back at the church. Marilyn was devastated, but the others fed on the repudiation like manna. Arlene was pumped, her face aglow with righteous indignation. "Let none of those scumbag politicos ever claim that they weren't given fair warning. We offered them the chance to thrash things out all civilized over one of their mahogany conference tables, but they stiffed us. So the gloves are coming off. Come Monday we're going to do things our way. They won't know what hit 'em."

None of them had the proper clothes for their plan B. It fell to the local Ottawa organizers to come to their vestimentary rescue. The Ontario girls would gladly have donated their own clothing to make up for the deficiency, but their counterculture closets yielded only denim, denim, and more denim, not at all what was required for a day of radical chic. So they pillaged their mothers' wardrobes and fanned out to hit the thrift stores. They negotiated the racks strategically, spurning the more recent styles in favour of outfits from the early sixties and even back to the fifties, retro garb that would drape the advance group in an extra layer of protective prim.

The Caravan girls were a disciplined bunch. On Monday

morning they prepared themselves from the ground up, shaving feminist gams that had never before made nice with a razor. Marilyn gauged all the hair in the sink with a professional eye, and there was plenty. If she were to gather it all up into a ball she'd have enough to crochet up maybe a dozen commemorative yarmulkes. But no time today. She was busy dolling herself up with the others. Marilyn was humbled that she, the most junior of the group, was being trusted with such a weighty assignment, included as a member of the special ops branch for the afternoon's offensive.

As the only ex-princess among them, Marilyn was undaunted by the dressing-up process, though she tried not to flaunt her expertise in front of the others who were having their issues. For the first time in donkey's years her Birkenstock sidekicks, who normally hung freestyle, were obliged to harness themselves into bras so they would point in the proper womanly direction. The girls all managed it, albeit not without grumbling. Why was it that men were allowed to dangle? Arlene put a lid on their bellyaching with a look. That gravitational discussion would have to keep for another day. They couldn't afford to get sidetracked.

Next up, panty hose. In their clumsy fingers, garnished with serrated nails since they bit them off for expediency, the mesh sprang runs before the girls had even yanked their stockings up as far as their knees. At the rate they were goring them, they'd soon have no hose left. The clock was ticking. Marilyn had no choice but to out herself. She moved in and instructed the others in the proper unrolling-from-the-toe technique. And with that small gesture Marilyn assumed control over the girls' toilette. She rescued her covey of amateurs as they fumbled to straitjacket their wild and woolly 1960s locks into Grace Kelly upsweeps and guided them in making pert bows of their lips while not colouring outside the lines.

What constituted beauty, Marilyn was moved to ponder as she shuttled from one girl to the next wielding a mascara wand in one hand and a spray can of Aqua Net in the other. Here she was philosophizing. Was there no end to her transformation on the road?

From the beginning she admired her companions their naturalness. Their hair was unperoxided, their faces unpowdered, their nails unpolished, just as God made them. This was not the standard of female beauty Marilyn had been suckled on. The women in her family were adherents of the brassy school. Back home her father used to look out the kitchen window mornings and expound on the wonders of the natural world. "Look kids," he'd say when he spotted a scarlet cardinal flitting from fence to fence in the yard. "See how the male of the species is the more brightly coloured to attract the female?" Marilyn's mother Bryna listened to nature boy's lectures, her glossed lips set in a moue of disapproval. The animal world had it ass-backwards in her estimation. Of the evolutionary model that positioned the male as the glamour puss while the female sat on the nest in a faded red *shmatte*, Bryna was a flat-out denier. Women weren't meant to be the shlumps. When Marilyn's mum went out there was no missing her. Her gold hoop earrings were big enough for Shamu to leap through and as for makeup, Bryna slathered it on like cream cheese on a deli bagel. And that was just for everyday. When she dressed up for a night-time do, she looked like she'd been plugged in. *Natural* was not part of her vocabulary.

Marilyn reeled her errant thoughts back in from her family in suburban Montreal and its be-sequinned matriarch. Enough with the daydreaming. She had to stay focused. The girls were on to the final touches and they needed her to cover their backs for every errant zipper, snap, or hook-and-eye. As wardrobe mistress it was Marilyn alone who had sign-off privileges. Only once the girls twirled round in front of her and received her blessing were they permitted to don their white gloves and head out to meet their fates.

For all that they were devoted to the cause, the prissy little gloves were almost more than the girls could stomach. Even the netted hats that they plopped like maraschino cherries onto their heads were somehow less repellent than the gloves. In an uncharacteristic show of sass, they hustled her to let them go without. Would it really make any difference? But their soft secretarial pool hands had morphed over the course of a journey that saw them digging cars out of ditches and pitching tents in the Manitoba mud. Didn't these gals ever look down? Didn't they see that their transfigured mitts belonged in overalls at the Esso service bay doing oil changes and rotating tires? Field Marshal Marilyn issued an ultimatum. Cover them up or ship out. They covered them up.

At last the troops were dressed. But before they could set off on their mission they required one crucial accessory to complete their ensembles. In a corner of the church basement, a folding table was covered with handbags set out in size-wise rows like fruitcakes-in-waiting for the parish bake sale. An Ottawa volunteer handed over to each girl the purse assigned to her with an air of solemnity that bespoke cached cyanide capsules. Once all of them were kitted out with their carry-on, they opened up their handbags and checked the gear within as assiduously as paratroopers. It was crunch time.

The demonstration on Parliament Hill was going full tilt when they arrived. The TV cameras were rolling and the press corps was out in force. The girls guesstimated the crowd as they pulled up; there must have been a thousand women, maybe even two, spread out across the lawns chanting, singing, and waving their placards. It was a wild, circus atmosphere. The turnout was better than the Caravanners could ever have hoped for, thanks yet again to their Ottawa hosts who grabbed whatever assignment was thrown their way and ran with it.

After Saturday's meeting with the Trudeau troika went phfft, the local girls took to the telephones and as directed mobilized women's groups in Toronto, Montreal, Hamilton,

London; any city within shooting distance of the capital. Their message was to the point; charter every bus that isn't nailed down and hightail it for Ottawa to come to the aid of your sisters. But they decided not to stop there; these chicks didn't need to be spoon fed. They prepped their knuckles with a few limbering-up cracks and kept right on dialing; they dialed with call-centre doggedness, they dialed until their fingers bled, targeting towns further and further out across the country until they had girls hitching down from Moosonee, hopping the train over from Quebec City, and flying in standby from as far away as St. John's and Banff. They hoped the Vancouver group had a war chest deep enough to foot the phone bill. It was going to be a whopper.

One alcove of calm, just to the rear of the Centennial Flame, set itself apart from the hue and cry. At that spot, in a simple dawn ceremony, the Caravanners had laid to rest the black slat coffin that accompanied them on their journey out from the Pacific. It was their Tomb of the Unknown Soldier. Like many of the women who filed by later in the day to pay their respects, Marilyn attached a specific name to its symbolic remains. To her the coffin was Jesse's, and she recited a silent kaddish before she disappeared to honour her shadow sister's memory with action.

In all the brouhaha, no one paid much attention to the shirt-waisted women who sniffed at all the unseemly rowdiness as they forged their way through the rabble to the entrance of the House of Commons. The Parliamentary commissionaires barely glanced down at the faux entry passes the girls tendered in their impeccably gloved fingers. So far so good. For this linchpin step the Caravanners dug their feminine wiles out of cold storage. Most of them weren't even aware they had any to draw on, but Marilyn, their secret weapon, their link with the unliberated, brought them up to speed. As she had advised them to do, they smiled their widest at the doddery guards hoping to distract them from their forged documentation.

The best they could come up with, most of them, was a rictus, inexperienced as they were at even elemental coquettishness. Eyelash fluttering they managed better. A scent of baby powder wafted from the group, wrapping them in a protectionist cloud of innocence. It was working.

One by one security passed them through the checkpoint that led upstairs to the Parliamentary visitors' galleries. Until it was Marilyn's turn. Inexplicably, as she paused before him, one of the guards popped out of his trance and remembered what it was he was paid to do. He requested, with all due courtesy, that Marilyn open her purse for a spot check. It couldn't all come crashing down on their heads now, could it? On her watch? Her failure to deliver would be more than she could bear. Marilyn had no choice but to unlatch her bag for inspection. The guard peered in at the contents. Instead of the neatly pressed hankie he was expecting, his eyes landed on a bottle of bleach. Luckily, the skull and crossbones on the label, coached with all the girls earlier in the day, knew enough to smile sweetly up at him. The commissionaire didn't say boo. It struck him as entirely plausible that über-housewives like the ones now filing before him might naturally be taken by a sudden urge to sanitize the Parliamentary toilets and he waved Marilyn and the rest of the group through with a ladies-right-this-way sweep of the hand. They were in.

They scattered themselves throughout the two observer galleries that faced each other choir loft style above the floor of the Commons. The girls shrugged their shoulders apologetically at the engaged citizens who were already seated as they bumped past their knees to assume their own places and listen to Question Period. Marilyn didn't find the debate quite so flat this time as during her previous student visit to the chamber. Probably because she couldn't catch any of the words being spoken over the roaring in her ears. Was she really the only one to hear it? Surely her neighbours on either side could make out her blood crashing against her skull like the Fundy tides, but they appeared oblivious to the din, completely homed in on the discussion down below. Their focus on the House floor served Marilyn well. It meant that they wouldn't see her shaking. She was suffering from delicate, ladylike tremolos to be sure, not landed trout fliperoos. No one would be tempted to stuff a towel in her mouth, but they were the shakes nonetheless. And to top it all off, she thought she might throw up. At least that symptom of her nerves run amok was indiscernible to the gallery. For now anyway. She had to pull herself together. She peeped discreetly at her fellow travellers. All the other girls had assumed an easy, attentive posture, heads tipped forward, legs crossed demurely at the ankles, purses on their laps, as if they were Mrs. Leave it to Beaver at the PTA. Marilyn took their cue and was able to reconnect with her inner chutzpah that had briefly decamped for a joyride around Ottawa.

At the two o'clock bongs from the Peace Tower carillon Arlene rose from her seat directly behind the carved wooden balustrade and made a megaphone of her hands. "Why should women be punished just because you can't control your honourable members?" The voices on the House floor cut out and all eyes turned in her direction. Before the MPs had a chance to assay the rogue loon in their balcony Marilyn leapt up on the opposite side of the hall. She used her Bat Mitzvah voice, trained to carry all the way back to the women's section. "My uterus is not government property." Sarah, back over on Arlene's side, launched herself from her seat with such vigour you could almost hear the sproing. "Abortion is our right." The parliamentary heads pivoted back and forth as if they were at Wimbledon.

"Women are dying."

"The operating room, not the back room."

"Babies deserve to be wanted."

"Free abortions on demand."

Sloganizing women were popping up like rabbits. The seats of their wooden chairs, bereft of their anchoring cheeks, snapped up with a bang, adding to the racket.

"Order, order in the House." The Honourable Speaker Geoffrey Boisclair shouted into the fray, but it had all the effect of a substitute teacher trying to rein in a kindergarten classroom riding a sugar high.

With the head of every MP fixed on the galleries, the girls reached into their purses and pulled out the heavy machinery; bleach bottles, untwisted coat hangers, cans of drain cleaner, vacuum cleaner hoses, knitting needles, letter openers, turpentine. They held their products high like TV pitchmen with their vegematics. Martha had wanted to throw their props over the railings to crash on the floor of the House at the end for effect.

"Think of the drama," she'd said when they were strategizing after the Trudeau snub.

"Think of the lawsuits. What if we conk someone on the head and knock them unconscious, or kill them even? These aren't water balloons, you know."

"It would be poetic justice."

The rest of the girls nixed her knucklehead suggestion. There was a place in every activist group for a hothead, but the House of Commons wasn't it.

The Speaker scrambled to reassert his authority, but he'd left his Bourinot's back in the bookcase at the office. He mentally thumbed through the chapters to see where this type of situation would fall. Unparliamentary language? No, that only applied to the Members themselves. He racked his brain to remember if there was an entry in the index under *visitors comma unruly*. Probably not, seeing as how it was a Canadian book.

He'd have to wing it. "Silence in the balconies. *Silence aux balcons.*" But the broads wouldn't shut their yaps. This was no surprise. He was used to being ignored. MPs talked over his head all the time like he was the pickle in the middle. He was convinced that they disrespected him because of that damned speech impediment that robbed him of the necessary gwavitas.

He tried another tack. "Empty the balconies." He wanted done with these blots on the face of womanhood who were ruining what should have been a placid afternoon umping a who-cares debate over radio station licenses.

The Commissionaires were enjoying the commotion like they would a catfight in a bar, but now they were being pushed to take some kind of action. The Speaker was waving them upwards. These guys didn't move fast. Their main responsibility, propping up the House doorframes, had flattened their feet and stiffened their joints over the years. They were rooted into the parquet like maple trees. Never had they been called on to eject a soul, least of all a woman. They followed the front porches of their bellies up the steps, straining to remember the security training they'd undergone back in the days when they still had hair.

Aloft, the Caravanners burrowed into their purses yet again as if the Speaker's do-something hand signals were intended for them. Out came the chains. These were no-nonsense chains, heavy grade, the kind used to restrain junkyard dobermans, none of those wimpy chains that lift up the flapper when you flush. I-mean-business chains. The girls wrapped them around their ankles in multiple figure eights and then padlocked themselves to their seats. They were quick about it. They'd rehearsed their Houdini knots all Sunday night.

The Speaker heard the clanking. He recognized the sound. Under other circumstances women in chains would perk up his day immoderately, but today he wasn't in the mood. The Commissionaires were stumped. Nobody had ever issued them chain cutters. They were equipped for their job like Mr. Jingeling, the security elf at Santa's workshop. All they carried were keys. They shuffled about in the balconies examining their navels. Arlene gave the signal and the girls commenced to chant. "Legalize all abortion now. Legalize all abortion now. Legalize all abortion now."

The MPs left their benches to get a better view of the tumult.

Liberals, Tories and NDP-ers mingled on the non-partisan central green carpet, heads canted back as if they were out birding. All the chanting from above affected the Speaker's style. "Wesume your seats, wesume your seats, wesume your seats," but repetition as a rhetorical tool did nothing to increase his authority. None of the elected representative sat back down at his bidding. In the midst of all the ruckus, the House maintenance men materialized with chain cutters. A cheer from the floor greeted their arrival. All this attention was foreign to them. They were used to modest gratitude when they tweaked an office thermostat that was stuck on the sauna setting, but normally they operated under the radar of the Parliamentarians. They threw their shoulders back, marched across the floor with a we'll-lick-'em gait, and mounted the stairs. Their enthusiasm soon faded. The protesters jiggled their legs and stomped their bound feet to hamper the chain crew's progress. Applying tools to moving targets wasn't the specialty of these men in grey overalls. The clogged drain traps and flickering fluorescents that were their stock in trade cooperated by being inert. Like surgeons they expected their patients to be safely anaesthetized before they made the first cut. It wasn't cricket to move in with the scalpel while the crash victim was still flailing on the gurney. Oh, how they now longed for the cozy anonymity of the boiler room.

God must have been listening to their prayers. Their shop steward, roused from his siesta, showed up in their wake and ordered his minions to cease and desist. Freeing radical nutcases wasn't part of their job description. He signalled them with an arched eyebrow to drop their equipment where they stood, and to the man they obeyed. Tools littered the floor harum-scarum like the detritus of a thwarted jail-break. The exit command from his second brow was de trop. His workers were already scuttering downstairs as fast as their steel-toed boots would carry them. The Speaker was envious. He wished that he had someone higher up on the Parliamentary totem pole who would come along and shoo him out of there, but he was flying solo. Too bad he didn't have a gavel like the Americans gave to their Speaker. Now they knew how to govern, those Amerikanskis. He could whack a head or two into line with one of those mothers. He considered the scene around him one last time. What the hell.

"This sitting of the House is suspended." No one heard him. His words were mashed to a pulp in all the tohu-bohu, but at least he'd done his duty. The history books wouldn't be able to fault him there, presuming they'd swallow his uncorroborated version of the events. The Honourable Speaker turned his back on the Chamber, the orderly conduct of which he had sworn to maintain, and bolted the mayhem in search of a restorative Johnny Walker.

The Commissionaires regarded each other. No way around it, this was their baby now. They picked the abandoned tools up off the floor and commenced to snippety-snip as if they were wielding secateurs to prune the rhododendrons. Their delicate manipulations made negligible headway until one of them landed three lucky chomps in a row, rousing his colleagues to put a bit more shoulder into the task, and in short order, schooled in the proper technique, they succeeded in unshackling the women. The guards herded the interlopers out through the front archway and led them well away from the building where they wiped their hands of them with the utmost relief. The girls were blinded by the explosion of camera flashes that greeted them. A bouquet of microphones blossomed in their faces.

"Ladies, ladies. Look this way."

"Over here. Give us a group shot. Pull in tighter."

"Come on girls. Can't you give us a smile? Tell the public about your Ottawa adventure."

"Ladies, I'm Erica Hart from CBC television. We're doing a live feed, coast-to-coast."

The diminutive reporter had elbowed her way up to the front of the scrum. "Were you aware when you started your protest today that no Canadian Parliament has ever been brought down by a disturbance from the gallery? Not once in its 103-year history? Could you comment on that?" Erica's parliamentary mole was pure gold.

In fact they were unaware that their operation was Guinness worthy, but the girls refused to address any journalists until their full complement had reassembled and at the current count they were one body short. Marilyn was still thumping down the stairs from the gallery. The youngest member of their brigade had done an exemplary job with her chain. It would have taken the jaws-of-life to disconnect her. In desperation, the chief commissionaire took his Swiss army knife out of his pocket and with its midget Phillips head unscrewed her chair from the floor just to be rid of her. Let them deduct the damn seat from his pay if they wanted. It would be money well spent.

Arlene turned to Erica Hart once Marilyn had limped up to assume her rightful place alongside the others. She was still tethered to her chair. It adorned the walkway beside her like a clubbed seal.

"It was not our goal to shut down Parliament, but to rouse it to action. We are demonstrating here today to draw the country's eyes to a national disgrace; to show the citizens of Canada that our government, through its gross neglect, has been complicit in the death and mutilation of thousands of women by forcing them to seek out underground abortions. We have crossed this country of ours and taken in the voices of its women at every stop we made. It is their message that we are delivering. Our government's treatment of females as a disposable sub-class has to stop now."

"But why are you targeting this government, the very one that decriminalized abortions performed in hospital?" Erica Hart had done her homework.

"The Therapeutic Abortion Committee plan that the Liberal government put in place is an insult to the women of Canada. The law is so narrowly defined that the number of legitimately needy women who benefit from it is infinitesimal. The government gave us the Therapeutic Abortion Committees, patted us on our heads, and expected us to go back to our kitchens, bake cookies, and shut up. But we won't be gagged any longer. On this day, May 11, 1970, we declare war on the government of Canada. Unless Prime Minister Trudeau agrees to legalize all…"

The Peace Tower clock started to chime three o'clock. At the sound Arlene cut off her oration mid-flow. She turned her back on the CBC reporter and craned her neck to look up at the Tower. Her fellow House ejectees turned and jacked up their heads in sync, shading their eyes. In no time, the thousands of protesters followed suit until everyone on the lawn shared an air-show posture.

"Erica, Erica, can you fill us in on what's happening?" Back at the Toronto anchor desk Andrew Peterson was looking at a dead shot of the Tower against a backdrop of blue sky. Those Ottawa clucks called this news?

"I can't figure it out, Andrew. Nothing's going on up there that I can see. No wait. Wait. There seems to be some activity on the parapet that surrounds the flagpole. Three people. No, correct that, four. Women it looks like from here, if I'm not mistaken. They're lined up, carrying something across their shoulders."

"Are you able to make out what it is from your vantage point, Erica? If they overpowered the guards to get up there, could it be a hostage? Or a body?"

"I don't know Andrew. They've set it down. It's out of sight now. But judging by the sheer size of the thing, I don't think it could be a person."

"Can you see what they're doing now?"

"They're working on the flag, I think. Yes. It's starting to go down. It could be," Erica hypothesized on the fly, "that they're planning on lowering it to half-mast as a way of honouring Canadian women who have died from abortions. That would be entirely in line with their principles." But the flag didn't stop at the pole's midpoint. It continued its descent all the way to the bottom where the flag detail unlatched it altogether and jettisoned it over the side. It drifted down till it sheathed one of the gargoyles that poked showily out from the Peace Tower at a viagran right angle. The heads of the perpetrators ducked out of sight for a few minutes while the cameras remained fixed on the denuded pole.

"Andrew, there they are again. Can you see them? They're hoisting a new flag of some kind up the pole. Something enormous from the look of it. That must be what they were carrying earlier."

The Caravanners high atop Parliament were heave-ho-ing on the halyard with all their might until their flag reached the top, but once it did, it hung limply in the still air, its folds hugging the pole like a sleeping bat on a downspout. This was a kink the girls hadn't foreseen. For all their meticulous preparations, for all their consideration of every eventuality, they hadn't accounted for the weather. The impotent flag-bearers stood at the base of the pole, cursing the elements, or lack of them, until a sympathetic wind kicked up out of the west and unfurled the new standard full-length against the sky.

"Its shape is very unusual, Erica. What significance do you attach to it?" Erica stewed internally. To think they gave that lamebrain the anchor spot over her.

"It's a uterus, Andrew. No doubt about it."

The shouts from the ground were deafening when the crowd saw the knitted ensign flying defiantly over Parliament. Marilyn stared up proudly. All the girls had done their bit on it of course, but the giant red maple leaf rib-stitched in the centre of the womb was her own expert handiwork. How long would it be allowed to wave, she wondered, before security broke through the barricaded door to the flag platform and yanked it down without ceremony as if it were just some muffler with a hormone disorder? And what would become of the flag that had come to life in the girls' hands, the flag they had worked on night after night all across the country in anticipation of this very moment, the flag whose progression, in Marilyn's mind, tracked her awakening to the world around her? If she had her druthers, it would come to its final resting place in a museum, duly labelled and explicated behind a protective pane of glass, like the Magna Carta. Then, the way her daydream spun it, she could pay a visit to the exhibit someday with her daughter who would laugh and roll her eyes to hear her mother reminisce about a time in the not-so-distant past when women didn't have property rights to their own bodies and telephones had dials. Marilyn treated herself to the vision for a minute or so, but then she redrafted it to jibe with reality. In all likelihood their flag would end up dumped out back in the Parliamentary garbage along with the shepherd's pie that had outlived its cafeteria shelf life.

For now, though, she stood on the grass with her sisters and soaked up the tintamarre that their precious flag inspired. The women crowding in on her from all sides whooped and howled, they sobbed and sang. Marilyn basked in the close-knit cacophony for a time, but the exhaustion and exhilaration of the past few days caught up with her then and there. She didn't faint but her mind temporarily checked into a spa and let itself blank out for a spell. She might have spent a few welcome out-of-body hours decompressing in a mud wrap if it weren't for one woman's piercing shriek. The pitch of that particular screech pressed buttons Marilyn didn't even know she had. It pulled its fingernails down the blackboard of her soul. That single scream perforated her eardrum with its intensity, and once it succeeded in popping a hole, barged in to her body through the aperture, grabbed Marilyn's very core in its fist, and shook her back to consciousness. It delivered its message in no uncertain terms. "Snap out of it toots. Your presence is required."

Evie's screams were by now so overamped that they had

the factory's ceiling baffles quivering. Delray had made the executive decision to arrive early, plunk in the middle of Marilyn's party, forcing the revellers to decamp to Jake's PDQ so they could guide Evie's baby into the world. Marilyn stood helplessly by, watching her daughter writhe on the rented hospital bed. The grandmother-to-be had no practical role to play now that it was D-Day. Her job title in the jury-rigged delivery room was Official Fretter. To this position she applied all her pent-up energy even though she knew it to be busy work. She had absolute faith in Arlene and Laura to get the job done. Evie wasn't so sure. For a woman about to give birth she was more than normally discombobulated. She looked up at the doctor palpating her abdomen. No reassuring white coat; she was suited out and pillboxed like Jackie Kennedy. And as for the bouffant, bespectacled, and be-chinned nurse who was taking her pulse, Evie could have sworn she was Dame Edna.

On top of being held captive in some crossover costume drama, here she'd penetrated the secret batcave of her father's factory for the very first time in her life. Evie'd never gone to work with her dad. Most of her schoolmates, the offspring of accountants, *shmatte* mavens, university professors, and lawyers, were intimate with their fathers' workspaces. On ped days their dads parked them at a free desk and put them to work stapling syllabi or boxing sweaters. Not Evie. She'd never made it beyond her father's outer office. It was too much sanitizing trouble according to her dad who was anal about such matters. So the sight of all the assembly lines, rollers, and clamps that manipulated the in-flight snacks was new and threatening to Evie in her vulnerable state. If she didn't watch out for her Delray, they might grab him, seal him in foil, and slip him into a galley cart with the pretzels and chips to be served up in the airspace between Montreal and Toronto. She had to remain vigilant. Laura glanced meaningfully over at Arlene. Mummy's pulse was racing.

While Evie was harbouring doubts about her medical crew, Marilyn was suffering comparable misgivings about this Moshe character who had shown up with her daughter. She checked the guy out, gangling, unprepossessing. A flyweight. He probably didn't have the nerve to refuse Evie his help when his turn came up in the prenatal rotation schedule she'd set up with her friends. Evie would snap him like a twig when the final contractions started to kick in. But in fairness to the shlemiel, he never left her side. For a guy who was only there because he'd drawn the short straw, he clung to Evie's hand, wiped her brow, and fed her ice chips as if he were the genuine article. Her Evie had accumulated a good reliable stable of friends in that crazy church she lived in, Marilyn had to admit. You could do worse.

The factory was empty of employees. Usually the outfit ran 24/7. It was a living breathing mechanism as Jake liked to point out to his family. He frequently invoked the human body as a metaphor for his beloved operation whose various components mimicked, in his mind, the essential functions of the body's main organs. They pumped, they transported, they cleansed, they reproduced. But when Jake got word while he was ladelling up the chili that Evie's water had broken, he pulled the plug on the whole shebang without a hic of hesitation. He phoned in to his night supervisor at the plant and instructed him to announce through the PA that it was a Jewish holiday he'd lost track of and everyone on site should take off *tout de suite* and stay home for the next two days to boot. Jake's employees loved the Jewish calendar sprinkled as it was with all those holidays whose gargly phonemes only the boss could pronounce but translated into a paid day off. As directed, they hotfooted it out of the factory, not wanting to offend the God of the Jews who was a vengeful God as everyone knew.

The workers' absence left plenty of floor space free for the rest of the Caravanners, the girls extraneous to the delivery.

They weren't meant to be on hand according to the master plan, but they'd held a quick confab in Marilyn's dining room while the others were heading off to the factory and decided to go along for the ride to lend support and send out positive vibes. Weren't they a team? They seated themselves away from the action, in the shadow of a stilled cookie conveyor, where they softly sang their old campfire songs, Arlene and Laura's spiritual doo-wop girls.

Considering it was a first birth, things were zipping along according to Dr. Arlene. Evie was grateful to hear it. She wasn't sure she could tolerate another chorus of Kumbaya. A contraction took hold of her. She strained against the bed as if one of her father's compressors were trying to squish her into a packageable rectangle. Laura lifted up the hem of the patient's gown and took a few subterranean measurements. Evie was dilated to the max. She could pop a pilates ball out from between her crooked legs. Any time now.

Delray got the message. He'd been living *la vida loca* in utero but the time had arrived for him to play the shit disturber on a grander stage. He did a few farewell back flips in his private pool and was about to go careering down the water slide full speed, revelling in his last bit of freedom. Delray was no dummy. He knew he was heading out into a world of no-no's, a repressive regime of seat belts, door-gates, and training wheels. This would be the last time he'd be allowed to undertake a manoeuvre as risky as this one minus a helmet and shin guards and he was determined to make the most of the opportunity. He floored it and headed down the birth canal. Photo radar would clock him in the red zone.

Evie had a contraction that ate all her previous contractions alive. Jake could kiss the security deposit on the rental bed goodbye. Evie's nails were furrowing the mattress as if she were tilling the soil for spring wheat. Her screaming was audible as far away as Vermont. Moshe, who had been whispering discreetly into her ear until now, was forced to yell out to her to be heard above her own wails. "Remember the pain, remember the pain," he shouted at the top of his lungs. It was a stupid thing to say, he knew, but worth a try. Moshe didn't believe for one minute that Evie would be able to coolly give up the newborn Delray once she saw him in the flesh just because she'd already run him through the postage meter for Amélie's address, whatever she claimed to the contrary. So he tried a new tack in his birth-coach chants. Enough of the daddy doggerel they'd taught him in prenatal class. He'd keep Evie focused on the negative. Maybe it would help her get past the rupture if he could encourage the agony of the birth to stay alive in her mind.

Evie raised her sodden head from the pillow and turned her Uzi on Moshe, spraying him head to toe with her spleen. "Shut up with that 'remember the pain' crap. Shut up! What are you, crazy?" she shrieked. Her pitch could shatter glass. "If I remember the pain then I'll never be able to have OUR baby when the time comes."

Everyone in the room froze, their eyes fixed on Moshe for a major re-eval. Even Delray put on the brakes halfway down. He sensed that the hands that should have been cupped between his mother's legs to receive him had petrified, so he'd damn well wait until they came to. He set his arms akimbo and stuck his knees out charleston style for added friction. At Evie's first post-delivery internal Arlene would feel the skid marks. In the entire battery of factory equipment, only the hinges on Moshe's jaw were operational, allowing his chin to drop to his belt buckle.

It was Evie who splashed them all with smelling salts to bring them back around to business. She'd started to bellow and heave, the sounds emerging from her throat earthy jungle floor grunts, fallen from the coloratura stratosphere where her earlier cries had been soaring. Her new timbre signalled to those in the know that it was all nearly over and done. Delray felt a swift kick in the tush that sent him barrelling down the rest of the way. So much for calling the shots. Arlene caught him as he erupted from his mother like a champagne cork. He was perfect.

Chapter 19

"I TRIED TO TELL YOU ALL THIS on the phone." Amélie cranked herself up to regurgitate her position for the umpteenth time. "I do not want the apartment." She pronounced each word separately and roundly, throwing a lot of mouth into each syllable, as if she were speaking to a rookie lip reader.

"Be that as it may, Madame, it is my duty as M. Médéry's notary to act on his instructions as laid out in his will, and it was his express wish that you inherit his condo."

"But what about my wishes? Don't they count for anything? We're retreading the same territory here. I already told you, over and over again, I don't need a second residence, and I have no intention of moving."

"It's a nice little starter property. Up and coming neighbourhood. Near all amenities. Some young couple will be glad to take it off your hands."

Amélie considered switching to English on the woman whose flat r's pegged her as an Anglo. Sometimes that's all it took to set a wobbly discussion back on four solid legs, but on second thought she was not really sure that language was the impediment. Her words seemed to be ricocheting off the notary's invisible flak jacket and splintering into their component letters which then spilled to the floor, puddling in an unintelligible alphabet soup. The notary wasn't misunderstanding Amélie's statements so much as willfully refusing to understand. "For the last time Maître," Amélie said. "I don't want to have to be put to the trouble of selling the property. I quite simply don't want anything to do with it." *For the last time* was a rash formulation to deploy so early on in the debate, a dead end locution, but this notarial battering ram had her so punch drunk that she let herself be hoodwinked into premature ultimatum.

"We just gave it a fresh coat of paint. The white opens the place up, don't you think?"

Now she was on to décor? The woman had segued like a Sherman tank over the hillock of Amélie's objections. For five straight days Amélie'd been under siege from Jean-Gabriel's notary, a holy warrior, persistent beyond all reason, bombarding her with phone calls at fifteen-minute intervals, robo style. Didn't she have any other legatees to harass?

To silence her once and for all the resistant heiress agreed to the notary's proposal that they meet up at Jean-Gabriel's condo to hash things out *mano-a-mano*. Amélie'd arrived fully armed with her business demeanor, honed to perfection after years of wheeling and dealing with the suits at head office. In full-blown corporista mode, when Mme. Turcotte stared an opponent down, he always blinked first. But somehow today it wasn't working. She must have left the ammo for her dart-gun eyes in her desk drawer back at the bank.

Agreeing to abandon her own turf was a colossal strategic blunder. Now she'd left herself defenceless on the Eastern Front, faced off against this bulldog with a briefcase and her spectral sidekick to boot. It would take more than two coats of cheap primer and a lick of paint to obliterate Jean-Gabriel's traces from the apartment. She could feel his presence bleeding through the latex like mould on the bathroom ceiling. Her breath was starting to come short and shallow in asthmatic chuffs. All she wanted was to get out into the fresh air, but the notary beat her to it.

"Why don't I step outside for a minute and leave you on your own to look around a bit?"

Amélie was grovellingly grateful for the offer of distance even if it did just postpone the inevitable. Down at the bank, Mme. Turcotte had earned herself a sobriquet, not that anyone who valued his job dared use it to her face, but it was out there and she knew it. Amélie the Great and Powerful. It was a good thing they couldn't see her now, downgraded to Amélie the Limp and Lily-Livered, wimping out ignobly under the pressure of this hyped-up paper pusher. She'd never get her street cred back. Amélie flipped the deadbolt shut behind her tormentor and locked herself in with whatever tufts of reputation that still clung to her.

Marilyn walked out of Jean-Gabriel's condo in her dun-coloured blazer that apparently did say *notary* after all. She hadn't tricked herself up in a disguise since her Caravan days of yore up on Parliament Hill and she experienced the same flutter today to see that her chosen ensemble had executed its intended flim-flammery. Her performance, on the other hand, she had no choice but to blast as a two thumbs-downer, sashaying between notary and real estate agent like a *farblondjet* understudy. In her own defence, though, Evie and Moshe had only supplied her with a bare-bones script. She'd wanted extra coaching but she couldn't press them to rehearse with her more, not as broken up as they were over the impending loss of their son. It would have been too cruel. They were barely hanging on, those two. So Marilyn was left to her own devices, and even if she was no Meryl Streep, she'd still succeeded in delivering Amélie to the apartment, however much her heart rebelled against her assigned task. Her role in this intrigue was played out.

Not a peep in almost twenty years, and suddenly this? Jean-Gabriel in a convent. She shook her head at the cockeyed juxtaposition. Six feet under and that man still had the power to give her a belly laugh. And to confound her. Amélie strolled through the rooms, revelling in the solitude, kicking the tires of his modest little condo. She ran the hot water in the kitchen sink till the pipes banged with the effort and fiddled with the stove knobs to wheedle them into cooperating with the burners. What was he playing at living in this Yugo of an apartment?

Scrimping. That was not Jean's MO. He'd leapfrogged over the whole struggling young artist stage. Success had found him while his moustache was still patchy on the ground and by the time she met up with him, envelopes bearing royalty cheques were flowing so regularly into his mailbox that they knew his address by heart. And his fame had only enjoyed a growth spurt since their parting, thanks in the main to her. She could still feel the weight of his shoe on her shoulder as he vaulted to new heights with *Amélie*, her wife-life lacerated in two acts.

Nowadays there was always a theatre marquee around town barking his name for some new production or other. Plummy CBC voices dramatized his plays on the radio waves, l'Opéra de Montréal libretticized them, and Les Grand Ballets Canadiens performed them en pointe. The only twist left was to do them on ice. He was still a cash cow, Jean.

So how had it come to pass that all that income had vaporized, reducing him to living in quarters too diminutive to hold his ego? Mme. Money-Manager stood in the middle of his empty bedroom and assessed what little she had to go on, her pocket abacus clicking. There had to be more to his estate than this runty flat. It was inconceivable that he'd blown all his assets in the years since she'd last seen him. The Jean she knew was generous with money, yes, but loose or careless, *jamais*. In their brief time together he'd been invited in on more ground floors than she could count, but get-richer schemes never seduced him. From her current financial perch she'd scanned enough portfolios to be able to qualify his investment style as schoolmarmish. He was a bond guy from the word go, only one rung up the fiduciary ladder from stuffing his savings in a sock. Jean saved his risky behaviour for other domains.

Apropos. Thirsty dependents. Now that was a scenario that could account for shrivelled capital, a just-so story that she'd seen played out time and again behind the closed door of her office. Had Jean spawned some scattered Jeannes and Gabrielles whose mothers had Outremont tastes? She tried that explanation out for size but her gut told her that it wasn't true. Or maybe she just didn't want it to be true.

An alternate theory started to hatch in her mind, one that booted her earlier one aside. An inkling it was, no more than that, but clingy. She could just imagine her Jean making some last-ditch philanthropic gesture to buy back his immortal soul, some megadonation that would seize him by the collar and yank him back from the brink *à la dernière minute.* Not his name on a hospital wing or a university pavilion, no; too posthumously me-me-me. It would have to be one of those children's causes to put a lock on his salvation, an orphanage in Bosnia, schools in the Sudan, a kiddie eye clinic in Gaza. The more she mulled it over, the more she was convinced that she'd hit on it. Jean had gone the payout route to land himself a cushy writer-in-residence sinecure in the clouds. Had he genuinely believed that Saint Peter wouldn't spot the black roots of his death-bed largesse and point him ever so politely in the direction of the down escalator?

Ah, what was the point of being shrewish at this stage in the game? Without an audience it lacked its old allure. She took a brief detour into magnanimity. They'd had their share of good times, the two of them. And she was hardly in any position to disparage his choices in life. Once her womb proved inhospitable, the rest of her body took its cue, shutting the doors and drawing the blinds, operating in perpetual penumbra. Their separation saw them each follow a warped path of their own designing.

A clunk from the direction of the living room distracted her from her musings. On top of it came a mewling cry. How had Jean ever been able to concentrate enough in this echo chamber to churn out any pages when you could hear the next door cat howling as clearly as if its litter box were in the adjoining room? Whenever he was holed up in his study on a writing bender, Jean demanded sepulchral silence, outer-galactic silence, cryogenic silence. Back then Amélie had come up with her own personal adjective to describe that capstone of noiselessness; those others just didn't cut it. Omelette silence was what she called it.

She could still see the mixture. All over the wall. Dribbling down in phlegmy strands. Yellowing the floor. Her favourite bowl in shards. She'd been cracking eggs too emphatically down in the kitchen while he was trying to tie up a tricky scene upstairs. That was her crime. Yet in this place the mitoyen walls were made of tissue paper and the pipes of cannelloni. For all the building's highfalutin heritage-plaque status Amélie'd seen pizza boxes more sturdily constructed. That the former nunnery was older than the country itself left her cold. *Justement*, it was probably the structure's pre-Confederation asbestos wadding that knocked Jean off prematurely. His health had always been robust. In more salubrious lodgings he might have banked a few more years under his belt.

Amélie's plain-Jane little row house rose up in her mind's eye. She very nearly hadn't bothered to go check it out the first time the real estate agent told her of its location; she wasn't looking to settle in that garden-gnome quartier, thank you very much. He struggled to dredge up some plusses, but the best the desperate realtor could come up with in trying to fix Amélie up with that faux-brick wallflower languishing on his list was that it had a good personality. His matchmaking skills, fumbly though they were, ultimately did succeed in uniting Amélie with 6738 rue de Montressis. Turns out the two were fated for each other. After so many years of steadfast companionship, Amélie would never think of trading in her beloved home that hugged itself around her like a pair of old slippers for Jean's wimpled flat. His rinky-dink condo, despite the building's hipster appeal, had nothing on her place, so solid, so true, but she sensed that if ever the two residences were to be introduced, Jean's would snigger at the blatant uncoolness of hers.

Amélie took umbrage on her home's behalf. The imagined mockery targeting her cherished little house was all it took to restore her starch. She'd just walk out of here. That's what she'd do. Enough playing the doormat. *Fini.* She squared her shoulders, treated the apartment to a firm good-bye, good riddance salute, and turned to leave, but on her way out through the living room she picked up a problem that demanded her attention, however desperate she was to put the place behind her.

On the street-facing wall was a hatch of some kind that she had barely registered before, coal-chute-ish in design, but hinged at the bottom. The utilitarian or religious purpose of such a strangely fashioned opening she could not divine in the few seconds she allotted her mind to toss it about, but what did it matter anyway what its original function was for the good *soeurs* who'd been cloistered here? All that mattered was that now its door was gaping inwards, angled down nearly parallel with the floor, inviting noise and sidewalk grit to make their way into the apartment unimpeded, not to speak of all those rats and pigeons out there of an exploratory bent. Anyone with a grain of sense would have long since had it sealed shut against the wind. Jean must have been losing it towards the end. Amélie could not make herself leave without dealing with it. It offended her sense of propriety, casting her mind back to her grandpapa Xavier who took to wandering around the house with the trap door hanging open on his union suit after mamie died, no matter who was there. It just wasn't right. Amélie went over to lift the door closed but when she bent down she saw that the niche that it formed with the wall was occupied.

He stopped squalling the instant she leaned in over him. At least she presumed it was a *he*. The baby was dressed up toasty warm in blue footsied pyjamas and swaddled for good measure in a hand-knitted grandmotherly blanket. Rebellious wisps of auburn hair sneaked out from under his acorn cap. One week old? Two maybe? A month? She didn't have enough experience with newborns to tell. In fact a grand total of none. Amélie picked the baby up and docked him on her shoulder to sniff. Did all babies smell of fresh-baked bread, she wondered? The infant nosed her up reciprocally. He was a curious little guy.

Amélie shifted the compact bundle against her chest this way and that, accommodating herself to its centre of gravity which seemed to rest in the diaper region. She cupped her right hand under that spot for extra support and it elicited a plastic-y crinkle. Her other hand, though an amateur of equal standing, somehow knew enough to cradle the head. Her hold on the baby seemed to her secure enough that she was emboldened to embark on a tentative test drive around the tiny apartment. The two of them took a few steps together without mishap so they ventured onwards, hugging the walls to maximize the mileage, moving at a stately pace. On their second lap he fussed a bit. Amélie interrupted their circuit and tried jiggling him up and down but her stiff, sink-plunger motion seemed to agitate him all the more. She panicked when she felt him revving up for takeoff. She had no moves left in her anorexic repertoire. That's when her hips took charge of the situation. Somebody had to. They commenced to sway from side to side. It was the lazy, sensuous hula of a different build of woman, a woman fleshier of form, with a cushiony belly and pendulous engorged breasts; a woman with her hair unbound. Gauguin might have tucked a gardenia behind her ear. A woman replete. After a few gentle swings back and forth in the hammock of her arms the baby calmed right down.

They resumed their promenade. At the front window they stopped to check out the sky. "What do you think Raphaël *mon bébé*? Those clouds look pretty dark. It's starting to turn nasty out. Will you be warm enough in that? *Hein, mon amour*?" How did her voice know to up itself an octave, resettling in that fluty acoustic range that baby ears so favoured? She kissed his cheek to mark her claim while awaiting his meteorological judgment. "Tell *maman* Raphaël. I wouldn't want you to catch cold." She experimented with a little tickle under the chin.

Raphaël studied her. She needed some breaking in, this one. He corkscrewed his lips to relay to her the message that he didn't give a hoot about the weather. His priority *numero uno* was to be served, and pronto. This, his first stab at communication with his adoptive mother was embarrassingly rudimentary. Charades he'd stooped to. Lower even on the semantic totem pole than *me Tarzan* but effective nonetheless.

Amélie took one look at his face and grabbed the raincoat she'd set down on the kitchen counter. Had it only been a half hour before? She bundled the baby up in its folds and the two of them scurried out of the apartment to scare up some formula and a bottle.

A gassy smile illuminated Raphaël's features. She showed real promise. He'd have her trained up in no time.

Acknowledgements

Thank you to my gentle but insightful first readers Joy R. Zaslov and Kendall Wallis. Many thanks also to Len Husband who led me to Inanna, and Luciana Ricciutelli who picked me out of the slush pile once I got there. Julie Barlow, Susan Doherty, Luigina Vileno, and Benoit Léger gave much needed advice along the way.

Above all thank you to Ron who always made me believe that it would happen. I'm grateful for your patience, your rejection buck-ups, and your meals along the way. I'm lucky I found you. Last but not least thanks to my son David, title coach and all-around good boychik.

Photo: *Marcie Richstone*

Phyllis Rudin has lived in the U.S., France, and Canada. Her award-winning short stories have appeared in numerous Canadian and American literary magazines. She lives in Montreal which serves as the landscape for all her fiction.